THE CHRIS-CROSS
EPISODE

THE CHRIS-CROSS EPISODE

Louie Elizabeth Parker

This book is dedicated to the memory of my late husband, Alexander <u>Alan</u> Crawford Parker. The thirty years we spent together in North East Scotland was truly a breath of fresh air.

louieelizabethparker.com

PART 1

THE KIDNAP

Family Tree

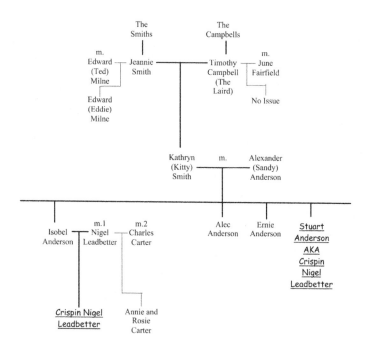

CHAPTER 1
London 1940

Crispin Nigel Leadbetter was born in the summer of 1940. His father had been killed in action in the Second World War, although at the time she gave birth to Crispin, his mother could not be completely sure of this sad fact. Just a few days earlier she had received a telegram informing her that her dearly beloved husband had been wounded, but the details had not been relayed. She knew, however, that such a telegram was all too frequently a precursor of the worst.

Not to be left on her own for the birth, she had gone to stay with her sister-in-law, Henrietta, in Guildford, about twenty-six miles from her home in Fulham. Originally from Aberdeen, Isobel had never really felt comfortable in the big city but, whilst her husband was with her, she was cosseted, moving in his affluent world, surrounded by his family, most of whom were at least showing some effort at making her feel welcome, if only for the sake of their dearest Nigel: a popular young man; charming; good looking with his blonde hair and piercing blue eyes. He was considered by the ladies to be 'a good catch' so there were more than a few gasps of surprise — disappointment even — at his choice of bride. Though fairly well-spoken and by no means rough, a girl from so far north was certainly not what those who knew him well had in mind. Nigel and Isobel were, however, happy together. Despite their differences, during their relatively short time together, they did appear to be a good match.

The baby, a beautiful boy with his father's blonde hair and blue eyes was, unmistakably a Leadbetter. His mother would have preferred to call him Alexander, which she could then have shortened to the typically Aberdonian 'Sandy', but the family would have been horrified and, of course, his father, about whom they still had no word, was not around to consult. Saddened by pending doom and weakened by the birth, Isobel was in no fit state for a confrontation so, following a family tradition, she allowed him to be christened 'Crispin' after his paternal grandfather and, for obvious reasons, added his father's name. She could do nothing about the Leadbetter.

When the baby was just three weeks old Isobel returned home with the young child. Within two days the dreaded telegram arrived. Devastated and not knowing what to do, Isobel returned to the home of her sister-in-law, hoping for some comfort; but the family were too much concerned with their own sorrow to sympathise with her predicament. They appeared not to understand her loneliness, how utterly bereft she felt in her loss: the death of her husband compounded by the separation, albeit of her own making, from her family hundreds of miles away. There could be no funeral, no real closure; and the war was very soon to come closer than they could have imagined.

It was perhaps a blessing that Isobel had a baby to care for and, for his sake, she was forced to keep going. The baby was also a distraction for the rest of the family. Henrietta would gaze upon him for hours on end, absorbed in her thoughts and no doubt comforted by the likeness to her brother she must surely observe in her young nephew. Nigel's parents, when they visited, so obviously devastated by the death of their son, seemed hardly to notice their daughter-in-law's distress. They did, however, coo and fuss over their grandson, remarking on his family features and bemoaning the loss on his behalf: "Poor, dear Crispin, whatever will he do; whatever will happen to him?" Did they not think his mother capable of caring for her child? Did they even notice her presence in the room? Henrietta's husband, Raymond, was a doctor — too involved in his work to share in their grief: he was shortly to become busier than ever.

September was upon them and, with the turning of the season, came the bombing, the Blitz. That the country was at war had been bad enough, but now it was right on their doorstep: it wasn't just the menfolk, who had been called to fight for their country, who were in danger: now everyone was a target.

The evacuation of civilians had begun several months earlier and, in a way, it would have made sense for Isobel to return to Aberdeen when Nigel went away. But their home was in London: it was convenient; it was comfortable and, until now, it had seemed the right place to be: but not so any longer. Isobel could not stay forever with Henrietta. Already she felt that she had outstayed her welcome. She realised she must return to Aberdeen but she kept her thoughts to herself. Although to a large extent she felt that she was merely being tolerated, she was not so sure how the family would react if she suggested that she was going to take Crispin away. In the end, Isobel indicated that she must go back to her home in Fulham — they could visit her whenever they wished. She was, in fact, formulating her own plan; her plan for the journey north with her young son.

Returning to Fulham two days after the first bombs fell in London was, Isobel realised, madness by any standards. Her in-laws were infuriated by her recklessness, but they were unaware of her real intentions, which would probably render her son much safer even than staying in Guildford.

Without a word to them, Isobel made preparations. Within a week she was on the train heading for Scotland. Exactly where she was going to stay she had no idea, but surely her family would give her shelter until she recovered from the trauma of recent weeks: until she felt stronger. She had every intention of making her husband's family aware of her relocation as soon as she was settled in her hometown.

CHAPTER 2
Aberdeen 1940

Arriving at Aberdeen railway station Isobel was unexpectedly deflated — what now? A question she would return to many times over the ensuing weeks. The excitement and, to some extent the guilt of making the decision, had overtaken reason. In all the upheaval she had not informed her own family that she was widowed or of the birth of her son, now almost six weeks old, let alone her intention to return home.

She hailed a taxi to take her the short distance to her parents' house in the Northfield area of the city but, as she cuddled the infant on her lap, she became increasingly anxious about her situation. She had been a petulant young girl, just eighteen years old when she met and fell in love with Nigel and, although they did not exactly elope, she *had* rushed off down to London and announced her engagement by letter some weeks later. Reluctantly, her parents had consented to the marriage, realising that nothing could be gained by refusing. Besides, they had to acknowledge that, provided things worked out, their daughter had done rather well for herself: Nigel was, after all, a fine young man. They had not attended the wedding. The cost of the journey to London was prohibitive and they could not afford accommodation in the big city. Now, three years later, here she was, very different from the teenager who could not get away fast enough, about to make a surprise appearance to the family she had effectively deserted. Circumstances had aged her beyond her twenty-one years. A mother herself, widowed and stunned by the reality of the war, she had been forced into maturity; but she was also alone and frightened.

With reservations, she dumped her case on the path and knocked on the door, gently at first, almost inaudibly, then louder. She heard footsteps in the hall. Was it her mother? Was it her father? Her heart raced.

The door opened and there, in the dimly lit hallway, stood a tall, slim young man; a stranger? She blinked, took a step back not knowing what to say, how to explain herself. Had she been mistaken; knocked on the wrong door in her anxiety? Surely not! Then slowly, reality dawned. She recognised the dark hair, the dark brown eyes — her younger brother, barely thirteen years old when she left, a schoolboy, 'a wee loon', now so grown up. He was looking down, not so much at her as the baby in her arms. "Yes?" came the deep voice, questioning her presence.

"Isobel, your sister, Isobel," she murmured, almost as if she didn't want him to hear. For a long moment he gazed at her, not quite taking in the situation.

"Ma," he called, summoning help, whilst his sister remained on the threshold. "It's Isobel," he added as his mother appeared behind him.

A stunned silence was followed by a scuffle, as his mother pushed past him to face the daughter she had not seen in almost three years. "Oh my, oh my goodness." Then, seeing the baby, she gently placed her arms around Isobel and drew her into the house.

Her brother, Ernie, picked up the luggage and, leaving it at the foot of the stairs, joined the reunion in the living room.

Da, puffing away at his pipe, now rose from his armchair in the corner of the room to welcome his daughter and the little fellow who was sound asleep and oblivious to the whole proceedings. Hugs and tears ensued as mother and father fussed around Isobel and the sleeping child. Then began the comments; the questions:

"How did you get here?"

"Where's Nigel?"

"When did you have the baby?

"Is it a boy or a girl?"

A whole barrage, before Isobel had the chance to utter a word.

"Whoa, one thing at a time," interrupted her brother, who realised that something dreadful must have happened for his sister to arrive unannounced on their doorstep. "How about a cup of tea?"

"I'd love one," Isobel replied, grateful for her brother's consideration. Ernie backed out of the room and into the kitchen to put the kettle on and make the tea. Tea: the answer to any crisis. In fact, in this household, the answer to everything.

"I'll take your coat," Ma offered.

Still grasping her child, Isobel managed to unfasten her coat with one hand. Her mother helped her take it off, then disappeared into the hall to hang it up. Meantime, Da returned to his armchair and continued to puff away at his pipe and drink tea from his own special pint mug.

Ernie returned from the kitchen with a cup of tea for his sister.

"Drink up, Isobel, and tell us what's happened, why you are here?"

"Nigel's d-d-dead," was all she managed to say before she began to feel dizzy and, still clutching Crispin, she sank onto the sofa and started to cry. Thoroughly exhausted from weeks of uncertainty and anxiety, exacerbated by the onset of the bombing raids, she sobbed as if her heart would break. Her family had no words to say; they were stunned at the news and sensed there was plenty more to come. In barely ten minutes it was as if their lives had been completely turned upside down. Having finished their evening meal, the three of them had settled round the coal fire, sharing the events of the day and looking forward to a game of cards — a favourite pastime at the end of the working week.

Ma moved over to the settee beside her daughter in an attempt to offer whatever comfort she could when, just at that moment, came the sound of a baby crying. Confused, Isobel looked up through her tears. Crispin was still asleep in her arms. She was disorientated, unable to comprehend what was happening. "That's Stuart awake," whispered her mother and, without further explanation, she rose from the seat she had only momentarily occupied, hurried out of the room, and up the stairs.

Totally dazed, Isobel asked, "Who's Stuart?"

"He's yer wee brither," responded her father, "did yer ma no mention in her letter writin that we'd had anither loon?"

"N-n-no," choked Isobel, "I'd no idea."

"Weel, he was born in July, ye ken. A rare surprise to us when we found out yer ma was expectin', never thoucht she'd hae anither at 'er age. But, he's a bonny wee loon. Got a good pair o lungs on him!"

Jerked out of her own self-pity, Isobel felt ashamed. She began to wonder; *had her mother mentioned it?* — she tried to think back over the last year: the events in her own life, her pregnancy, the onset of the war, her husband posted abroad, the birth of her son and the death of Nigel. There was so much that she hadn't written home about, making out that life in the big city was good. Well, for a time it had been, but the last year had been a nightmare. Still, surely she would have remembered her parents' news?

"Aye, we've had oor hans fu' this last few weeks, that's for sure," commented her Da, "and noo this!"

"I- I'm so sorry," Isobel stuttered, between sobs, "I'd no idea, a-and, now here I am with all my troubles."

"Dinna be sorry aboot us Isobel. Stuart's a richt wee smasher, broucht a fair amount o joy tay yer ma and me. Niver seed 'er so happy — not after you went off." At this Isobel's tears flowed faster than ever.

"Och, now, now, dinna fech thee sen. Aye, things have bin hard, but the wee bairn's bin a blessin' and we'll sort things out. Somehow we'll manage."

At this point, her mother re-appeared, "That's him settled again, the noise down here must have wakened him."

"Well, what's all this about Nigel?" Her mother enquired. "Killed in action, I presume. This war really is taking its toll."

"I just got the news about a month ago, although I'd already had a telegram to say that he had been wounded. That came a few days before Crispin was born."

"Who?" came the puzzled tone from her father.

"Crispin, our son," she emphasized, forgetting how foreign that would sound to her parents.

"Fit? Ye canna ca' a loon Crispin, nae in this part o the country, whativer will folk mak o that?"

Hardly disguising a grin, Ernie, piped up, "We'll just call him Chris, no-one needs to know."

Even in her sorrow, Isobel was gaining a good deal of respect for her young brother. He had not simply grown in stature; he had matured beyond all recognition. He was thoughtful, understanding and appeared to have developed some common sense — an unusual attribute for a sixteen-year-old.

"Come now, Isobel," her mother coaxed, "tell us what's worst, you've obviously had a difficult time this past few weeks? How's the rest of Nigel's family? Have they helped you?"

16

Isobel began to relate the sorrowful tale. She explained that, though not blatantly unkind, she felt intimidated by her London relatives who seemed oblivious to her plight. However, she added that they too were wallowing in their loss and that the war was ever closer to their doorstep. Their home in Guildford, being away from the centre of London, would hopefully avoid the worst of the bombing, but when she had returned to her own house in Fulham a few days ago, having decided to return to Aberdeen, London was filled with the stench of burning: this final visit to her home had confirmed the need to make a rapid escape.

She ended by saying that she was anxious to seek out suitable accommodation for herself and her son, but asked that she might stay until she sorted this out.

It was only now, in her parents' meagre yet cosy abode, that Isobel began to consider the suffering that they had endured over the years. Glancing from one to the other, for the first time in her life, she recognised their pain — a pain that must surely be reignited as they listened to her tragic tale.

Sandy

Her father, Alexander (Sandy) Anderson, was born in Glasgow at the turn of the century where *his* father, Thomas, worked at John Brown's shipyard. Their home was on the top floor of a tenement block. The three rooms were spacious, a blessing with a growing family, but high ceilings made it difficult to heat. A range in the kitchen-cum-living room provided the focal point for the family in the winter: it was the only heating and also the only means of cooking. Sandy was the eldest son. It was his job to carry coal up the two flights of stairs, a tough task for a young boy. Nevertheless, he was a willing helper and, despite his tender years, he noticed how hard his mother, Lizzie, toiled in the home: washing; ironing; cooking; cleaning; polishing. Also, she must take her turn, on hands and knees, scrubbing the shared staircase and landing. Every other year saw the arrival of another baby, another mouth to feed and more work. Sandy's only escape was school, which he loved, and where he excelled. Reading was a particular joy to him but, like most working-class families, there was little access to reading material in the home. Whenever he did get the chance to go out to play in the backcourt[i] or the street, he remained at his mother's beck and call: running errands; bringing in the washing; keeping an eye on his younger siblings.

Life was hard, but Lizzie was not one to complain. As long as she could put food on the table and they had a roof over their heads, she could manage. So far, they were a happy family, content in each other's company. Sadly, things were about to change.

Thomas, who had always been a meticulous timekeeper, began arriving home late. He claimed that he had to work overtime, but there was no bulging pay packet to show for these extra hours; on the contrary, less

---

[i] A shared yard to the rear of the tenement.

money was available. Like many of his fellow workers, Thomas was in the habit of dropping into the pub for a quick pint on payday but, until now, that had always been his limit. Lizzie was uneasy about this transformation in her husband's habits and attitude: the stale smell of beer on his breath confirmed her suspicions — there *was* no overtime. He was visiting the pub most days on his way home from work, staying for longer and consuming more and more beer.

Each Friday when he handed his pay packet to his wife, it was smaller. When Lizzie questioned him, he became angry, telling her she was a useless housekeeper and she would just have to manage: this was not the man she had married! She came to dread the sound of his footsteps on the stairs; afraid of his moods, his outbursts, and, ultimately, his violence. He would demand that his dinner was on the table straight away, no matter when he came in. He grumbled if it had been warmed up — he didn't like it warmed up! He complained about the children, there were too many. "It's time these boys were earning their own living," he shouted, referring to their two oldest offspring, "Sandy's nearly twelve, it's time he was away from the school, and Bobby's just wasting his time."

"But he's only ten," objected his wife. She daren't say too much. There were the four girls to consider and, as yet unbeknown to Thomas, another child on the way.

A few weeks later, weary from lack of sleep and pathetically thin, Lizzie trudged into the city. She needed to enquire about the possibility of placing some of her offspring into a children's home for, in truth, she could no longer sustain her family, not on the pittance she now received from Thomas. Once the rent was paid, there was little left for anything else. After much deliberation, it was agreed that the authorities could accommodate her two middle daughters — as a temporary measure. It was suggested that Sandy and Bobby could be boarded out: there was a demand for growing lads in the Aberdeenshire area where they could work on a farm, earning their keep. Lizzie was not happy about sending her sons away, but they didn't mind too much. Sandy was constantly the target of his father's ill-temper. A new life — a new adventure — would surely be no worse than what he had come to endure in recent weeks. Bobby was reluctant, but he too was suffering at the heavy hand of his father. At least he would have the company of his older brother. Meanwhile, their eldest daughter, Peggy, would stay at home. She was just eight years old but already proving to be a good helper.

Lizzie had tried hard to reason with Thomas, but he was oblivious to her needs and that of his family; he only seemed to care about himself. Perhaps with four of them away, he would regret his actions and mend his ways. Wishful thinking maybe, but she had to hope. The stress of watching her family taken from her, albeit at her request, was almost too much for Lizzie to bear.

As Sandy and Bobby set off for a new life many miles from the only home they had ever known, their tears were soon replaced by excitement when they boarded the train for the long journey north. Neither had ever been away from the noise and bustle of urban life. Seeing the rolling hills and the green fields as they left Glasgow behind, they began to look forward to living in the country. It was several hours before they arrived at Aberdeen Railway Station. There they had to change trains for a town further north, where they were met by the farmer, their new foster father, who took them the short distance to the farm in a horse drawn cart.

As foster children, they were accommodated in the farmhouse, as part of the family. The farmer, Mr Grant, and his wife were friendly enough, but it was obvious from the start that they would not tolerate any nonsense. After supper, a bowl of thick tattie soup, they were shown to the attic bedroom that they were to share, and a bathroom on the first floor. They were given suitable clothes for the following day when they were set to work on the farm.

At first, much of their time was spent fetching and carrying, but gradually they were expected to take on other tasks: 'mucking' out hen houses; collecting eggs; feeding the pigs. There was never a shortage of work. Often, they were expected to lug heavy loads of produce across the rough fields, toiling hour after hour in all weathers. However, with good wholesome meals, they soon toughened up to meet the demands of their employer. But, carrying heavy loads in his early teenage years, took its toll on Sandy. His back was badly hunched from the effects of the burdens he had been expected to carry before he reached physical maturity. Yet, despite this, he was always cheerful. Towards the end of the First World War, he met Kitty, his beloved wife.

Kitty

Until the age of ten, Kitty had enjoyed a relatively carefree childhood, living in a little cottage in the country with her mother and father, two brothers and a sister; or so she thought. When Kitty was five, her sister, Jeannie, married and moved into a house in the village with her new husband. She frequently called in at her old home and, along with her husband, Ted, they would join the family for tea on a Sunday. One Sunday, about five years after they were married, the couple announced that Jeannie was expecting a baby. Everyone was delighted. Later, whilst chatting to her mother, Jeannie made a comment that caught Kitty's attention. "I was beginning to wonder whether I would ever be able to have another child."

Another child? Kitty, a curious girl, was puzzled by her sister's remark. Maybe she had misheard her. Jeannie had always been a part of Kitty's life: she didn't remember her having a baby.

She tried to forget about it, but when she arrived home from school the next day, she was still mulling it over. Her mother was alone in the kitchen, without hesitation, she confronted her. "What did our Jeannie mean... 'another baby?'"

Her mother appeared startled at first. She tried to brush the question aside, but Kitty persisted. At last, Ma gave in. She motioned Kitty to sit down and with the words, "Perhaps it's time you knew the truth," she unravelled the story of Kitty's birth, revealing that she was, in fact, Jeannie's daughter.

For a few moments Kitty was too stunned to move, then she let out a scream and crying, 'No, no', she fled to her room, collapsed on the bed and wept.

It was a long time before Kitty came to terms with the revelation that her 'mother' was actually her grandmother. What should she call her? Was she supposed to call her 'Ma', as she had always done, or 'Granny' or, in her anger, 'Thing'. She felt betrayed: who could she trust? Then she thought… if Ma isn't Ma, then Pa isn't Pa. Who is my Pa? Who else knows? Her brothers? Well, if her sister was her mother, then her brothers were her uncles! Oh, what a muddle!

When she asked about her real father, her 'granny' said she didn't know, which was the truth; although, at first, Kitty did not believe her. Over the following weeks, Granny tried to console her granddaughter, to reassure her that she was loved, that they had done what was best. She tried to explain that Jeannie was so young, they had wanted to protect her. But Kitty wasn't listening. No longer the happy little girl playing in the fields or down by the seashore, she became moody and, often, bad-tempered. She kept her distance from Jeannie, making excuses whenever 'her sister' came to the cottage. It was only when Jeannie gave birth to a baby boy a few months later that Kitty accepted her situation. She acknowledged the new addition to the family as her brother, refusing to be an aunty. She was not willing to continue the lie.

Then, something else happened that changed the course of Kitty's immediate future. When she was about twelve years old, Jeannie received an important missive in which she was informed of a legacy to be used for her daughter's education. The trustees, acting on behalf of the unknown benefactor, arranged for Kitty to attend an elite all-girls school in Aberdeen, where she would board during term-time. Her grandparents were reluctant at first, but Kitty was excited at the prospect. Deep down she was still hurting from what she felt was a betrayal; the thought of this opportunity appealed. She welcomed the chance to get away. It was not unusual for daughters in farming communities to attend such an establishment. Kitty knew of girls from her primary school who had gone away to attend a 'posh' school in the city. Sons, on the other hand, needed to toughen up, so would remain at the local school.

With uniform, stationery and spending money, all supplied via the trustees, Kitty attended the school in Aberdeen for the next four years, returning home most weekends and holidays. It was a dual existence, but one which suited her. She made friends easily, dropping her country accent to conform to the expectations of teachers and fit in with the other girls. However, at heart, she still loved her home in the country. At this time, the First

World War was raging in Europe, but Kitty's life and that of her relatives was little affected.

Sandy and Kitty

It was a beautiful spring day in 1918 when Sandy and Kitty first met outside the village store in East Bay; he, a rugged farmworker with dark, curly hair and a twinkle in his eye; she, a slim attractive brunette, with sharp, though not unduly harsh features. Their eyes met, lingering just a second longer than a cursory glance, but nothing was said. The second time, a week later, they bumped into one another inside the shop. When, on the following day, they encountered each other a third time, he invited her to a barn dance at a neighbouring farm. She accepted. Seeing him three times in such a short space of time seemed more than mere coincidence.

They were married soon after the end of the war, both still teenagers, and moved into a farm labourers' cottage. Isobel was born in 1919. Two boys, Alec and Ernie, followed in 1922 and 1924.

Sandy's hard work on the farm had not gone unnoticed. Entrusted with some of the essential skilled tasks during the war years, he had unwittingly made himself indispensable, and thus avoided conscription. However, despite this, in 1933 he moved the family to the city. Farming was tough and, though well respected, Sandy had no real future. More importantly, he wanted something better for his young family than was available in the countryside. Ironically, at the age of fourteen, their eldest son, Alec, had decided that life in the country was exactly what he wanted. Whenever he could he cycled out to East Bay to stay with Grandma Jeannie, where he enjoyed the freedom and the fresh air. One weekend, having left school, he rode off to East Bay and didn't come home. He started working life as a delivery boy at the grocery store but frequently cycled four miles to help out at a local farm. That, he knew, was where his heart lay.

....

A muffled cry from the bundle in her arms brought Isobel abruptly back to the present. She wanted to hear more about what had been happening to her Aberdeen family in the last three years, but she could barely keep her eyes open and it was time to feed Crispin. Seeing how tired her daughter looked, Kitty said it was time for bed. Tomorrow was Sunday, so they would have time to discuss the future once they had all had a good night's sleep. Isobel indicated that she would manage on the settee in the living room, but Ernie immediately quipped that she would do no such thing. "You can have my room tonight; we'll sort things out in the morning. I'll sleep down here." There could be no argument.

With two young babies in the household, no one was having the luxury of a long lie the next morning. When Ernie left for his paper round at six o'clock, the house was abuzz with activity. However, the boys, both only a few weeks old, were fast asleep by mid-morning, giving Kitty and Sandy time to explain their current circumstances to their daughter.

Before Isobel had left home, Ernie was attending the Grammar School. He had proved to be a bright lad, doing well throughout his primary school and passing a 'qualifying' exam, securing a bursary, which enabled him to attend this fee-paying establishment, rather than the local academy. But he needed a uniform, a PE kit and items of stationery. His parents were not in a position to provide all of these extras, but they were determined that he should not be denied the opportunity. It was, after all, the very reason they had moved into the city. When they had arrived in Aberdeen, Sandy had no problem gaining employment, but only as a dockworker — a labourer. He had no trade, no relevant skills. It was better paid than the farm work but still poor, especially as living in the city was more expensive than in the country.

Kitty, who herself had benefitted from a privileged education and, as a result, gained employment in a bank before her marriage, understood the importance of giving their son a chance. She now sought employment. It wasn't easy but, eventually, she was successful. The manager of a local branch of one of the big banks was impressed by her education and previous, though brief experience. He offered her a job: she was delighted. Isobel, who had already left school, was employed as a clerk in the purchases office of a large department store in the city, so her income added to the family budget.

When she went down to London to marry Nigel, her contribution ceased, but it was not a disaster for the family. For more than two years things had gone smoothly. Then, a few months ago, Kitty discovered she was pregnant. Determined to keep Ernie at school, she worked until the baby was due. She was hoping to return to her job quite soon. Ernie also helped out, distributing newspapers each morning before school and working as a butcher's delivery boy on a Saturday.

In the meantime, Sandy's health was deteriorating. His hunched back, caused by carrying heavy loads in his younger days, was giving him pain and discomfort, along with arthritis in his knee joints. Six weeks ago it had reached the stage when he was no longer fit to work at the docks. He was reduced to temporary work at the local grocer's and even that was hard for him, having to stand all day. At around this time the family had received a letter from a former neighbour whose son had been offered a job at a bakery in Aberdeen. He would be working shifts each night from Sunday to Thursday: would they be able to take him in as a lodger during the week? In their current circumstances, this was a request they could hardly refuse: it would add a little to their weekly income, but it meant their spare room was now reserved for Jim for most of the week. He arrived each Sunday evening, dropped off his belongings (his mother did his washing at the weekends) and went straight to work. He would arrive home in the morning and sleep for most of the day. Ma would make him 'supper'[ii] before he set off for another twelve-hour shift.

Hearing her parent's tale, Isobel felt guilty for burdening them with *her* problems: the loss of her husband and the birth of their son. However, at least she had her own income, meagre as it was. Her parents agreed that she must take some time to settle her affairs: to contact her bank, her solicitor and her London family, using their address for communications. Later in the day, after a traditional Sunday roast dinner, they discussed the sleeping arrangements for the next few weeks — not that there was much to discuss. Ernie insisted that he would sleep on the settee in the living room. Isobel would search for a place of her own and look for work. She was grateful to her parents: thankful for the warmth of a real home after the trauma of the last few weeks.

Before the winter set in, Isobel decided to visit her maternal grandparents (or, rather, great-grandparents) and introduce them to their new great-great-grandson. She might also see Grandma Jeannie and other members of her family.

It was a sunny September morning as she boarded the bus to East Bay, alighting a short distance from the coastal village, to walk the half-mile or so to Granny and Grandpa Smith's cottage. She had not gone far when she heard the sound of a bicycle bell warning her of its approach from behind. Seeing the woman carrying the

---

[ii] Supper was the main meal of the day, served in the early evening

baby in her arms, as well as a sizable bag, the lad on the bike stopped to ask if she would like some assistance: he was delivering groceries from the shop in East Bay to some of the local country folk. When she said she was going to visit her great-grandparents in the nearest cottage, he gave her a strange look — they were his great-grandparents too. Then it registered — she was his older sister who had married the 'posh' army officer from 'down south'. "I'm Alec, your brother Alec," he announced. He told her to put her bag on the top of the basket attached to the front of the bicycle and walked along the road beside her. They had very little time to catch up with news of the intervening years, before reaching the cottage.

Granny was delighted to see her. Grandpa had gone for a walk, probably along the cliff tops: the couple, though well over eighty, were both healthy and active. Kitty had written to them to let them know about Isobel's return and inform them of her current circumstances, so the visit was not a total surprise. Alec was not able to stay and chat: he had several other deliveries to make. He had worked at the grocer's when he first left home four years ago and still helped out from time to time, but his main job was at the farm where he was learning all the skills required in every aspect of dairy and agricultural work. However, he could not escape conscription: now eighteen years old, he knew he would be called up to serve quite soon. Alec offered to come back in the morning to accompany Isobel to the village, where she intended to visit Grandma Jeannie and her husband, Ted.

Isobel had a lovely day with her great-grandparents. She enjoyed being in the countryside, where she had spent much of her childhood. After London, it was a breath of fresh air. Great Granny and Grandpa made her so welcome, insisting she stay the night, for which she had come prepared! It was a pleasure to taste Granny's Scotch broth and delicious mince and tatties — good wholesome Scottish food. In the evening they made toast in the traditional way: the bread suspended on a toasting fork close to the flames of the open fire. The couple made a fuss of their great-great-grandson, who Isobel had introduced as Chris, taking the sensible advice from her younger brother, Ernie.

In the morning, her brother, Alec, arrived as promised. This time he sat the baby in the basket at the front of the bike. The motion soon sent him off to sleep. Alec left the mother and child at Grandma Jeannie's, to return to the farm for the rest of the day. Jeannie's house was at the end of a terrace looking out over the bay. Though not as quaint as Granny's cottage, it was cosy and had its appeal, not least for its scenic views. Jeannie and her husband, Ted, had welcomed Alec into their household when he had decided, at the age of fourteen, that he wanted to be in the country. They were devastated at the thought of him joining the forces to go to war. How empty their house would be without this lively young lad to cheer up their winter evenings! Their son, Eddie, had left home in his early twenties, moving to the nearby market town with his bride. He had followed in his father's footsteps working alongside him in the hardware store which, since Ted's recent retirement, he now managed.

Listening to Isobel's tale, her grandmother suggested that she would be safer in the country than in the city, where she was currently trying to find work and accommodation. Even with Alec, there would be plenty of room for her and Chris. "Think about it," she urged.

"But I need to work," Isobel responded. "I have my widow's pension, but I would struggle to survive on that."

"With so many men away, I'm sure you'd find something," her grandma commented.

As Isobel sat on the bus with her baby son on her knee, she thought about Grandma Jeannie's words. Maybe it would be a good idea. The bombs in London had frightened her. Aberdeen, though not as threatened, was also a target. Her parents were settled in the city and, with Ernie showing such promise in his studies, they had no intention of moving. Their home was cramped. Ernie could not be expected to sleep on the settee forever. Her mind swayed one way and the other. What should she do?

She decided to keep her thoughts to herself for the time being, until she was clearer in her own mind about the idea. In the meantime, she wrote to Nigel's parents in London to explain her decision to move back to her home city, at least for the duration of the war. It was almost two weeks since she had made the journey — longer than that since she had seen them — and she suspected that they might have tried to get in touch with her at her address in Fulham: they would not be pleased.

Her solicitor had already responded to her letter informing him of her change of address. The house in Fulham had been in her husband's name but, on his death, the mortgage was cleared and the property transferred to her. Under normal circumstances, she would have been tempted to place the house on the market, but these were not normal times. Without asking for his opinion, he had come to the same conclusion and advised her against such a decision. She had already transferred her bank account to her local Aberdeen branch. The allowance she had been receiving from her late husband's salary was now replaced by a widow's pension. This would have to cover some costs on her London home as well as her living expenses in Aberdeen: there was, therefore, not much room for manoeuvre. But Isobel considered herself fortunate: thanks to the willingness of her Ma and Da to accommodate her, and the good nature of her younger brother, she was not destitute.

In early-October, the family had a visit from Alec. He had cycled into Aberdeen from East Bay, despite the dismal Autumn weather, to let them know that, as expected, he had received his call-up papers: he would be leaving home next week to join the army. He was not happy, although he had resigned himself to the fact. He stayed overnight with his parents and siblings, sleeping on the floor in the living room, giving him time to say his farewells to the family. Before settling down for the night, he managed to have a word with his sister in private. The manager of the grocer's in East Bay was elderly. He was desperate for someone to take over the running of the shop. As both owner and manager he was living in a flat above the store, so he would always be around to supervise as necessary. Both he and Grandma Jeannie felt this would be an ideal solution to Isobel's problems. After all, she had worked as a clerk for two years before getting married, so they were sure she would be able to deal with the paperwork involved.

Isobel admitted it was an ideal opportunity. Her grandma had already told her that she would be more than welcome to live with them. They would take care of the baby once she found a job: there would be no problem!

To Isobel, this seemed an offer too good to miss. She felt guilty. Since her trip to East Bay a week earlier she had failed to mention her grandmother's proposal. So far, Isobel had only made a half-hearted attempt at finding work in Aberdeen. Maybe, deep down, it was a reluctance to remain in the city with her son that had caused her to hesitate in her search for employment.

"I really will give it some serious thought," she confided in her brother. They were all sad at Alec's departure. The dreaded call-up was the fate of the majority of young men in the country. Though some were excited by the prospect, Alec certainly was not.

Isobel penned another short note to her in-laws, since she had not had a response to her first letter. Again she gave the address of her parents, as well as an indication of her immediate plans.

Later that day she told her parents about her grandmother's offer and the possibility of a job at the local shop in the coastal village. Like their daughter, they agreed that it made sense.

CHAPTER 3
A Safe Haven

Within a few days, Isobel and her young son were on the move once again. Da accompanied her to East Bay to help with her luggage. Jeannie and Ted were delighted.

As Alec had explained, the proprietor/manager of the shop was elderly and in poor health, but he was anxious only to hand over the running of his business to someone responsible and trustworthy, as well as competent: Isobel was very young for such a position. He expressed his concerns — though, in truth, no one else had come forward as a suitable candidate. He was willing to give her a trial.

Isobel herself had reservations. She had not worked for three years: she was out of touch. However, Grandma Jeannie had every confidence in her granddaughter. To her, she was a feisty young lass who'd not baulked at the idea of leaving her Aberdeen home to make a life more than 500 miles away amongst strangers: she was a survivor; she could do it! *Just do it*, Isobel murmured to herself, as she awoke on the first morning of a new life.

Mr Braithwaite, her boss, was a no-nonsense person, yet he was probably just as nervous as she was on that first day. He wanted his business to continue to thrive — he hoped young Alec had been right to recommend his sister. Such a shame that the lad, like so many others, had to join up: he hoped this dreadful war would be over soon. Much to the relief of both Isobel and Mr Braithwaite, the first week went well. Then tragedy struck…

Mid-way through the second week, Grandma Jeannie came rushing into the shop in a state of panic — her tear-stained face drained of all colour. One look at her sent Isobel into a state of alarm — whatever was wrong? Where was Chris? She tried to ask, but no words came. Mr Braithwaite, seeing that something was seriously amiss, guided the two women into the room at the back of the shop and returned to the counter to serve a customer who had entered just behind the distraught grandmother.

Although not what Isobel had feared, in no way was she prepared for the horrific revelation that finally crossed Jeannie's trembling lips.

"It's Stuart," she sobbed, "He's gone!"

Stunned, Isobel sat down at a table, adjacent to where her grandma was already seated, head in hands. For a few moments, a deep silence hung in the air, before Jeannie continued: "I've just received a telegram from your Ma. Stuart was taken from his pram this morning. The police have been informed. That's all I know."

"I must go to Ma," Isobel stated.

"No, no, I'll go. You have your job and Ted will watch Chris. If it's all right with Mr Braithwaite I'll try to get to a phone box in the morning and ring you here, at the shop, to let you know what's happening."

This did make some sense; although quite how she was going to concentrate on her work she was not sure. It was already mid-afternoon and, tomorrow being Wednesday, was a half-day. She would have to get through it.

By the time Isobel arrived home just before six o'clock, Jeannie was already on the bus on her way into Aberdeen. Chris was awake and ready for his evening feed, while Ted was trying to keep him amused. The evening passed in relative solitude. Despite Ted's attempts to engage in conversation, they were both wrapped in their own thoughts — hoping that Stuart would be found safe and well. How could this be happening?

Isobel could not sleep for thinking of the wee boy's face: his cheeky grin, his liquid blue eyes and the slight trace of light, sandy-coloured hair. Bleary-eyed, she attended to Chris in the morning, before struggling to the shop. Thank goodness she only had to be there until lunchtime! Mr Braithwaite was surprised to see her at all: if it wasn't for the promised phone call from Jeannie, he doubted she would have made the effort. Still, he was grateful for her presence, although wondered whether she would be able to manage: she didn't look good.

As the morning slipped by, Isobel became increasingly anxious for news. Every time the phone rang, she jumped. It was almost closing time before Mr Braithwaite called her to the phone to speak with her grandmother. Stuart had been taken from his pram around eleven o'clock the previous morning. Kitty had taken him with her to the shops and, on her return, left him in the pram by the front door, while she went inside to unload the groceries and prepare the lunch. Although almost the end of October, it was a bright, sunny day. It was normal for babies to be left outside in their prams to benefit from the fresh air, as long as they were well wrapped up. Within minutes of the discovery, neighbours were searching the area. Kitty had rushed to the local post office to make the emergency call to the police. So far, the child had not been found. The whole family was devastated. Kitty was in bed, too traumatised to move. Sandy was pacing the living room, unable to settle and Ernie, along with volunteers from the neighbourhood, was scouring the surrounding area, fearing the worst. By the time the pips went, ending the three-minute call, Mr Braithwaite was locking up having seen off the last of the customers. "You need to get off to your granddad and your baby," he said. "You can take the whole day off on Saturday if you want to go to see your ma and pa." —Isobel was grateful for this kind gesture but wondered how she was going to manage over the next two days, although being at work would provide a distraction.

Somehow the family got through the next few weeks, though it was a sad time for them all. The gloomy winter days and the thought of their other son, Alec, currently in army training in England and destined for goodness knows where, compounded their misery. Isobel managed to go through to Aberdeen to see her parents twice before

Hogmanay, but only for a few hours and, so far, without her own son — she would wait until her parents asked to see him, not wishing to add to their distress. However, as the new-year loomed, Jeannie suggested that Kitty, Sandy and Ernie come to East Bay for a couple of days. It was hardly going to be a celebration but, at least, it would get her daughter and family away from the city. The fresh sea air might do them some good.

When her parents arrived, Isobel was tentative — how hard was this going to be for them? Chris, now five months old, was propped up on cushions in his playpen, gurgling away happily. As Kitty approached, he stretched out his arms in anticipation. Isobel breathed a sigh of relief as her mother bent down and picked up the child in a loving embrace: the ice was broken — Kitty smiled.

As the war in Europe raged on, the family learned to live with their loss. Kitty went back to her job; Sandy struggled, working part-time at the grocer's, and Ernie excelled at school, gaining a place at the university to study medicine — far outstripping the expectations of an ordinary working-class family. Hopefully, it would all be worthwhile. Isobel, as Alec had predicted, ran the shop in East Bay proficiently. Mr Braithwaite was able to relax in his retirement, knowing that his business was in safe hands.

It wasn't until January that it occurred to Isobel that she had not received a response to the letters she had sent to her in-laws in September and October. However, apart from giving her parents' address, she had revealed nothing of their circumstances and only a vague reference to her own — that she intended to remain in Scotland for the duration of the war. Maybe her late husband's family did not regard her brief communications as worthy of a reply. Still, she had expected some acknowledgement. Perhaps she should write again; tell them that she was now settled in the coastal village, give her new address and let them know how their grandson was thriving. There was no point in disclosing anything of the tragedy that had befallen her family in Aberdeen: they would not be interested. So, out of a sense of duty rather than concern, Isobel penned another short missive. After all, they were Crispin's grandparents. Two weeks later the letter was returned with an official Royal Mail stamp and the words '*Not Known at This Address*'.

Somewhat stunned, but not overly upset, Isobel thought it a little strange that they had not made an effort to let her know they had moved. They had been obsessed with their grandson in the weeks following Nigel's death: what had changed?

The weeks turned to months and the months to years as the war dragged on. Crispin, or Chris as he was known, was a healthy, happy little boy. Although she was his great-grandmother, Jeannie was not yet sixty and, both she and her husband Ted, were fit and remarkably energetic. When Chris was small, they would fasten him into his pushchair and walk along the coastal path to the adjoining bay, then watch as he rummaged in the rock pools for all sorts of treasures — pebbles, shells and even tiny crabs. Chris loved the beach.

Several times a week Jeannie would take him to her parents' cottage, following the road round by the church, then onto the single-track road for the half-mile to their home. They adored their new great-great-grandson. Even as they approached their nineties they would listen to his chatter and, in turn, tell him tales of their own experiences as children way back in the 1860s and 70s.

CHAPTER 4
1945

It was a bright sunny day in the late spring of 1945. There was excitement in the air, even in this remote part of the Aberdeenshire coast, as people celebrated the end of the war in Europe. In the midst of all this, with dancing and laughter in the main street of the village, Chris tumbled down some stone steps, landing on his head and knocking himself out. He let out a short screech as he fell, then lay motionless on the path, blood seeping from the top of his head. In the furore it was a few moments before anyone noticed the young lad, though he was only a few feet from his mother's side. The atmosphere changed abruptly as Isobel shouted for help and a crowd gathered around the unconscious child. Ted raced towards the shop yelling to Mr Braithwaite, who was standing outside, to phone for an ambulance. No time was wasted in making the call but it was a while before the emergency vehicle arrived. Isobel went in the ambulance with her son.

The blood was a result of a graze to Chris's head as he hit the rough pavement: it was not as profuse as it looked. However, it was a few days before he regained consciousness. The damage to his brain was serious in the short term: the injury left him temporarily paralysed, unable to walk or talk. The whole family was distraught — Isobel was in shock. She was not allowed to remain overnight with her son, who was transferred to Aberdeen Royal Infirmary; but, for two weeks, she stayed with her parents so that she was able to visit each day. For the next three months she spent the weekends in Aberdeen, but returned to East Bay to work during the week, knowing that Chris was being well cared for in the hospital, with visitors every day. His uncle Ernie, currently training as a doctor, kept a watchful eye on his nephew, looking in on him regularly.

He had another visitor, an elderly gentleman — a stranger. He always came outside the normal visiting hours. The staff treated the man cordially, appearing to know who he was, welcoming him onto the ward. He never told the boy his name, nor did he bring him gifts, other than friendship. But they enjoyed each other's company.

Chris slowly learned to walk and talk again, supported by a devoted physiotherapist and encouraged by the hospital staff. They were charmed by the courage and determination of the delightful little boy. When he was finally discharged from the hospital, he was well on the way to a full recovery.

During this difficult time, there was another worry for the family as they waited to hear from Alec, who had been posted to India in the early years of the war. At first, letters were exchanged regularly, but Alec's letters stopped abruptly when his regiment was sent into Burma. In January 1944, having heard nothing for almost two years, Kitty received a letter from her son, from a transit camp in Deolali, India. He said he had been taken ill in Burma, brought back to India, and spent some time in hospital in Dacca, before being transferred to the camp. He had received more than fifty letters from home in one batch, some more than a year old, so it might take some time for him to answer them all! But, he emphasised, there was nothing to worry about; he was enjoying the camaraderie as he waited for another posting. At the time of writing, he had no idea where he would be sent.

On the big day of celebration, 8th May 1945, (subsequently known as VE Day) to commemorate the end of the war in Europe, the Japanese were still fighting, as the war in the far east continued to rage: *jungle* warfare, the most horrific of all, as the world would learn later. The family hoped and prayed that Alec had been spared a second 'tour' into a war zone. Throughout the next two months they became more anxious than ever until, in July, with no prior warning, he arrived at his parents' home in Aberdeen. He had a few weeks' leave before returning to barracks. He was finally demobbed in February 1946.

Alec was devastated at hearing the news of the disappearance of his young brother Stuart, taken from his pram. The family had not made any reference to this in their letters: they felt that their eldest son had enough to deal with. In any case, there was nothing he could have done about it. He was doubly shocked to hear of his nephew's recent accident. Anxious to see him, he set off to surprise the young lad on what was his fifth birthday.

Chris was delighted at the appearance of his uncle, who turned up in army uniform — he wanted to know everything about the war. Alec, however, did not relay the horrors of his time in Burma but told his young nephew many stories of life in India and the antics of his army pals. Chris listened, wide-eyed, at these amazing tales. He decided he would join the army when he grew up! Alec walked or cycled to the hospital every day to see Chris. When the boy went home to East Bay, his uncle went with him and stayed until his leave ended.

Now that the war was finally over, it was time for Isobel to make another decision. Chris had recovered from his accident, but the whole incident made her realise how dependent she was on her family. Nevertheless, they could not stay with Grandma Jeannie and Ted forever: she needed her own home with her son. Perhaps it was time to sell her London home and buy a house in Aberdeenshire, close to those who had given her such support in her time of need.

Since the return of her undelivered letter to Nigel's family in London in 1941, she had heard nothing from them. Perhaps she could try once again to make contact — though why should she? They had her address but they had not bothered to get in touch: why should she be concerned? Then it occurred to her — the third letter she had sent had been returned, but had they received the other two? Although she would prefer not to be involved with the family at all, Chris might feel differently when he grew up. She knew from her mother, Kitty, how hurt she had been when she discovered that Jeannie, whom she had always believed to be her sister, was actually her mother: she had felt betrayed. Added to the hurt, Jeannie had never revealed the identity of the father. Isobel's situation was not the same but, if she failed to make contact with her husband's family, Chris could see it as a betrayal. She must, at least, make an effort.

Isobel contacted her solicitor in London. Her house in Fulham had escaped damage in the Blitz and could now be sold. In the meantime, she could stay there for a week or two, visit Henrietta in Guildford, and find out what had happened to Nigel's parents. Maybe she should have tried to contact her sister-in-law when she had not had a response from her parents-in-law, but there was so much going on in her life at the time.

Grandma Jeannie and Ted were always willing to look after Chris, who, at five years old, having recovered from his accident, had just started school in the village. A new assistant had begun working at the shop six months previously and was proving very competent. She would take charge whilst Isobel was away.

CHAPTER 5
London 1945

The train journey south seemed to take forever. Isobel was tentative — what state would her house be in having lain empty for almost five years? A neighbour had offered to keep a watchful eye on the place for her, but that was such a long time ago. As for meeting with her in-laws, that would be another hurdle.

Before leaving the train, Isobel placed the house keys in her coat pocket. She raked out some change for a taxi to Fulham and summoned the assistance of a porter to take her luggage to the taxi rank.

As she stepped out of the car at her house, she was surprised to notice the lounge curtains twitch slightly. She struggled through the gate and up the path, placing her case on the ground while she retrieved the key from her pocket ready to open the door. She was shocked to hear the click of the latch drop just as she was about to turn the key — she was locked out! All went silent from within. She knocked on the door; she rang the bell; she even shouted through the letterbox — all to no avail. Her heart was beating fast as she retreated down the path and out through the front gate onto the deserted street. Now what? The neighbour with whom she had left a spare key might know what was going on. She crossed the road and walked along a few yards, hoping to find out. Much to her relief, Mrs Wright, who recognised the weary traveller straight away, opened the door almost immediately.

"Come in," she said, giving her, what appeared on the surface, a cordial welcome. "How nice to see you. Would you like some coffee or tea?"

"I would appreciate some tea," Isobel responded, quickly finding her London manners. Mrs Wright showed her through to the lounge, having indicated for her to leave her rather large suitcase in the hallway.

It was a few minutes before Mrs Wright returned with a tea tray complete with cups, saucers, plates and a three-tier cake rack filled with cakes and scones. All well and good, Isobel thought, but she just wanted a cup of tea and an explanation. It was already obvious that her 'generous' host had some explaining to do. Isobel waited patiently for Mrs Wright to speak.

"I'm sorry," she began. "I wanted to contact you, but I had no idea where you were. It has been a very difficult time and, well, the truth is…"

The preamble was painful. It was as if the woman was stalling, playing for time. Isobel was beginning to feel cross. Exactly what *was* the truth? It was blatantly obvious that strangers now occupied her home — who were they? It was equally obvious that Mrs Wright knew all about it. Since Isobel's key still fitted the lock, her house had not been broken in to. With gritted teeth, she listened to more and more 'ums' and 'ers' before eventually learning a little about the 'truth'.

Mrs Wright's nephew, his wife, and their two children had lost their home in the Blitz. Fortunately, they had been sheltering in a Tube station at the time, otherwise they would all have been killed: their house had received a direct hit. The family had nowhere to go so, having the key to Isobel's property, this 'benevolent' aunt had suggested they take up residence. After all, the place was vacant and they were homeless. This happened more than four years ago — they had been there ever since.

At first, Isobel sat there open-mouthed, in disbelief. Thankfully, she had the presence of mind to excuse herself to use the 'convenience' thus suppressing the burst of outrage she felt rising from within. Giving herself sufficient time to calm down, she returned in a steadier frame of mind. It was wartime, she reasoned; the family had been made destitute. What would she have done? "I need somewhere to stay tonight," Isobel voiced, rather more abruptly than she had intended.

"You are very welcome to stay here," Mrs Wright responded. "I have a spare room. I am so sorry. If only I had been able to contact you, I'm sure we could have worked something out." Being practical and having little option, Isobel accepted the invitation of a bed for the night, though she almost choked at the idea of thanking the woman.

Isobel wasn't quite sure how to react to this individual. What would the family have done if she had not entrusted her house keys to this neighbour? Had they thought about the future? What were their plans? The war had ended several months ago — surely it must have occurred to them that they could not stay in her house indefinitely. Come to think of it, was this arrangement (or rather, the lack of it) legal? Were they paying rates? Isobel was fairly sure of the answers to these questions, but she intended to ask anyway. Mrs Wright suggested Isobel might like to 'freshen up' after her long journey. She invited her to join the family for dinner at half-past seven. It was now six o'clock. After showing Isobel to the guest room on the first floor, Mrs Wright left her. She said she would be downstairs in the kitchen preparing the meal if she needed anything.

Isobel slumped down in an armchair in the corner of the room to contemplate this disturbing turn of events. She was cross with herself for feeling annoyed that her neighbour had offered the house to a family in their time of need — wasn't that a good thing to do? But something did not seem quite right. Why had they stayed there for so long? Why were they still there?

A few minutes before mealtime, Isobel made her way back to the lounge. Mr Wright was sitting by the window reading a newspaper. He rose from his chair as she entered, greeting her with a smile. He explained that they were waiting for their son, who was due home at any moment. "Please, sit down," he said. "Ian won't be long."

For what seemed to Isobel a very long 'few' minutes, Mr Wright attempted to engage her in polite conversation, whilst avoiding the issue of the unauthorised occupancy of her home. It was with some relief that the sound of voices, emanating from the kitchen, indicated the arrival of Ian, and the imminent announcement that dinner would be served. Perhaps it was simply the awkwardness of the situation, but Isobel found the formality exhibited by this household a strain. It was far removed from the relaxed atmosphere in the homes of her parents and her grandparents in North East Scotland.

Isobel did not recall having met Ian when she had lived in Fulham. He was tall with short dark hair, brown eyes and a serious look, which Isobel found rather intimidating. He must be about her age. Apart from Mrs Wright, who invited Isobel to help herself to the vegetables, no one spoke as they sat down at the dining table — the only sound was the clanking of the dishes and the clinking of the glasses. Ian appeared to be weighing things up. Finally, he broke the silence, forcing his parents to disclose the true facts behind this awkward predicament.

"So, you're the owner of the house across the road," he declared, "This must have come as quite a shock! Have my parents explained the extent of their involvement in this fiasco?"

Isobel did not quite know which way to look, let alone what to say. "Er, not exactly," she eventually managed, half under her breath.

"Mmm," Ian responded, turning to his mother and father, "Well, perhaps now is as good a time as any to begin."

Although Mrs Wright's outline of the story of the homeless family was true, the details, now revealed in the presence of their son, were much more damning. It was obvious that their actions did not have his approval. Ian, it transpired, had graduated in Law. Whilst he was away from home, serving as an officer in the army during the war, the distraught relatives, his mother's nephew and his family, had begged the Wright's to take them in, knowing that they had plenty of space in their house to accommodate them. Mrs Wright, in collusion with her husband, neither of whom wanted their peace to be destroyed, offered the homeless family 'the house across the road.' Furthermore, they had come to 'an arrangement', which suited both parties. The young family were led to believe that their aunt and uncle were acting as letting agents for the property. They understood that the money they were paying to her covered the rent and the rates when, in reality, they were squatters.

Isobel was aghast at this intrigue. She had trusted her neighbour to keep an eye on her house, never thinking of such a consequence. She wished now that she had taken a little more time to think things through before she had left her home. Had she placed the property in the hands of her solicitor, he may have been able to let it out on her behalf. However, it was a difficult time: she had needed to depart in hurry. Thank goodness for Ian, otherwise she may never have been made aware of the truth. But what was she to do now? She looked, pleadingly, at this young man for some suggestion as to a way forward. He, in turn, is waiting for his mother to come up with a solution to the problem. Clearly, she had been the instigator, albeit with the support of her husband.

Before any more was said, Isobel announced that she had written to her solicitor before leaving Aberdeen. A meeting with him had been arranged for the following morning.

Having only recently taken up a position as a junior partner with a firm of solicitors in the city, Ian was anxious to preserve his reputation. He did not want the misdemeanours of his parents to affect his future standing in the profession. In his opinion, covering up for them in the presence of the rightful owner had not been an option. It could potentially be much more damaging than exposing the facts. However, he wanted the mess cleared up without a fuss; without the heavy-handed involvement of the law.

"Sort it!" he demanded, glaring at a red-faced Mrs Wright, who had the grace to apologise to her guest and victim of her criminal activity.

Ian added, "When we have finished our meal, I wish to have a word in private with Isobel."

For the next half-hour, Ian attempted to help Isobel feel more comfortable, encouraging general conversation about her life in Scotland. He then led her through to the lounge where they could speak, confidentially, about the best way to tackle the problem of the illegal occupancy of her property.

Though maintaining a serious look, Ian appeared a little more relaxed. He began by apologising for his forthright approach at the dinner table which, he admitted, must have caused her considerable distress. However, under the circumstances, he felt he had no option. It was obvious that he was angry with his parents, but how much this stemmed from sympathy for Isobel, and how much a bid to save his own name, was debatable. Whatever the case, Isobel did not intend to allow her fate to be determined by *any* member of this family, no matter how much they appeared to be on her side.

"I will see my solicitor in the morning, as planned, and seek an estate agent to place the property on the market. That was the initial purpose of my visit."

This blunt approach appeared to have the desired effect. For the first time, a very faint grin crossed Ian's lips, conveying a less harsh side to his character.

"In the meantime," she continued, "I have nowhere to stay."

"I'm sure you could stay here," Ian responded.

"No," came a further blunt attack from Isobel. "After this evening, I would be very uncomfortable with that."

Ian could appreciate her point. He realised that having recovered from the initial shock of discovering that her house had been 'commandeered', she was not a person to be crossed. They continued by discussing the practicalities of the next few days. Ian offered to make enquiries about bed and breakfast accommodation for her. He, or rather his parents, would cover her expenses for the duration of her stay. He suggested that they meet for a late lunch in London the following day so that he could give her an update on any progress made. He agreed that her house should be placed on the market as soon as possible, but requested that she delay a visit to the property by the estate agent until his cousin vacated it. 'The middle of next week' was all the leeway that Isobel was prepared to give. She explained that she had other business to attend to. She did not want to extend her stay in the capital beyond a fortnight.

Isobel was tired. She excused herself and retired to the solitude of her room. Meanwhile, Ian would discuss with his mother the eviction of her nephew and his family from 'the house across the road'. So far, they were unaware of the return of the rightful owner although, after Isobel's attempted entry into what they regarded as their home, they must have realised that trouble was brewing.

Weary as she was, Isobel was not oblivious to the raised voices coming from the room below. *I just want to be away from here*, she thought.

The next day, with a mixture of resentment and relief, she escaped from the home of the shamed couple. As she made her way to the Tube station, she passed her house, resisting the temptation to hammer on the door and demand entry. Once in the city centre, she headed for the left luggage desk at the railway station. She didn't want to trail around London burdened with a heavy suitcase.

The Tube was alien to Isobel, but she realised that it was by far the most convenient way of getting around the city.

Her first stop, before meeting with her solicitor, was a café in the station. She had skipped breakfast with the Wrights, declining her host's offer, in her haste to get away. Now she could sit down and relax with a cup of tea and some toast. She needed to consider exactly how to approach this consultation without giving too much away, neither admitting nor denying that the property was currently occupied. Ian had advised that it would be much better if his cousin were to move out of the house without a fuss — that way no one else need be involved: he hoped they would agree. The alternative, he explained, could result in a long, drawn-out battle to have the family evicted. However, suppose they decided to 'sit it out'. Where did that leave her? She was glad that she had given Ian an ultimatum. Although she wanted to trust this man, she could not be certain of his motives.

The solicitor sat behind a desk in a dimly lit office. Files and papers were strewn across every surface, with cardboard boxes stacked on the floor. How on earth anyone could function amid this chaos was beyond Isobel. Nevertheless, he greeted her with kindness and her file was, miraculously, on top of a pile on his desk. Isobel had little recollection of her previous encounter with this elderly gentleman. On that one occasion, she had been too distressed to take notice of his appearance or his surroundings. All further communications had been by letter.

The ensuing discussion went rather better than Isobel could have anticipated. She explained that she was now settled in Scotland. She was intent on purchasing a home of her own, thus requiring that the London property be sold as soon as possible. He asked if she had considered renting it out to provide a steady income. If so, he could direct her to a reputable agent to act on her behalf. Isobel shuddered! "No," she confirmed, emphatically. "My life is now in the north." She did not add that her experience in the south had brought her nothing but trouble and heartache.

"I quite understand," he responded sympathetically, "You've been through a lot. Aberdeen is your home. It's just that selling a house is a big decision — I like to be sure my clients are aware of the options. Please forgive me."

Isobel appreciated the concern of this fatherly figure: his gentle tone was reassuring.

"Well," he continued, "selling houses is not my remit, at least not the actual sales part. I can direct you to a reputable estate agent unless, of course, you already have one in mind?"

"No, no," Isobel assured him. "I would be most grateful for your recommendation."

Isobel came away from the solicitor's feeling a good deal better. She had avoided any awkward questions, although she felt a little guilty that she had not revealed the potential problems that she, and he, might have to face. Still, with luck, that situation would not arise.

Her next call was to the estate agent that her solicitor had suggested. It was close by, so she was able to walk the short distance. *Deep breath!* she thought, as she entered the building — *this could be tricky.* It was Thursday. She wanted them to know that she was anxious for a quick sale, yet she needed to put off a visit until next Wednesday. *Did that make sense?* With fingers crossed, she went up to the young woman at the desk.

"Can I help you," she asked, peering at her client over the top of a pair of horn rimmed spectacles, which gave her an officious appearance.

"I have a house in the Fulham area that I wish to place on the property market," came Isobel's response, in an attempt to match the self-important tone of the receptionist.

"Of course, I will take the details and arrange for my colleague to visit. I'm afraid we are rather busy at the moment, so he will not manage to come out until the middle of next week."

"That's perfect," Isobel stated, with some relief.

The particulars were taken and an appointment made for a visit the following Wednesday morning at ten o'clock. If the family who had taken over her house agreed to leave quietly, they would surely be away by then? Where they would go was of no concern to her: that was their problem.

The morning's work concluded, Isobel had no need to rush before meeting with Ian for lunch. She hoped that his morning had been equally successful. Since it was a bright, sunny day she walked back to the main station, enjoying the opportunity for a little exercise. As she strolled across to the agreed venue for lunch, she heard a clock strike two. Ian was standing by the entrance of the café. He greeted her with the mere hint of a smile before opening the door, indicating to her to pass through ahead of him. Although spacious with a rather formal atmosphere, it did not pass as a restaurant. However, it was pleasant enough.

Ian began by saying he had booked her into a hotel close to the station, with instructions that the bill be forwarded to him. It was within easy access, by Tube, to anywhere in London. He had not felt comfortable about leaving her in a bed and breakfast, without recommendation.

"Where is your luggage?" he queried.

"It's in the Left Luggage department at the station," she replied.

After ordering lunch, Ian proceeded to speak about the further confrontation he'd had with his parents after she had retired for the night.

"I left them in no doubt about the consequences should they fail to ensure that your property is vacated this weekend. Mother argued that it was just not possible for her nephew to find alternative accommodation at such short notice.

'In that case,' I told them, 'I will move out. That will allow more than enough room for them to stay here until they find a home of their own. It is exactly what should have happened a long time ago.'"

"And what will you do?" Isobel asked.

"I don't know, but I'll think of something," he quipped. "I wasn't intending to be there for much longer anyway. But after this, I *have* to get away — I really am disgusted with the pair of them."

"But they're your parents!" Isobel interjected, concerned that, in his haste to support her, he was damaging his relationship with them.

"I'm adopted," he stated; an element of disdain in his voice.

He quickly changed the subject, asking Isobel about the meetings with her solicitor and the estate agent. He seemed pleased — confident that she had made the right decision. It would add fuel to any further altercation with his parents. If they faltered at all in their dealings with 'the nephew', he would personally challenge his cousin.

Isobel was beginning to have a little more confidence in this man than when they had first met less than twenty-four hours earlier. He asked how she intended to spend the next few days. His question jolted her out of her current dilemma, to the reality of what she had anticipated would be the greater of the two challenges she faced in coming south. But now was not the time to enter into any details, so she simply said she intended to visit her late husband's family. He realised, by her manner, that there must be more to this than she was prepared to convey: he chose not to pry.

On parting, Ian suggested they meet in the foyer of her hotel at six o'clock on Sunday evening when, no doubt, there would be plenty to discuss. He didn't know where he would be staying but, if all else failed, he might have to book into the same hotel for a few days!

Isobel went immediately to collect her case from the railway station and, from there, to check into the hotel. Although old, it was clean and well maintained, with breakfast included. It was a place where she could be comfortable. She had to detach herself from the trauma of recent events and focus on her next obligation — to find the family she didn't want to find. It was what she must do for the sake of her son. Sooner or later he would ask questions about his father. She regarded it as her duty not to lose contact with her late husband's family.

The following morning, as soon as she had finished breakfast, Isobel set off to the railway station to catch a train to Guildford. Being a little unsure of her bearings, she confirmed directions at the information desk. As she recalled, Henrietta's address was a good fifteen-minute walk from the station. She decided the exercise would help her to relax before facing her sister-in-law for the first time in five years.

Two youngsters, probably in their early teens, were leaving by the front gate as Isobel drew near to the house. She smiled as they passed. Walking up the garden path towards the large semi-detached building, her stomach churned. In the past Henrietta had never welcomed her with open arms: she could not imagine that things would be any different now. Filled with a sense of dread, she pressed the doorbell and waited — and waited. Eventually, she heard the sound of heavy footsteps followed by the turning of a key. Clearly, it was not Henrietta. It must be her husband, Raymond. But it was not Raymond. It was a tall, heavily built man, not unlike Raymond in stature, though there the similarity ended. However, there was something vaguely familiar about this figure. Had she seen him somewhere before?

"I'm Isobel Leadbetter. I'm looking for Henrietta…" she stopped abruptly. She could not recall the surname of her sister-in-law. Had she even known it? "Henrietta and Raymond," she continued, trying not to sound foolish. "This is the last address I have for them."

"I'm afraid you're out of luck. We've been here for almost five years. I've no idea where the previous occupants went. We never met them."

"Oh-oh, I see. They didn't leave a forwarding address?" she pleaded.

"No, they left in a hurry. I'm sorry, I can't help you," he confirmed, already closing the door before she had a chance to apologise for troubling him. She turned around and headed for the street. A cold chill passed through her body as she secured the sneck on the garden gate. For the second time in two days, she noticed the surreptitious twitch of curtains and felt the eyes of strangers boring into her soul. Quickening her gait, she passed the front of the house, walking in the direction of the town centre. Something was seriously wrong!

In the main street, she found a tearoom where she took refuge to consider her next move. Nigel's parents lived in Farnham, or at least that was where they used to live. Since her last letter to that address had been returned, she decided there would be little hope of finding them there. However, she had to try. Maybe they had departed in less of a hurry than their daughter!

She finished her tea, paid the bill and made her way back to the station. She had never been to Farnham before, so hoped someone would be able to direct her to the address where she might discover her parents-in-law. Finding the address was not a problem — finding her in-laws was another matter. They were not there and, once again, the current residents were unable to help, although this time Isobel sensed that the gentleman who answered the door was sincere. They had bought the house just three months ago, but not from the Leadbetters who, he believed, had vacated the property several years earlier. He appeared genuinely sorry that he was unable to help.

Isobel returned to her hotel in the centre of London, disconcerted with her efforts. Surely the whole family could not disappear? After the fuss they had made of Crispin when he was born, why were they no longer concerned for him? He was their only link with their deceased son — it made no sense. Well, she'd done her best, considering she never really wanted to see them again. But Isobel didn't like unsolved mysteries. The disappearance of her baby brother shortly after she had returned to Aberdeen unsettled her: the mystery surrounding his kidnap adding to the loss. And what about her grandfather, Kitty's father? Who was he? Where was he? And now, she wondered, where were Nigel's relatives? She sat in an armchair by the window, gazing out on the street below — pondering. Would any of these puzzles ever be solved?

Suddenly, her reverie was interrupted — someone was tapping on the bedroom door. She must have dozed off, for the noise startled her — seeming, at first, to come from far away. It was a moment or two before she shook herself awake, rose and crossed the floor to answer. A young lad stood a yard or so back from the threshold: he announced that there was a gentleman in the foyer asking to speak with her. "Tell him I will be down in a few minutes," she responded, without thinking to ask for the name. She must still be half asleep she mused — *how silly of me*! Well, only one person knew where she was, so it didn't take much figuring out. She brushed her hair, freshened her lipstick and made her way down the stairs. Sure enough, Ian was standing close to the reception desk — the trace of a grin crossed his face as he met her gaze. There was even the hint of a twinkle in his dark brown eyes.

"Done," he said. "They're on their way."

"Goodness, that was quick!" Isobel exclaimed. "How did you manage…?"

"Let's go for a cup of tea," he said. "I'll tell you all about it."

They made their way to the nearest tearoom, just around the corner from the hotel. "Mother was dithering," he began. "When I arrived home from the office yesterday, she had made no attempt to confront the family, admitting that she couldn't face them. So, I summoned the support of friend — the local Bobby — and we tackled the problem head-on. I think my cousin and his wife had an inkling that something was amiss when they saw you approach the house with your luggage, then cross the road to our house. I was apologetic but told them the truth — that my mother had allowed them to stay in the property without the permission of the legal owner, who had now returned: they must vacate the premises immediately if they wished to avoid prosecution.

They invited us in as, unsurprisingly, they were upset and wanted further clarification of their position. They insisted that they had accepted my mother's offer of your house in good faith, assuming everything was above board. For more than four years they had given her money to cover the rent and rates, on the understanding that she was acting as an agent. I responded with raised eyebrows… they appeared to get the message! I suspect they were suspicious from the start, but it suited them to accept my mother's word. Presumably, they were paying less than the cost of an official rental, whilst over the years my mother has, no doubt, accumulated a nice little nest egg from the deal."

Isobel was astonished at the no-nonsense approach Ian had adopted towards the problem. Nevertheless, she remained sceptical of these illegal tenants. "Will they move out without making a fuss?" she questioned.

"Oh, they'll go all right. Jeremy, my policeman friend, emphasised the seriousness of the situation: if he were to return to the property it would be in uniform, in an official capacity. To help them on their way, I gave them a key to my parents' home where, I said, they could stay until they found alternative accommodation."

"And what about you?" Isobel asked.

"I have arranged to move in with a friend for a few weeks until I find a place of my own. He has a car and has offered to help me move from my parents' home. I'm quite relieved to be going. I'll make sure I retrieve the key to your house from my cousin. If it's all right with you, I can try to arrange for cleaners to go into the house on Monday or Tuesday. It's short notice, I know, but I'll do the best I can. Also, might I suggest that you stay at your house on Tuesday evening to oversee the visit from the estate agent on Wednesday?"

"I appreciate all of your help," Isobel replied. "It would be reassuring to feel that the house really is mine. It is where I had expected to be staying when I arrived on Wednesday."

"Well, I have a busy weekend ahead," he said. "Perhaps we can meet as planned at six o'clock on Sunday evening. If you're agreeable, I will take you out for an evening meal? Hopefully, your house will be vacated by then, so we will have something to celebrate."

Isobel accepted Ian's invitation. She was greatly relieved at the news of the 'eviction': at least that was one problem solved. Returning to her hotel room, she felt extraordinarily tired. Her initial thought was to collapse into bed and sleep, but it was not yet 6:30. She decided to make an effort, freshen up and go down to the hotel restaurant for a meal and maybe even a glass of wine. It had been a long day.

The weekend loomed ahead. Isobel had not anticipated having time to spare but, for the next two days, there was nothing she could do except look forward to meeting Ian on Sunday evening. Not until that moment had it occurred to her that she actually wanted to spend time with this man. *Don't be silly,* she told herself, dismissing the idea. She turned her attention to making the most of the next few days in Britain's capital: there was plenty to see and do.

On Saturday evening she wrote a letter to Grandma Jeannie, letting her know that, despite a few hiccups, she had made arrangements for the sale of her house. She omitted all reference to finding the place occupied when she had arrived — that would wait until she returned home. She was a little more specific about the unsuccessful search for her in-laws; said she hoped to travel home next weekend as planned, and sent lots of hugs and kisses to her son, along with a rough drawing of a steam train. Chris had been so excited about 'Mummy going to London on a train'. It was all he talked about during the week before she left.

Ian was waiting in the foyer at six o'clock on Sunday evening. He'd had a busy two days: moving out of his parents' home, assisting in the removal of his cousin from the 'house across the road' and involving the help of his friend to clear up after they had left. He recouped all keys to the property, leaving nothing to chance. Also, he had managed to engage a team of professionals to give the place a thorough clean: they were coming on Monday morning. He was relieved at how smoothly things had worked out.

As Isobel walked towards him, he noticed how composed she looked. He greeted her with a smile: he too was more relaxed. They made their way to a nearby restaurant where he had booked a table for two. As they were shown to their seats it was apparent that the pressure of recent days had lifted. Relieved of their problems, they took advantage of this opportunity to get to know one another a little better...

Ian had graduated from the University of London and trained as a lawyer, gaining a little experience before war broke out. He joined the army as an officer, spending some time in France, where he was shot in his left shoulder. It had rendered him incapacitated for a while, but had healed well. As a result, he had returned to the UK to take up responsibility for recruitment. He reckoned that the injury probably saved him from a much worse fate.

Isobel told him that her husband too had been an officer in the army. He had joined before the war, intending to spend a few years in the forces before joining his father's accountancy firm. Sadly, he had not been so lucky, losing his life around the time of the birth of their only child. The house in Fulham was meant to be their family home but, following his death, she had decided to return to her native Scotland. She had made this journey south to resolve two issues: selling the house and finding her late husband's family, who had not answered her correspondence. So far, she had not traced them.

Ian listened intently to the traumas Isobel had faced in her life. He concluded that his life had been much less stressful, despite his time in the army, and having to contend with his deceitful adoptive parents.

The evening passed quickly. They were both reluctant to part company but, inevitably, the time came when they must say good-bye. Ian asked Isobel when she intended to travel back to Scotland. She replied that her original intention had been to return next weekend but, with the house sale in the hands of the estate agent, she could go home sooner. She was not keen to spend any more time than was absolutely necessary in her old home — not with the Wrights living opposite. Ian understood. He offered to extend her hotel booking so that she could return after the estate agent visited her property, and remain for the rest of her stay in London. He expressed his wish to meet her again before her departure, but

Isobel was not sure. Was it a good idea to become involved with this man when it would make their inevitable separation all the harder? The answer was definitely not but, as is so often the case, the heart is stronger than the head — she gave in to her emotions. They agreed to meet again after he finished work on Wednesday.

On Monday morning Isobel decided to pay an impromptu visit to her solicitor. She would let him know that she had consulted the estate agent, alert him of their impending visit to her property and of her intention to travel north at the end of the week; but that was not all...

As she entered the building, she heard voices coming from his office. She waited for several minutes after his clients had gone before approaching his room and tapping gently on the door.

"Come, come in," he called. "Ah, Mrs Leadbetter, what can I do for you?"

She updated him on recent developments as she had planned to do — from now on they would have to conduct all further business by letter. As she turned to leave, she asked casually: "By the way, do you still act for my sister-in-law and her husband — Henrietta and Raymond?"

"Ah, now —- that would be the Dobson's." He looked up at her for confirmation.

"Yes," she said, with more confidence than she felt.

"Now then, if my memory serves me correctly, they moved to Oxford at the beginning of the war — he's a doctor, I believe."

"That's right," Isobel responded.

"M-m-m," the solicitor continued, "funny business! I thought they might ask me to deal with the sale of their property in Guildford but they mentioned something about an exchange with a friend or a relative — I'm not sure. In any case, they no longer required my services: they would be appointing a local firm to act on their behalf in the future. I always got on very well with Raymond. Have you seen them since you arrived?"

"No, no. I've been quite busy sorting out my house. I've not had time to get that far."

As she left the office Isobel considered what her solicitor had said. *I knew there was something familiar about that man in Guildford,* she thought: *he was at our wedding.*

Her question had resulted in more information than she had expected, considering that she was not sure they had had the same solicitor in the first place. She now had a name and a possible location, although the family could have moved again. Realistically, however, she was not much closer to finding her relatives. What she had gained from this small piece of research was the knowledge that they did not *want* to be found. Her trip to Guildford, in the light of the solicitor's comments, proved that. She was almost sure that the man who came to the door was Raymond's brother. She had given her name, so he knew perfectly well who she was. He had turned her away abruptly. A trip to Oxford at this stage would be futile — she would need to be sure of the facts: she would need an address. As for the Leadbetters — her parents-in-law — where on earth were they? She remained mystified as to why none of them wanted to see Nigel's son.

Isobel waited until Tuesday afternoon before making her way to her house in Fulham. For her own peace of mind, she needed to see the place and, of course, she had to be present to meet with the estate agent the following morning. It was with mixed feelings that, for the second time in less than a week, she approached the home she had once shared with her beloved Nigel. This time there was no twitching of curtains. Her key turned easily in the lock. She was greeted in the entrance hall by the distinct smell of polish. Exploring the house brought tears to her eyes. Overwhelmed by memories of her short marriage, she allowed herself ten minutes to ponder over the past, before making a thorough check of the property. On opening a large package that had been left in the lounge she was surprised to discover freshly laundered bedding and towels: items she had left when she departed five years before. It seemed that Ian had thought of everything. A few essentials had been placed on the dresser in the kitchen; sufficient for an evening meal and breakfast in the morning.

Satisfied that her old home was quite respectable for the estate agent's visit the next day, she went out for a walk. On her return, she had tea and settled down for the evening with a book.

She awoke early on Wednesday morning, leaving plenty of time to tidy up after breakfast before the agent arrived. Mr Smith, a smartly dressed man in his mid-fifties, arrived on schedule. He had a quick look over the whole building, inside and out, prior to assessing each room individually, taking measurements and making notes. When he had finished, he accepted Isobel's offer of a cup of tea, allowing time to discuss the details of the sale's procedure: she gave him the spare key that the cleaners had posted through the letterbox. The agent was confident that a buyer would be found before too long.

It was with a sense of relief, yet some sadness, that Isobel turned away from her house in Fulham for the last time, returning to her hotel in the city centre.

The evening with Ian passed pleasantly — maybe too pleasantly. Isobel was drawn to this man: a stranger until a week ago. Ian's manner, even his looks, were in stark contrast to the son who had tackled his parents so frankly on her behalf. He smiled now. His features had softened; he spoke in gentle, sincere tones. He wanted to keep in touch — to see her again. Isobel, if she were to admit it, felt the same, but she was cautious. "My life is in Aberdeenshire with my family and my son," she stressed, eyes diverted so that he could not detect her true feelings. But she could not hide them from him. He sensed her emotions; he pleaded for an answer.

They strolled back to her hotel, where they stood in the entrance hall, both reluctant to part. "At least give me your address so that I can write to you?" he begged whilst, at the same time taking a sheet of headed notepaper from the inside pocket of his jacket. "This is my office address where you can always get in touch. I can let you have my new address as soon as I'm settled if you give me yours...." He tailed off, as he produced a small address book and a pen from the same inside pocket. Isobel no longer had the will to resist. He kissed her lightly on the forehead before turning towards the busy street. He didn't look back. Isobel stood for several minutes, gazing in the direction he had taken, before turning into the hotel. *What a week!* she thought, as she began packing her case in preparation for her long journey home.

CHAPTER 6
October 1940

As the couple alighted from the train at Aberdeen railway station, they followed the crowds along the platform, walked passed the hissing steam engine, and out of the station by the main exit. They had no difficulty locating the Station Hotel where they booked under the name of MacFee for two nights, with an option to extend their stay if necessary. They were both feeling grubby from the long journey in the cramped third-class compartment. By choice they would have opted for first-class but, on this particular occasion, it was essential to remain as inconspicuous as possible. The hotel was a necessity: their choice, being next to the station, perhaps more likely to have a higher turnover of clientele than others. In a further bid not to draw attention to themselves, they found a restaurant away from the hotel for their evening meal.

The next morning the pair set off early — they intended to use the day to become familiar with the area between the city centre and a housing estate to the north that would be their focus. 'Mr MacFee' donned a cap, to him an unfamiliar accessory. His wife wore a headscarf, dressing down her old grey woollen coat — she felt shabby, although she wasn't sure how much of a disguise it represented. Still, neither of them was likely to be recognised in this godforsaken outpost. 'Mrs MacFee' carried a holdall. It contained a few items they might need before they returned to the hotel, although neither imagined the job would be done that day: this was an opportunity to assess the surroundings and to snoop. Blending with the locals was what was important, especially in the estate to which they were headed: not the kind of lucrative area from which they hailed.

A half-mile from the station, unsure of their bearings, they asked directions. They had great difficulty understanding what the man said. Just as they were about to give up, he pointed towards a bus stop, shouting out three numbers and saying any one of them would do. With all the stopping points, the bus took about a quarter of an hour: they made a careful mental note of the route, hoping they would find their way back on foot if necessary. The bus came to a halt in a square surrounded by shops. All of the remaining passengers alighted, so the two strangers followed suit. "Now which way?" they uttered simultaneously, looking at one another as if their spouse had the answer. Neither thought it a good idea to ask. "We'll wander around for a while: it can't be too far away," the husband suggested. With the street and the house number firmly etched on their minds, they walked for the next fifteen minutes trying to look purposeful. Finally, they found the road they were looking for.

The houses were all semi-detached council properties. Each had a small front garden with a path leading to a door. Outside one or two of these doors, there was a pram: not an unusual sight in the 1940s. As long as babies were well wrapped up it was considered beneficial for them to be outside, especially when the weather was bright and sunny as it was today. As they progressed along the street, a woman pushing a pram turned into a garden about a hundred yards ahead. The couple slowed their pace and watched as the mother lifted a shopping bag from the top of the pram, bent over as if tucking up her baby and entered the house, closing the door behind her. Nearing the house, to their surprise, the couple saw that it was the number they were looking for. At the gate, the pair turned to face each other, nodded, opened the gate and walked the few yards up the path. While her husband appeared to knock on the door, his wife carefully lifted the infant out of the pram and popped him into the holdall. The couple walked back down the path, closing the gate behind them, and casually strolled to the far end of the street where they turned right towards the city. Neither spoke until they were well away from the estate. The baby, soothed by the swaying of the bag, remained fast asleep.

'Mr MacFee' went into the Station Hotel alone. He collected the case from their room and proceeded to the reception desk to check out. He claimed that a friend had offered to accommodate them that night but said he was willing to pay for the two nights since it was now after the normal check out time. The receptionist was very pleasant: she only charged for the one night and said she hoped to see them again sometime. Emerging from the hotel he made his way to the ticket office at the station where his wife had already purchased tickets to Edinburgh — the train was due to leave in twenty minutes — at mid-day.

As they settled into an empty compartment in a third-class coach, they grinned at each other. So far, the day had exceeded all expectations. Their original plan to kidnap the young child was far more complex than the reality of the operation. They could scarcely believe their luck at seeing the pram left out at the front of the house just as they were approaching. But they had been cautious, avoiding the temptation to flee from the estate at speed: it worked. Nobody had noticed anything unusual about the shabbily dressed couple, who refrained from quickening their pace until they had crossed Anderson Drive, the city's ring road, and were well on their way to the centre of the town.

....

About half an hour after leaving her baby son in his pram, while she put away the messages and set about that morning's chores, Kitty went out to check on him. By the time she had raised the alarm, informed the police and given a statement, the abductors were well on their way to Edinburgh with Crispin Nigel Leadbetter by their side... or so they thought!

The train was pulling out of Dundee before the little hostage awoke. 'Mrs MacFee' exited the compartment and made her way to the toilet, where she extricated the baby's bottle that she had tucked away between her ample breasts that morning to keep warm in case it was needed: it was filled to the brim. Back in her seat, she lifted the baby from the holdall — he was now making his presence known. Two middle-aged women, who had boarded the train at Arbroath, were looking on with concern. Maria Dobson, the real name of the person behind the façade, knew exactly how to handle a baby: she had two young children of her own. Holding the little hostage close to her, she carefully eased the teat into his mouth. Her initial concern was soon alleviated as she realised the child was familiar with the bottle. However, Maria was struck with another uneasy feeling. Now that she had her first good look at the babe in her arms, he did not appear quite as Henrietta had described. "He's the image of his father," she had said, referring to his blue eyes and his blonde hair. This youngster did have blue eyes, although they were a pale liquid blue, not the deep blue that her sister-in-law seemed to remember. When she removed the knitted bonnet with the wide peak that had covered much of his face, as well as his head, a hint of sandy coloured hair was beginning to appear over the otherwise bald expanse of his scalp. Maria's stomach churned as she turned to look at her husband. She dared not speak her thoughts; not with other passengers seated opposite who seemed to be focussing all of their attention on the little mite. Frederick Dobson, the erstwhile Mr MacFee, looked questioningly at his wife, with a slight shrug of his shoulders. Either he did not notice the discrepancies or he regarded them as insignificant. When the couple discussed the issue later in the day he commented, quite correctly, that close relatives often read more into a new baby's features than is credible, and the said features can change dramatically over the first few weeks. Maria acknowledged his comments — but the eyes still troubled her.

When they arrived in Edinburgh, the couple went straight to the information desk to enquire about hotel accommodation for the night, preferably within walking distance. Continuing to London that day would have meant arriving very late at night — not a wise move given the relentless bombing of the city by the Germans and the blackout restrictions. However, they did need to buy train tickets to travel to London the next day. As a precaution, in the light of their criminal activity, they had not purchased London tickets in Aberdeen.

The overnight stop gave them the chance to attend to *Crispin's* current needs, as well as prepare bottles for the next day. Besides, it provided an opportunity to relax after the exploits of the day.

Despite *Crispin* waking twice during the night, the couple felt refreshed the next morning, ready to face the remainder of the journey south. When they finally arrived in London, they took a taxi to Guildford, to the home of Raymond and Henrietta — Frederick's brother and sister-in-law. Part of the deal surrounding the kidnapping was the agreement to exchange properties. Frederick and Maria would take up residence in this large house in Guildford, whilst Raymond and Henrietta would move into his brother's house in Oxford. In the meantime, the Leadbetters were about to move from their home in Farnham to a village in the Oxfordshire area. Stuart Anderson was thus destined to be raised as Crispin Nigel Leadbetter by the unsuspecting grandparents of his nephew — the real Crispin Nigel Leadbetter. Mission accomplished...

Frederick and Maria were relieved to have completed the dastardly deed. Much to their surprise, Raymond and Henrietta were both at home. Raymond had been asleep, following a harrowing night on duty at the hospital, but was wakened by the sound of the taxi as it turned into the driveway. Bleary-eyed, he descended the stairs to join his wife, greeting their very welcome guests who had carried out the onerous task at such speed. They could hardly believe how efficiently the plot had been executed. Until her parents moved into their new home, probably within the next few days, Henrietta would take responsibility for her supposed young nephew. As if on cue, her charge let out a sudden cry.

Taking him from the arms of her sister-in-law she cradled him gently, seeing him for the first time since Isobel had left her home when the child was barely five weeks old. She let out a short gasp as she removed his bonnet. Was this really her nephew? The child, as she remembered, had a mass of blonde curls. This baby was practically bald, and the hair that was beginning to grow was a light sandy colour. And the eyes — there was something different about the eyes. Henrietta was puzzled. In her confusion, she let the shawl fall from the baby's shoulders revealing a blue matinee jacket: it was, without doubt, the jacket her mother had knitted for Crispin. The accusation that had been on the tip of her tongue — that they must have kidnapped the wrong baby — failed to escape from her lips. Looking again, she beckoned Raymond, "He's changed; he doesn't look like the same child. What's happened to his blonde hair — and his eyes — his blue eyes?"

Raymond glanced over the bundle she held, "Of course he's changed — all babies change, especially in the first few weeks. They often lose their baby hair and, as for his eyes, they're definitely blue."

"But they're not the same blue, and I'm sure he looked more like Nigel," she persisted.

In truth, Raymond had never taken that much notice. He was still tired and beginning to feel impatient with his wife. "He may not look quite like his father, but there is a distinct resemblance to his mother," he said, crossly. "My brother has done as you asked; now maybe Frederick and Maria would like a little refreshment and some time to relax. I'll put the kettle on. Judging by the noise Crispin's making I think you need to get on and pay him some attention."

Having dismissed her doubts, given the assurance of her husband, Henrietta set about caring for her small charge. It was, after all, several weeks since she had seen him and, despite his altered features, once he was fed and washed, with clean nappy and fresh clothes, he was just as contented as she remembered.

It was not until they sat down to enjoy an evening meal that Frederick and Maria relayed the whole story of their journey north and their good fortune in finding 'Crispin' asleep in his pram by the front doorstep of the house where Isobel was living with her parents. "And did you actually see her?" Henrietta asked.

"Not close up," Maria admitted. "She was wearing a dark coat and her head was covered with a scarf, just like most of the other women we saw in the neighbourhood. She was the same height and build as I remembered from the wedding."

"And you're sure she didn't see you?"

"I'm certain. We were a good distance away when she turned into the garden, and she didn't turn around as she went into the house. There were very few people about in the street but I'm sure no one else gave us a second look: we were very discreet."

Raymond and Henrietta were amazed at how the whole job had been carried out with such ease.

"Still, we have to be cautious," Henrietta remarked, with concern. "Isobel is sure to be suspicious and maybe come looking. The sooner my mother and father move and we exchange homes the better. Everything has gone well so far — we mustn't let down our guard now."

Henrietta and her parents had masterminded the abduction. In their smugness, they justified these actions with reference to Isobel's irresponsible return to her home in Fulham during the first days of the Blitz. Maybe Nigel's widow should have informed them of her real plan — her desire to return to Scotland — but would that have made any difference? No doubt they would have found some other excuse to justify their heinous crime. Had Frederick and Maria not discovered the pram, placed outside the house at the very moment they were passing, the kidnap may never have taken place. No one could have anticipated that single stroke of luck, which served to avoid the complexities of the initial plot — a scheme that involved following and recording Isobel's movements over several days. Although a more thorough approach may, at least, have resulted in kidnapping the real Crispin Nigel Leadbetter!

CHAPTER 7
A new home for Stuart

When Henrietta's parents moved to Oxfordshire, they collected the child they believed to be Crispin and took him with them to their new home — *his* new home! Henrietta and Raymond who had, so far, failed to produce any offspring of their own, would not be too far away once they relocated to Oxford: they had agreed to play a role in their nephew's upbringing. As for Frederick and Maria Dobson — they were delighted at the prospect of the impending move, which would place them closer to Frederick's office. Their two children were currently staying with an aunt who lived out in the country: she had agreed to care for them whilst the war was raging.

Priscilla Leadbetter purchased a beautiful new pram for her grandson, along with several other items that she considered necessary for such an important addition to the family. She and her husband, also Crispin, would be candid about the circumstances... or almost! Their story: their son, Nigel, had been killed in the war and his wife, sadly, had died shortly after giving birth! So, 'Crispin Nigel Leadbetter' would grow up with this lie, believing himself to be an orphan — unaware that he held his own secret. Would the Leadbetters ever discover that they were the victims of their own wrongdoing?

Priscilla was never so concerned as her daughter about the seeming change in her grandson's appearance. True, she had drooled over the new baby, but it had been through the tears she shed for her son. Nigel's own mop of blonde hair at birth had disappeared soon afterwards, although his second and permanent crop was also blonde. This baby's current near bald state, showing the first signs of a light sandy growth, did not trouble her. She was a little disappointed that he had lost what she remembered to be a look of Nigel but, as Raymond had pointed out to Henrietta, there was no mistaking the resemblance to his mother.

Stuart, from now onwards referred to as Crispin Nigel Leadbetter, appeared quite contented, just as they would expect. He was well cared for: clothed, fed and loved. But something was missing from the baby who had been so cruelly taken from his home with his real parents, Kitty and Alexander (Sandy) Anderson…. He'd lost his cute, cheeky grin.

The house in the Oxfordshire village, where Crispin Nigel Leadbetter resided with his supposed paternal grandparents, was a spacious detached property with a large garden. For a child whose early life was spent during the war years, he was fortunate — he had his own nursery: a large room with plenty of space to play. He had lots of toys and books, a swing in the garden and a brand new tricycle, given to him on his third birthday. His grandfather had a car, which was used for family outings and visits to Aunt Henrietta, with whom Crispin often stayed: she continued to dote on her young nephew, spending hours reading to him and playing board games.

Crispin enjoyed these visits, loving the special attention he was afforded, along with a much less strict regime than was in place at his home. His grandfather was especially stern, often frightening the child with his formal approach.

When he was four years old Crispin was taken to the church in the village where he attended the Sunday school. This was his first opportunity to mix with other children: he loved it. At home he was often lonely, being left to amuse himself. The company of playmates was something that had been missing from his life.

Soon after his fifth birthday on 5 August (although he was actually born two weeks earlier than that), he started school in the village. He was delighted to see some of his friends from Sunday school. For the first time in his short life he experienced a feeling of joy, although, as yet, he still did not quite manage a smile.

With the war only recently ended, Crispin was not the only child in his class to have lost his father to the war effort. He was, however, the only one to be an orphan, having lost both his parents. Priscilla and Crispin (senior) had always told the boy that they were his grandparents, although the difference was not really apparent to him until he became conscious of his classmates and teachers making constant reference to 'Mummy' and 'Daddy'. It was then that he began to ask questions about his parents. At first, his guardians were reluctant to tell him too much but, with constant pestering, they brought out a few photographs of their son, Nigel, often with his sister, Henrietta.

For a while this sufficed, until one day about a year later Crispin again became curious. He wanted to know more; he wanted to know about his mother. Then, for Crispin, the bombshell came — his mother had died when he was born. This, in his head, meant that he, somehow, must have caused her death. For several days the young lad recoiled from the family, spending even more time alone than usual. He cried and cried until, three days later, his grandfather declared he had had enough. He strode into the nursery where his grandson was curled up on a couch, still sobbing. Although not normally a violent man, Crispin Leadbetter was, increasingly, showing a darker side to his character, particularly in relation to his grandson. Drawing the belt from his trousers he dragged the terrified boy to his feet and proceeded to leather him until the tears turned to screams. Hearing the racket, Priscilla burst into the room. Holding up her hands in horror, she cried out. "Stop, stop, there is no need for that!"

With his face the colour of beetroot, Mr Leadbetter turned to his wife who, for a split second, feared that he was going to turn the strap on her. In fear, she cowered back towards the door. Crispin ran to her for protection as his grandfather continued his outburst with angry words.

"No grandson of mine behaves like that," he roared. "I will not have him crying like a girl. The sooner he goes off to boarding school the better!"

With those words he brushed passed his wife and his terrified protégé and stormed out of the room, flinging his belt down on the nursery floor.

Stunned, Priscilla Leadbetter, who was not usually one for soft words, led her grandson to the couch, where they both sat down for the next half hour. It was the longest time this woman had ever given to the boy, marking a change in their relationship.

"Did I kill my mummy?" the child asked, after a long silence.

"No, of course you didn't," she stated firmly.

"But you said she died when I was born."

For the first time since the kidnap, Priscilla questioned the actions of that October day, almost six years ago. At the time, she had been devastated by the death of Nigel. What had gone through her head to imagine that taking another son from his mother would compensate? Now, she would have to live with this lie for the rest of her life. What would Nigel have made of his parents' deeds? Despite how the family had felt about Isobel, she knew that Nigel loved his wife dearly. A sense of shame coursed through her body, interrupted by a little voice beside her…

"Granny – what did Grandpa mean about me going to boarding school?"

Priscilla explained to him that when he reached the age of seven, he would go away to a school where he would stay throughout each term, returning home for the holidays. Now and again they might visit him in his school, and he would be able to come home for at least one weekend during each term. She added that this was quite normal, especially for boys. His father had attended such an establishment, and also his grandfather, so Crispin would be following in the family tradition. Instead of being even more upset, as she had expected, Crispin's face lit up.

"I can go away?" he asked.

"Yes," his grandmother confirmed.

It was with this thought in his head that the young Crispin coped with the next year. True, his grandmother showed more kindness, but it could never compensate for the actions of his grandfather: Crispin hated the man. As far as possible he avoided him, which was not too difficult. Crispin Leadbetter senior was out at 'his business' — an accountancy firm. His working days frequently extending into the evenings. The young Crispin would breathe a sigh of relief when his grandfather was delayed beyond the time of the evening meal at seven o'clock — a meal that he had been expected to attend from the age of five, and which he dreaded. One false move whilst at the table and he would be sorely reprimanded: sometimes expected to apologise for a misdemeanour he did not know he had committed. On several occasions, he was sent to bed before the meal was over. Manners were everything in this household: children were 'seen and not heard'. Crispin dared not speak, conversation being the prerogative of adults only. No wonder he was relieved when his grandfather was absent, when he could relax and, since the beating, chatter with his grandmother.

Around his seventh birthday, Granny and Aunt Henrietta took him into London for a day, to be fitted for his new school uniform. He was sad to say good-bye to his friends at the local school but looked forward to starting a new life in September. He had visited the school earlier in the year with both his grandparents. At the time, they were formally introduced to the Headmaster, Mr Scott, a tall straight-backed gentleman who greeted them with a welcoming smile. Crispin was then passed into the care of an older boy, a prefect of eleven years old, who would be leaving at the end of the term: he had been given the task of showing Crispin round. They visited a classroom, the library and the gym, before crossing the campus to one of several houses where, as a boarder, he would reside.

"Do all the boys live at the school?" Crispin asked.

"Mostly," came the reply, "although there are some day pupils and several who return home each weekend."

"And, what about you?" Crispin enquired. "Are you a boarder?"

"Yes," he said, "and I think that's best. There is so much to do for those of us who stay here. Day pupils miss out on a lot of the fun. You need to be tough, mind. We play lots of sports, the rougher the better. I like rugby."

Crispin didn't know what rugby was — they only played five-a-side football at his local infant school, but he liked that. Granny tut-tutted a lot when he came home with filthy shorts stuffed into his shoe bag along with even dirtier socks and gym shoes. Altogether, Crispin liked the sound of this place.

Meanwhile, Mr and Mrs Leadbetter had afternoon tea with Mr Scott and the housemaster who would be responsible for their grandson. The Headmaster was somewhat taken aback, though not totally surprised, by Mr Leadbetter's attitude towards the system. The man made it clear that he expected the school to 'knock the boy into shape'. He needed assurance that his grandson would be strictly disciplined. Listening to him, Mr Scott began to wonder what sort of little monster he was admitting to his school! Unlike Mr Leadbetter, and many of his colleagues in the public school sector, he was not 'old school'. He did not support the idea of beating his pupils into submission. Yes, he expected high standards, but he was not a violent man. He knew that, with like-minded staff, his methods worked, and he was confident that they would continue to do so. He listened to this client with concern, nodded in the right places and assured him that the boy would excel in his care. Satisfied, the Leadbetters were shown to the reception area where they waited for their grandson who, for all his tender years, knew better than to exhibit the excitement he felt at the prospect of attending this school. The smile, that had disappeared when he was just a few weeks old, remained locked behind the sullen façade he had shown since he had been abducted from his true home — his real family.

CHAPTER 8
Boarding School

It was a long summer as Crispin waited to escape from his grandparent's home — his only respite, the trips to see Henrietta and Raymond where, on one occasion, much to his delight, he was allowed to stay for a few days.

At last, the big day arrived. His trunk had been forwarded a week earlier, a bag containing the rest of his belongings was loaded into the car — they were ready to go. But, before they set off, his grandfather issued a stern warning:

"I have had words with your Headmaster. If you cause trouble you can be sure that we will hear about it," he said threateningly.

Crispin had no intention of causing trouble and, if he ever did, he decided at that moment, he would run away!

The journey to the school took almost two hours. Crispin sat in the back, in silence. When they arrived at the reception desk in the main school building, a secretary checked their details and escorted them to the house that would be Crispin's term-time home for the next four years. She informed them that his trunk would be beside his bed: the housemaster would be along in a moment to show Crispin to the dormitory. At last, it was time for him to say good-bye to his grandparents. His grandmother gave him a hug and whispered, "Be a good boy." His grandfather shook his hand as they parted. He said nothing.

Crispin stepped outside to watch as the pair made their way to the car park — he wanted to be absolutely sure that they were on their way! As he turned back to the house, the faintest indication of a smile crossed his lips. Most boys, especially those as young as Crispin, would be upset about leaving their home for the first time, but Stuart Anderson was not. He might be Crispin Nigel Leadbetter, but he had always had the strangest feeling that he didn't belong with this family.

The housemaster, Mr Clark, came hurrying down the stairs to greet the new boy, who was gazing curiously around him. The foyer, with its high ceiling and oak panelling, exuded an atmosphere of grandeur. Photographs of groups of boys who had occupied the house in the past adorned the wall directly opposite the entrance. A glass case to one side held trophies awarded for various achievements.

"Ah, Master Leadbetter, I believe. I'm Mr Clark, your housemaster. I'll show you to your dormitory: it's on the first floor — follow me," he instructed. Crispin hurried after the housemaster who, with long legs, took the stairs two at a time. The lad managed to catch up with him half way along a corridor leading to a dormitory where several new boys were already settling in. Addressing them, Mr Clark introduced Crispin, adding that only two more newcomers were expected.

"We'll have lunch together in the refectory when they arrive. In the meantime, carry on unpacking — leave your empty trunk at the end of your bed to be collected and placed in the storeroom later today."

As Mr Clark disappeared out of the door at the end of the large dormitory, Crispin gazed around at the seven boys already in the room, six of whom were momentarily focussed on him, but soon returned to the task in hand. The boy nearest to Crispin urged, "We have to unpack before lunch."

Seeing the other boys putting their belongings into the locker and drawers beside their beds, Crispin followed suit. All the while, one boy was lying on his bed, head buried in his pillow, quietly sobbing. Crispin was tempted to go over to him but decided to sort out his belongings first. He had almost finished when the housemaster returned with the two remaining boys — identical twins! Crispin had never seen twins before, let alone identical twins. For a few moments, he was mesmerised. No sooner were they introduced, as George and Henry, than he had forgotten which was which!

"I'll be back in fifteen minutes to take you across for lunch," Mr Clark announced, as he once again exited the dormitory. The twins had been allocated the two beds closest to the door leading into the corridor.

Having completed his unpacking, Crispin approached the boy who still lay curled up on his bed, sobbing.

"I'm Crispin," he said, "what's wrong?"

"Nothing," the boy replied.

"Then why are you crying?" Crispin persisted.

"Don't like it here — want to go home," he answered stubbornly.

"But, how do you know? You've only just arrived."

"I just do."

"What's your name?" Crispin enquired.

"Sam, I'm Sam and I don't like it here."

"Will you stay with me when we go for lunch?" Crispin asked. "I'll be your friend." At this Sam stirred. He turned around and looked up at Crispin.

"O-o-okay," he mumbled, "but I still don't like it here."

Lunch was served in the large refectory over in the main school building — a room that could accommodate all pupils and staff although, so far, only the first years, including day pupils and staff, were present. The fourth years were due to arrive in the afternoon, and years two and three the next day.

When lunch was over, the new recruits were taken to the main hall where the Headmaster, Mr Scott, addressed them. The housemasters then gathered together their own groups, including day pupils, and escorted them to their house for a guided tour, ending in the common room. All three houses had four dormitories — one for each year group, with ten boys in each. Also, there were four first-year day pupils in the same 'House' as Crispin.

After the housemaster's talk, the boarders trooped back to the dormitories where they changed into their P.E. shorts and singlets. The rest of the afternoon was devoted to physical activities, together with the first-year boys from the other two houses: as it was a fine day they were outside.

Crispin stayed with Sam, who cheered up as the day progressed; there was no time for moping around. It wasn't until the lights went out that sobbing could be heard once again, coming from his direction.

The next day, the second and third-year pupils arrived. Formal lessons began for the first and fourth years, while the rest of the students were settling in.

With lessons, prep, meals, sports and a variety of pursuits for the boarders, there was little time for any of the boys to feel sorry for themselves, but Sam was often miserable. Crispin did his best to comfort him but, even as the term progressed, his friend had bouts of distress. It wasn't until the Christmas break drew close that he began to brighten up, showing a less forlorn aspect to his character. For Crispin, it was quite the opposite. It was only now that he realised just how miserable and lonely he had been at home. For him, the school was wonderful... he had company; he had friends.

That's not to say that Crispin's new life was all perfect; like most seven-year-olds, he got into some scrapes, suffered plenty of scratches, cuts and bruises, and didn't like his arithmetic teacher — well, he just didn't like arithmetic. Maybe he had an underlying aversion to the subject, given that his grandfather was an accountant. Although it had never been discussed, as the only male descendant, Crispin was, automatically, heir to the family business: 'The Leadbetter Accountancy Company'.

Crispin could never put his Leadbetter existence completely behind him. He dreaded that first Christmas holiday as much as Sam looked forward to it. During the last week of the term Sam, emerging from his own misery, noticed that Crispin was less cheerful than usual.

"Aren't you looking forward to the end of the term?" he asked.

"I would much rather stay here," came the reply. "I will be counting the days until we come back."

Sam was aghast, "What about your family? You must want to see them?"

Crispin was the only first-year boarder in the house who had not seen his family during the term. They had not come to visit him as his grandmother promised they would. But Crispin was not upset; he was relieved.

"I don't care about my family," he admitted.

Seeing the puzzled look on Sam's face, Crispin poured out his hatred for his grandfather telling, for the first time, of the terrible night when Crispin Leadbetter had beaten him with the leather belt because he had cried.

"Why were you crying?" Sam asked. He wanted to know more.

"I found out that my mother had died when I was born. My father was already dead: he was killed in the war. When they told me that my mother had died too, I thought it must be my fault — I couldn't stop crying."

"So, you were beaten for being upset?"

"He didn't just beat me; he shouted at me: he was red with rage. He said he would not have me crying like a girl. Granny was nice to me after that, but I still don't want to go home. Sometimes I think they're not really my family."

"Gosh, Crispin, I'm so sorry. I don't want to be away from my family, but I suppose it really isn't so bad here. I'll try not to be such a baby next term — I promise."

On the very last day of the term, the whole school attended a Christmas Carol Service in the school hall to which parents were invited. As soon as the service ended the boys were formally dismissed for the holidays. They collected their bags from their house and met their parents in the foyer. In his usual formal manner, Mr Leadbetter shook his grandson by the hand. Granny smiled sweetly but waited until they were away from the other boys, before giving him a hug, not wishing to embarrass him in front of his friends.

As with the last car journey, three months earlier, Crispin sat in silence on the back seat. They arrived home to a late lunch prepared by a part-time housekeeper who had been employed since Crispin had left. After lunch, Crispin was summoned to the lounge, where he was 'interrogated' about the term by his grandfather. Except for arithmetic, which was 'satisfactory', Crispin's grades and comments were commendable. It was, however, arithmetic that Mr Leadbetter was interested in.

"What's this, boy," the man bellowed, the colour already rising in his cheeks. Crispin was too scared to open his mouth.

"Answer me." He demanded.

"I-I-I did my best, Sir" Crispin stuttered.

"It's not good enough. I hope you felt the hand of the Headmaster for this."

Crispin was stunned. He remained silent.

"Well, did you?"

"No," he admitted.

After further questioning, Crispin Leadbetter senior was not impressed. A hint from Crispin that he was happy at the school further enraged him.

"I am not spending all this money for you to be happy. I will see Mr Scott at the beginning of the term. If this continues, I'll have to see about moving you elsewhere."

With these words, he stormed out of the room leaving both Crispin and his grandmother speechless for several minutes. Only at the sound of the front door closing, and the car turning out of the driveway, did Mrs Leadbetter make an attempt to comfort her grandson.

"Your grandfather is having a difficult time at the office," she stated, in an attempt to justify her husband's foul temper which, in Crispin's eyes, was even worse than it was before he went away. Crispin said nothing.

"Would you like to tell me about school?" Priscilla coaxed.

In just a few hours, her grandson had reverted to the lonely child who had left home in September. For several minutes he didn't respond — he didn't even move. He was scared; mortified at the thought that his grandfather might remove him from the school that he so loved; the place that, in just three months, had become his home. Even the idea of the whip was less painful than that.

Eventually, he murmured, "I was a good boy Grandma; I tried really hard; I did all my lessons; I did as I was told."

He wanted to tell her all about his friends, about the fun they had together, about some of the pranks they got up to. But, after his grandfather's harsh words, he knew better than to reveal any more truths about life at the boarding school. His grandmother was sure that he was holding back, that he would never share that life with them. It made her sad, and added to the guilt of taking him from his mother. How she wished she could turn back the clock. Isobel may have returned to her home without telling them of her plans, but she had written to them — she would never have kept Crispin from them. They should have responded to her letters, not discarded them.

Her husband had always been stern: he was a strict disciplinarian, running a tight ship at his accountancy firm; but he was never as severe with their own two children as he was with Crispin. What was he thinking?

Changing her approach to Crispin, she suggested:

"How would you like to visit your Aunt Henrietta tomorrow? Maybe you could stay there for a few days."

Relieved, but not daring to show any excitement, Crispin nodded and stated politely, "I would like that, Grandma."

Henrietta was delighted to see her young nephew. She said he could stay right up until Christmas day when the whole family would be gathering for a traditional Christmas dinner.

Glad to be away from his grandfather, Crispin was able to relax. Henrietta fussed over him: she took him everywhere with her; visiting friends; shopping; walking in the park. He helped her decorate the Christmas tree, and even made mince pies. He found the constant attention a little irritating at times, but his aunt obviously cared about him. Anything was better than being 'at home'. Uncle Raymond, when he was not at his surgery, also had time for him. He would take him to the park armed with a football to practise kicking, dribbling and throwing. His uncle praised his nephew's newly acquired skills.

So, by the time the Christmas Day festivities were over, more than a week of the three-week break had passed. Crispin's aim now was, as far as possible, to avoid the company of his grandfather. The next three days could be a real challenge since Crispin Leadbetter senior would not be returning to work until Monday. However, young Crispin did have an unexpected respite from his nemesis…

CHAPTER 9
Friends

Mrs Roberts, a widow who lived in the village, was now very much a part of the Leadbetter household. Every morning during the week, she arrived at nine o'clock to clean, attend to the washing and prepare lunch. This arrangement worked very well during the school term, but the holidays were proving difficult. Mrs Roberts had a son, Jamie, a year older than Crispin. From Boxing Day through to the New Year, Mrs Roberts had no one to look after her son, who was too young to be left on his own. Furthermore, Mrs Leadbetter required the services of her home help over the coming weekend: she had invited guests for dinner on Saturday evening. She suggested that Mrs Roberts bring the child with her. Mr Leadbetter had not been pleased with the idea, but his wife had persuaded him that, with Crispin at home, the two could be company for one another. Reluctantly he agreed, as long as they stayed out of his way and had lunch in the nursery.

Crispin recognised Jamie from the local primary school. He was in the year above him although, being a small village school, they had shared the same classroom and had the same teacher. Mrs Roberts, of course, had to accept responsibility for both of them whilst she was there, but that was not a problem. Crispin was delighted to have the company and Jamie was equally thrilled at having a playroom with so many toys, jigsaw puzzles, books and writing materials. When the weather was fine they were allowed to go outside, where they could play hide-and-seek amongst the bushes.

Jamie wanted to know all about the boarding school so, at last, Crispin had an audience — someone to share the secrets of his rough and tumble experiences. Jamie was intrigued as he listened to all the antics his friend got up to. The idea of keeping these things hidden from the wicked one', as the two of them now referred to the formidable Mr Leadbetter, made the stories even more attractive. Crispin, encouraged by his new friend, often exaggerated his tales and, with heads together, the pair conjured up ever more implausible stories, thereby creating a close bond between them. By the end of the Christmas break, they were firm friends. Nevertheless, Crispin was still anxious to get back to school. He dreaded his grandfather coming home in the evenings. Whenever he was in his presence, he was in constant fear that he would say or do something that would upset the man. He could never forget the night of the beating: the angry face; the stern words. If he'd done something really bad or been very naughty, he would have accepted his punishment, severe as it was, but Crispin couldn't think that crying for his mother was a crime.

....

Having avoided the heavy hand of his grandfather over the entire Christmas vacation, Crispin almost felt safe in the back seat of the car, returning to his beloved school — how was he to know that the crunch was yet to come?

As he retrieved his P.E. kit and satchel from the boot of the car, instead of bidding goodbye, his grandparents accompanied him back to his House before turning towards the main school building.

"I have an appointment with the Headmaster and your maths teacher," Mr Leadbetter announced, with a steely smirk. "Extra arithmetic for you, young man. From what I hear, you spend far too much time cavorting about on that sports field."

Crispin's heart dropped into his stomach — or so it seemed. He felt hot tears welling up. *Don't cry, please don't cry*, he told himself.

"Yes sir," he said, before disappearing through the main door, into the foyer. For a moment he thought his legs were going to give way beneath him. In sheer panic, he had forgotten to say cheerio to his grandmother. It was too late now. Still, why hadn't she warned him? She must have known of his grandfather's intentions.

Instead of rushing up the stairs to the dormitory, as he had envisaged since he had left at the end of the last term, he took each step slowly, deliberately. He trudged the length of the corridor, not knowing how to greet his friends. As he attempted to make a discreet entrance, white-faced and visibly shaking, one of the twins — he still wasn't sure which was which — swung round:

"Golly Leadbetter old chap, whatever is the matter with *you*?"

Crispin managed to reach his bed before his legs finally buckled and he sat down heavily, with a sigh of despair.

"Gracious," piped up the other twin, "you look as if you've seen a ghost!"

By this time all eyes were on Crispin, all pressing for an explanation. Crispin wasn't going to cry. He had made it up the stairs and, looking around, he knew he was with friends.

"My grandfather's gone to see Mr Scott. He's furious about my arithmetic report."

"Who, Mr Scott?"

"No, no, my grandfather," Crispin clarified.

"What did you get?"

"C+ and satisfactory."

"I got C and average," said Henry.

"Mine was C+ and satisfactory," said George

"C and 'fair'," came another voice from across the room.

Comparing notes, it seemed that everyone had C grades with satisfactory, average or fair from Mr Fairbanks, the maths teacher. Except, that is, Cecil.

" I had B+ and 'very good', he boasted."

"Swot!" came the response from all the boys, in unison.

Cecil was the class swot. The other boys tried to bully him, but Cecil took not the slightest notice. When one or two of them had tackled Crispin for wasting his time trying to befriend Sam, Cecil had come to the rescue: "My dad said to ignore the bullies." His advice had worked.

Crispin gained some comfort from his classmates. Considering he disliked the subject so much, he thought he had done rather well.

Half an hour later Mr Clark, the housemaster, entered the room with instructions that lunch would be served at the normal time, followed by a whole school assembly. In the meantime, he called Crispin to follow him to the main building. All eyes were once again on Crispin as he trotted after Mr Clark.

"Poor fellow!" George exclaimed. (The twins had an older brother who attended a senior boarding school — they were proudly copying the speech of the big boys).

Scuttling along behind the housemaster Crispin had, once again, turned a deathly shade of pale. He guessed that he had been summoned to the Headmaster's office and trembled at the thought of the consequences. *Would Mr Scott take out his cane? Would he be expelled?*

"Don't look so worried," came a reassuring tone from the Headmaster who was looking down at Crispin with a kindly smile. "Your grandfather has left."

"Y-y-yes, Sir," Crispin managed to utter, still quivering.

"Your grandfather seems to think that you are a poor scholar, especially in arithmetic, but I have assured him that is not the case. You have worked very hard. Mr

Fairbanks is willing to give you some extra tuition if necessary, but he is perfectly satisfied with your work. Would you like some more arithmetic work?

"Not really, Sir." Crispin had to be honest with this man.

"How about half an hour a week, after lessons on a Monday. Then I can tell your grandfather we're helping you."

"Yes Sir," said Crispin.

"Off you go then, we'll have you top of the class by Easter."

Although not happy about having to face Mr Fairbanks for another half-hour every week, the outcome could have been much worse. He had a feeling that the Headmaster was on his side.

As Mr Scott watched the boy leave his study, he was overcome by a surge of anger. He had not been happy about the confrontation with the boy's grandfather, for there was no other word to describe the boldness of the man, entering his domain and challenging his integrity and that of the staff. Fortunately, he had succeeded in quelling the situation, primarily for the sake of the child. Mr Leadbetter's attitude had been a matter of concern to him since their first interview before Crispin entered the school the previous summer. The man, he concluded, was a bully. Crispin was a good student, a diligent worker but, thankfully, as far as Mr Scott was concerned, not perfect. From what Mr Clark had revealed, the boy had been involved in a few pranks during his first term, and tended to be a little rough on the games field, but his thoughtfulness towards the once timid Sam had also been noted. There was really nothing untoward about Crispin's behaviour to cause alarm. The extra arithmetic tuition he had suggested was simply a way of placating Mr Leadbetter, in the hope that he would be less aggressive with his grandson.

Crispin returned to the dormitory, where nine inquisitive youngsters were anxious to discover the outcome of Crispin's unfortunate ordeal.

"Did you get the cane?"

"Have you been expelled?"

"Gosh, was it really awful?"

The walk across the campus had given Crispin the chance to recover from the events of the morning. By the time he entered the house the colour had returned to his cheeks. For the time being, he was safe. The attention from his friends, with their desire for gruesome details, almost persuaded him to goad them, to tell them what they wanted to hear; but he declined and, instead, revealed the truth. It was, after all, his grandfather who was 'the wicked one' and no exaggeration would be required to expose the dastardly deeds inflicted on him by *that* man. So far, only Sam was aware of Crispin's suffering at home — but, after this, he would happily share it with the others.

Crispin replied honestly, "Mr Scott said I always work very hard, but my grandfather does not have the same opinion. I have to have some extra tuition in arithmetic from Mr Fairbanks."

"So you didn't get the cane?"

Crispin detected the disappointment on the faces of the group, but he didn't take it to heart — they were always game for a bit of excitement, even if it was at the expense of each other.

"No," said Crispin firmly. "Mr Scott was really nice: he even smiled."

"Well done, old chap," quipped Henry (or was it George?) whilst giving him a friendly pat on the back, just as the bell sounded for lunch.

It was much later in the day before Crispin was quizzed about his grandfather, as he knew he would be. Every boy in his dormitory gathered round to listen to his stories about 'the wicked one'. He began with the night of the beating, relaying in graphic detail the whole experience: Mr Leadbetter drawing out the leather belt from his trousers to strike him — time and again the implement lashing down on his small frame.

"Why, why did he do that?"

"I was upset when I found out that my mother had died when I was born." He didn't tell them how much he'd cried, but added, "I was only six." He had their sympathy. To big boys of seven and eight, six-year-olds, still at infant school, were mere babies. More comments and questions followed:

"How awful for you, old chap!"

"What's all this about your arithmetic grades?"

"Did your grandfather beat you again?"

Crispin told them about the day he had arrived home for the Christmas holidays — how 'the wicked one' had ranted and raved at him about his poor grades, threatening to send him to a stricter school. On that occasion, he was sure it was his grandmother who had saved him from another leathering. He said he had no idea his grandfather had arranged to see the Headmaster that morning — not until he got out of the car, delivering further threats.

"I don't like the sound of 'the wicked one'," remarked Graeme — a quiet-spoken lad — from his position behind the twins. He didn't normally say too much but he was clearly horrified at the revelations about Crispin's home life.

"I've had the strap from my father," came another voice from the background.

"And what did you do to deserve that?"

"I played truant from Sunday school with my friend Dick. We ruined our best clothes climbing trees and splashing about in puddles: it was super fun. Everything was going so well until a policeman caught us stealing apples from a garden."

"Whose garden?"

"Well, as it turned out, it was his garden."

"Golly, what happened then?"

"He took down our names and addresses — he said if we tried any funny business, he would cart us to the police station. He marched us home to our parents, who had been out looking for us for ages. My dad was very cross and gave me one stroke of his belt. He said if I ever stole again, I would have to go to a home for naughty boys. I didn't much fancy that idea."

More tales of exploits were shared amongst the boys. All of them, including Sam, were happy to be back with their friends.

Crispin was annoyed at having to spend an extra half-hour in the classroom on Monday afternoon with Mr Fairbanks, whilst the rest of the first year was out on the sports field. However, it wasn't quite as bad as he had anticipated. Without having to keep the rest of the class in line, the maths teacher was more relaxed with his one pupil. He encouraged Crispin, saying he just needed to keep practising his multiplication tables and get quicker with his sums.

Crispin's life at the boarding school continued fairly smoothly over the next four years. There were a few ups and downs, of course, but no major hiccups, and nothing to warrant a consultation with his grandfather: Mr Scott saw to that. Crispin paid a little more attention to arithmetic, although he never liked the subject. The thought of one day taking over his grandfather's accountancy business — the reason for the outbursts should he show any signs of poor performance in the subject — horrified him. This miserable prospect was brought to his notice long before he left the junior school, but Crispin had learned early in life not to challenge the overbearing Mr Leadbetter: that would have to wait until he was older. Crispin had no idea what he wanted to do when he grew up, but of one thing he was certain — he was *not* going to follow in his grandfather's footsteps!

As each school holiday loomed, Crispin dreaded the thought of going home. His saving grace was his friend, Jamie, who was always delighted to see him. As they grew older, they were allowed to roam beyond the garden gate. There were plenty of open spaces, meadows and woodland close to the village, where they could play, out of sight from prying eyes. On wet days, they would seek refuge in the nursery or, if Mrs Roberts was 'off duty', they could go to Jamie's house. But both boys were wary of 'the wicked one'. Crispin might get up to some mischief at school, but at home he would avoid trouble at all costs. Likewise, Jamie had been warned. His mother was cautious, fearing for her job if she did not keep both the boys under control.

Unlike most parents, Crispin's grandparents did not visit the school often. There was never a voice amongst the spectators to cheer him on at the school sports. It was an area of the curriculum that did not interest Mr Leadbetter, who regarded it as wasting time that could be spent within the confines of the classroom. However, they did attend the closing ceremony at the end of each school year, expecting to see their grandson high on the list for awards. Mrs Leadbetter was always pleased with the boy's achievements, but her husband scowled at his obvious prowess on the sports field.

With this aspect of Crispin's school life causing him some anxiety, Mr Leadbetter was giving serious thought about taking him out of the public school domain. Now, coming to the end of his junior school years, he could send him to the local grammar school which, by all accounts, had an excellent reputation. The money saved on fees could be spent on private tuition out of school hours and at the weekends. This way, he could keep a closer eye on his grandson: he had always been distrustful of the boarding school — Mr Scott, he decided, was far too lenient.

Had Crispin been made aware of these plans he would have been horrified. Fortunately for him, Crispin Leadbetter senior discussed this idea with his wife before approaching the grammar school. Mrs Leadbetter was not in agreement: she had established a fully active lifestyle since moving to Oxfordshire. Her social calendar was filled with meetings and events. She could not *possibly* take on the extra responsibility that would be incurred by having her grandson at home permanently. Besides, she pointed out, it was during term times that they were able to get away on holiday together: Mr Leadbetter enjoyed these breaks with his wife. Priscilla was not completely heartless as regards her grandson. In a way, she would have liked to see him a little more often, but she feared for the wrath that her beloved husband might bring to bear upon the boy. So, where *would* they send him?

"Maybe he should continue his education at the high school linked to his current junior school," she suggested a few days later. She did not add that she had spoken with her grandson and that was what he wanted: Mr Leadbetter was not in the habit of allowing Crispin to have his own way.

"I'll speak with the Headmaster before I make my decision."

Initially, he contacted Mr Scott, who spoke very highly of the senior school, known rather grandly as a college. Crispin would have to prove himself competent in the forthcoming examinations, which could result in a bursary that would help towards the fees. Crispin Leadbetter senior was not interested in charity, but neither would he turn the offer down. "We'll see how he gets on," he replied, still not convinced of the boy's ability, despite his constant impressive grades. "Can you supply me with the name of the Headmaster of this college?"

"Of course," Mr Scott responded.

As soon as he replaced the receiver, after furnishing Crispin's overpowering grandfather with the details, he rang his 'friend' Mr Smith, the Head of the College, to warn him to expect a call from the formidable Mr Leadbetter. "Best to present him with a hard-line approach, particular in Mathematics," he suggested. "The boy, by the way, is a first-class student."

Predictably, Crispin excelled in his final primary school examinations and, along with most of his classmates, continued to the high profile boarding school just a short distance away. He was delighted but, as always, mindful of how he presented himself to his grandfather, careful not to show his excitement, addressing him as 'Sir'.

So, in 1951, Crispin began the next phase of his education. No longer at primary school, he was allowed to make the journey alone on the train, relieving him of the uncomfortable silence sitting in the back of his grandfather's car. When he listened to the other boys at the school, he concluded that his so-called family were hardly worthy of the name. True, Henrietta was always kind but, as he grew up, there was less to occupy him on his visits. Reading and playing games with her were less attractive than being with his friend, Jamie. He rarely saw his Uncle Raymond. As for his grandparents, with each vacation, he felt more like a stranger in their home. His grandfather, though still demanding, was less aggressive; satisfied that he was making progress, especially in Mathematics. Crispin was sufficiently astute to ensure he attained good results in the subject, despite never having a great love for figures. *Keep the man happy,* he told himself through gritted teeth. One day he would *show him.*

CHAPTER 10
Chris

Isobel returned from her trip to London in September 1945. She was exhausted from travelling as well as the events of the week. Her quest for Nigel's family had left her confused — it didn't make sense. The unforeseen circumstances regarding her house in Fulham were truly bizarre. But strangest of all was meeting Ian Wright. For the first time since Nigel's death, she found herself attracted to another man, and it seemed obvious that Ian was attracted to her. She realised, of course, that the situation was impossible; telling herself that he would soon forget about her, any notion of further involvement would pass. Nevertheless, it had raised her awareness that another relationship was possible. After all, she was only twenty-six years old.

For the time being Isobel continued to stay with Grandma Jeannie and to run the local shop: she could make no other arrangements until the sale of her house in Fulham was secured.

....

Unlike his Uncle Stuart, who was raised as Crispin Nigel Leadbetter, the real Crispin Nigel Leadbetter was very comfortable at home with his mother and close family in Scotland. He had the advantage of a large, supportive extended family, all interested in his wellbeing. He attended the local primary school along with his friends from the village. Like his uncle Stuart, he enjoyed sports — the rougher the better — but, ironically, his favourite subject was arithmetic. The war years had seen an influx of residents to the village: families who, like Isobel, chose to move away from the more dangerous environment of Aberdeen. Many now returned to the city, resulting in a sharp fall in the population. When he was nine years old the village school, where he was a pupil, closed. Along with his friends, he had to attend a country school over a mile away.

East Bay was a relatively safe place for a young boy to grow up. Chris spent many hours on the beach, scouring the rock pools, making dams, watching the fishing boats. Even when still quite young he was free to walk along the rough road to see his great-great-grandparents in their cottage a half-mile or so from the village. There were great aunts and uncles and cousins, all living close by. Sometimes he thought he must be related to everybody. If he ever got up to mischief, Grandma Jeannie and Ted always seemed to know about it before he arrived home! His grandparents, Kitty and Sandy, visited regularly from Aberdeen and, during the school holidays, he sometimes went to stay with them. He liked it best if he could travel by train from the nearby market town.

Chris's real 'heroes', however, were his uncles, Alec and Ernie. He was thrilled having his Uncle Alec to stay at East Bay for a few weeks in 1945, before returning to his base in England, to await his official release from the army. "Will you come back to stay with us?" Chris asked. But Alec would make no promises. He needed to give some serious thought as to what to do with the rest of his life. His brother, Ernie, had achieved more than his working-class family could ever have imagined. His parents, especially his mother Kitty, who had herself benefitted from a first-class education, was thrilled by the success of their second son. But they were equally proud of Alec who had fought for his country in the most horrific circumstances imaginable. His father, Sandy, had moved his family to the city to give them a chance in life, but Da's heart was in the country. Perhaps there was a chance that his eldest son could make a life for himself away from the city, as had been his intention before the onset of the war. He would certainly encourage the lad if that was where he saw his destiny. Like his father, Alec was drawn to the outdoor life. He was a hard worker, he was tough and he was intelligent, despite having left school at the first opportunity.

Whilst on leave, Alec cycled out to the farm where he had worked before he was called up. The manager was delighted to see him: many young men never returned.

"Is this you home for good?" he asked.

"Sadly, no," came the sombre reply. "I must return until I get my final discharge papers. I don't know when that will be."

"Well Alec, whenever that is, I can promise there will be a job for you here. And," he added, "I'm sure I can organise accommodation for you on the farm."

Alec hesitated. Although he appreciated the offer, he needed time to think. Work as a farmhand was fine, but he was no longer a young lad — he didn't mind the labour but he wanted more than that. After five years in the forces, having spent years in India and survived the treacherous conditions of jungle warfare in Burma, he was more ambitious at twenty-three than he had been at eighteen. Mr Wilson, the manager, registered the uncertainty in the young man. Reading his mind he urged:

"Well, promise you'll come to see me as soon as you're back; I'm sure I can make it worth your while!"

Mr Wilson was more certain than he was letting on...

....

Although Chris undoubtedly fared much better than his counterpart in the south, it was not all plain sailing. Having close relatives across the generations brings heartache as well as joy. When Chris was eight years old his beloved Granny Smith (his great-great-grandmother) suffered a stroke, from which she never recovered. Three months later she died. She was ninety-four. His great-grandmother, Jeannie, tried to persuade her father, Grandpa Smith, to come to stay with them in the village, but he refused. A stubborn old man of ninety-five and almost blind, he was adamant that he was perfectly capable of looking after himself: arguing with him was useless. Jeannie or Ted visited each day taking him home-made broth, stew and freshly baked bread. Jeannie's brothers and their families were also regular visitors. When the family was not around, neighbours kept a watchful eye on him. In the end, though, all this attention did not save him.

It was late one evening when the family living next door detected the smell of burning. Willie, the man of the house, rushed outside to see smoke billowing from the open front door of his neighbour's cottage. He headed for the entrance shouting "Fred, Fred, I'm coming," but the smoke was so thick he fell back, choking.

"Get away from there," came the terrified scream of his wife. Another neighbour, hearing the din, rushed off to the telephone box to call the fire brigade. By that time the entire community, the occupants of the small hamlet, were out of their homes, watching in horror as flames were seen to fill the living room of the end cottage. In an attempt to hold back the blaze before the arrival of the fire engine, water — collected in every available receptacle — was thrown into the hallway. In scarcely ten minutes a fire engine turned into the rough track that led to the group of cottages.

They arrived in time to save the neighbouring cottage from damage, but not the life of Frederick Smith. From the evidence gleaned once the fire was extinguished, it seemed that he had been sitting in his favourite armchair, puffing away at his pipe, and fallen asleep. The smouldering contents of the pipe must have set his clothing alight: the old man had no chance. There was little left of him from which he could be identified.

It was a sad demise to a long and mostly contented life. Nothing could be salvaged from the ruins of the home where Jeannie and her brothers, as well as Kitty, had been raised. Chris sorely missed his aged relatives. He would often wander along the road and down the track to rummage through the wreckage of the cottage, recalling happy days that he would cherish forever in his memory.

Within a year of the deaths of Granny and Grandpa Smith, another tragedy befell the family when Jeannie's husband, Ted, was taken ill with Leukaemia. Jeannie spent six months caring for him at home or visiting him in the hospital in Aberdeen. He died in December 1950.

....

Isobel's plan to purchase a property for herself and Chris, using the proceeds from the sale of her house in Fulham, did not materialise in the way she had planned. The transaction was completed in October 1946, leaving her a healthy bank balance: more than enough to purchase a superior home in the north-east of Scotland. However, now that she had the money, Isobel was not sure what she wanted to do. Chris, at six years old, was settled at the village school, obviously enjoying his idyllic childhood. Isobel too, was happy. She loved her job at the local store, where there was never a shortage of company. Furthermore, where else would she have such willing childminders? A large fancy house might be fine, but not at the expense of the ties she had established with family and friends in East Bay.

A further source of concern was Ian Wright. Away from his presence, Isobel concluded that pursuing the relationship was not feasible. She had already left her beloved Scotland once for a man — a venture that, with the onset of the war, had ended tragically. Was she really prepared to give up a much more established lifestyle for the sake of another man? Maybe it had been foolish of her to agree to correspond with Ian, but she was flattered by the attention. Besides, in the aftermath of the war, there was a shortage of eligible young bachelors. Her mind swayed one way and the other: her marriage had resulted in the birth of a son — wasn't that enough? On the other hand, should she deny herself the prospect of a future relationship?

Isobel returned to London once more in connection with the sale of her house: to sign the final papers and ensure the transfer of her affairs to her Aberdeen solicitor. Before the trip, she had decided to settle the situation with Ian: she would meet him; she would tell him that there could be no future for them as a couple; she would make it clear that her life was in Scotland. However, the conversation she had so carefully worked out in her head did not go according to plan. When they met at the railway station in London, having communicated by letter but not seen one another for a year, she sank, helplessly, into his open arms.

This time, without the pressures encountered on her previous visit, and only one consultation with her solicitor, there was time to relax, to visit some of the attractions, to see a show and to converse at leisure over an evening meal. Rather than ending the relationship, the result was a closer bond. Still, Isobel was adamant that she would not leave her northern home. Much to her surprise, Ian announced that he would move north. It would involve some further study on his part, to gain an understanding of the differences between English and Scottish law, but it was not insurmountable. It was obvious that he had given this idea much thought. Nevertheless, Isobel felt a responsibility. Fighting against her emotions, she argued that he must visit Scotland; he must be sure that the decision was right for him before he made a commitment. Once again, as she sat on the train during the return journey, she pondered the futility of moving forward with the relationship.

PART II

THE BENEFACTOR

CHAPTER 11
The Meeting (July 1900)

Over the years someone else had taken a special interest in the fortunes — and the misfortunes — of the Anderson family. His name was Timothy Campbell.

Timothy was the son of a laird, owner of an estate in Aberdeenshire, just a few miles to the west of East Bay. He was educated at a boys' private school in Edinburgh where he boarded during term-time. He later attended Aberdeen University, graduating in Law. As a youngster, he spent most of his school holidays on the estate, where there was never a shortage of things to do. When he was sixteen, he invited a friend from school to stay with him for the month of July. With his friend for company Timothy, though anxious to show him around the estate, was also keen to explore the surrounding area. Together they cycled along the coast as far north as the fishing port of Peterhead, and south to within a few miles of Aberdeen. One day, early in the holiday, they met up with a group of young teenage girls in one of the coastal villages. Timothy and his friend, James, were not used to the company of girls, but that didn't put them off. Boldly, they approached; trying to appear casual, as if meeting with the opposite sex was an everyday occurrence. Visitors to the villages along the coast were not unusual. Families from towns and cities would rent accommodation for a month or even longer, but usually they came with younger children who were eager to spend the summer days playing on the beach. Two teenage boys, almost young men to the girls, were quite a novelty. And these boys were different from the 'loons'[iii] who went to their school — these boys spoke with 'posh' accents. After a while, some of the girls wandered off saying they had to be home for dinner, but two of them hung back. They also must make their way home, but they lived more than half a mile away from the village.

"You could walk along with us," suggested one of the girls. Timothy was strangely attracted to her: she was quite tall and slim with blonde hair; she responded to his gaze with a coy smile. The other girl was shorter, with a mass of dark curls and an infectious laugh: she captured the attention of James. The four of them strolled out of the village, round by the church, and proceeded along a rough track — the boys pushing their bicycles. They parted at a place where a narrower track, off to the right, led to a group of small dwellings — home to the girls, who lived in cottages next door to one another.

"We'll come back to see you?" Timothy offered — more a question than a statement.

"We go down to the village most mornings to take eggs to the shop," the dark-haired girl responded by way of agreement.

Over the next two weeks, the boys were regular visitors to the village. Sometimes they left their bicycles

---

[iii] A colloquial term for a young boy

there while they headed off on foot, along the coast, in one direction or the other. They met the girls, often in a group — chatting casually; skimming stones across the water or walking along the rugged path to an adjoining bay. On two occasions Timothy managed to sneak off with the blonde girl, hiding in the tall bracken away from the others. A week before James was due to leave, the girls announced that there was a Ceilidh on Saturday evening in the village hall. Youngsters from all around the countryside were expected to be there. The boys were excited. Who knew what opportunities lay ahead? Timothy's heart raced at the thought of any opportunity to meet 'his girl'.

The big night arrived. Eagerly the two boys, spruced up in their Sunday best, cycled to the village: they had high hopes. The hall was packed with country folk; both young and not so young, anticipating a wild night of song and dance… they were not disappointed.

Well into the evening, when most of the crowd were intoxicated with the music and the revelry, Timothy and his attractive blonde sweetheart (for in his head he was giddy with love — or was it lust?) slipped out into the warm summer evening. The sun was sinking low in the sky — the air was still.

They walked up to the little church at the edge of the village and there, on a grassy patch between the gravestones, Timothy Campbell had his way with this innocent young girl, barely fourteen years old. She, in turn, delighted in his kisses and took pleasure in 'she knew not what' — for she was uneducated in the ways of men and women. Timothy, though up to that time a virgin himself, was well aware of this activity. His need was desperate, but he was kind and gentle with his maiden, and would long afterwards cherish those precious moments of lovemaking until, that is, he came to realise the consequences of his selfish deed.

Back at the village hall, the pair slipped inside, unnoticed by the crowds who were still whirling around the dance floor as energetically as ever, though not for much longer. All too soon the evening came to an end: it was hardly dark as everyone spilt out into the street, filling the night air with noise and laughter. Many were heading out of the village in the same direction as Timothy and James, and their two friends. At the church, to the disappointment of the boys, several turned off the road to take the same path as the girls, leaving them little choice but to say a brief farewell and continue on their way. "Come on, you two," shouted the others in the group, "we can't wait for you all night." Timothy said little as he cycled the four miles home with his friend. And, as for Jeannie, she had a warm feeling inside but said nothing at all.

James departed two days later, having spent four glorious weeks wallowing in the fresh air in this northeast corner of Scotland. Living in a castle on an estate was thrilling: meeting the girls and going to a ceilidh made it his best holiday ever.

Timothy spent the rest of his vacation helping on the estate: his father, the Laird, was anxious that his son should know about the workings of the land, and that he meet with the three managers, each responsible for many acres of farmland. There were only two occasions when Timothy succeeded in escaping for long enough to cycle to the village in the hope of seeing 'his girl', but there was no sign of her or her friend. He was saddened at not having the chance for a proper good-bye.

Getting away from the estate during the mid-winter break would, he knew, be impossible, so it was the springtime before he was able to go in search of her. Yet again she was nowhere to be seen, but he did catch sight of her friend with the dark curly hair — he couldn't remember her name.

"Hello," he shouted, walking briskly towards her, "Is Jeannie anywhere around?"

"Well, hello to you," came the bright response, followed by a frown. "I'm afraid you're out of luck. Jeannie went away before Christmas to stay with an aunt and uncle who needed some help running their shop. I think she'll be home soon as I believe Mrs Smith, that's Jeannie's ma, is expecting a baby; so she'll want Jeannie back to help with the little one."

"Oh," was all Timothy could manage, disappointed.

"And what about that handsome friend of yours?" Jessie queried. "Will he be back?"

"I-I-I'm not sure," Timothy stuttered. "Please tell Jeannie I've been looking for her. I'll be back in July."

"I'll tell her. And you bring your friend along too," she urged.

Timothy wandered away, despondent. He retrieved his bicycle from where he had left it leaning against a wall, and rode slowly back home.

CHAPTER 12
The Baby

As promised, Jessie passed the message onto Jeannie when she returned from her aunt and uncle's just a few days after Mrs Smith had supposedly given birth to a baby girl. The baby's name was Kathryn, to be known as Kitty. Jeannie looked very pale and thin; her beautiful blonde hair had lost its healthy sheen: there was no sparkle in her eyes.

Jessie was shocked at the appearance of her friend, "Whatever have you done?" She asked. "You look awful."

"I'll be fine," Jeannie retorted, "I'm just tired, that's all."

Jessie wasn't the only one to be concerned. Mrs Smith couldn't believe the state of her daughter. Yes, at fourteen she'd just had a child, but even that didn't account for Jeannie's deterioration since she had been sent away four months earlier.

"I didn't know Ma, honestly, I didn't know it was wrong. I'm sorry, I'm so sorry. It hurt having the baby, it hurt so much. The mid-wife was really cross with me. She said I was bad. Aunt Mary said I was a real naughty girl."

Jeannie's mother was horrified. Although she had sent her daughter away 'in disgrace', it had been for the good of them all. Jeannie was so young, too young to be having a baby, too young to take responsibility for a child. This way was best. Ma Smith would tell her neighbours and her friends that the baby was hers — no one need know. Well, hardly anyone. But, her sister, Mary, had to know. She knew Mary would be angry, but she'd expected her to have some compassion for her niece and, with a shop to look after, she had said she would welcome some help around the house. She had not thought for a moment that Mary would have Jeannie fetching and carrying heavy buckets of coal, or down on her hands and knees scrubbing floors, right up until the moment she went into labour. Aside from that, the girl was half-starved.

Mrs Smith tried to console her daughter, but Jeannie cried and cried. She cried until there were no tears left. Once she had calmed down Ma coaxed, "Come now, we have a baby to look after. She will be your little sister, but you must help me. First, let's get some food into you and some fresh air to bring back your rosy cheeks."

A few weeks at home saw Jeannie return to good health — a little older and a good deal wiser than the innocent child of last summer. Now, at least, she knew what not to do.

When Ma Smith had first suspected that Jeannie was pregnant, she quite naturally asked who the father was, but Jeannie was confused — she simply told the truth: she didn't know. She had no idea what she had done to be having a baby. When she was eventually made aware of the facts, she realised that the father could only be the 'posh' boy she had met in the summer. Other than his first name, she did not have a clue as to who he was or where he came from, so she still insisted she didn't know. Besides, she liked Timothy, and she didn't want to get him into trouble. Furthermore, even if she did know more about him, she was too young to be married. None of her friends supposed for a moment that Jeannie's little sister was her daughter so, for the time being, all was well.

Jeannie's friend told her that Timothy had been looking for her and would come to the village in July. Jeannie was unsure about meeting him but thought he ought to know about the baby. After all, he was the only person she could tell. Each morning in July she made her way down to the village in anticipation of seeing him. By the middle of the month — when she had almost given up hope — there he was, sitting on a wall, waiting for her. She sauntered up to him, not quite knowing what to say. As she drew near, he stood up and gazed into her eyes. There was a connection, but he sensed straight away that she had changed: there was something very different about her — a maturity, in stark contrast to the young teenage girl he had met a year ago.

"We need to talk," she said. Her tone was serious. "Somewhere quiet," she added. "I'll walk up to the graveyard. You can meet me there in ten minutes."

Strange he thought, as she stepped into the shop to deliver a basket full of eggs before passing him again, giving just a casual nod, and proceeding towards the church. Ten minutes later he was standing beside her at the very spot where they had made love on the night of the ceilidh.

"Your friend told me you were away but would be home to help your mother with her new baby. So, you have a little brother — or a sister?" he questioned.

"Neither," she responded. "Everybody thinks that I have a baby sister, but she isn't my sister — she's my daughter — our daughter."

Timothy backed away from her, totally at a loss for words.

"That night," Jeannie continued. "That night, right here. I didn't know what we were doing. I didn't know what it meant. By Christmas my tummy was starting to swell. Ma asked me all sorts of questions; then she told me I was going to have a baby. She wanted to know who I'd been with, who had done this to me. There was only you and I didn't know your last name or where you lived, so I said I didn't know. I didn't even say your first name. I wasn't sure whether I would ever see you again, and I didn't want you to get into trouble. I thought you cared about me."

Timothy was stunned. He tried to piece things together in his head. The baby was born in April, so that was nine months after the event. Nine months, he knew, was the length of time it took for a baby to be born. He believed Jeannie; but what could he do? He was only seventeen; he was still at school. His father was the Laird — he would be furious if he were to find out; he might even banish him from the estate. As if sensing his fear, Jeannie said, "It's all right, I won't tell. I won't tell anyone that you're her father. Everybody thinks the baby is my sister. I promise; I won't tell."

Listening to Jeannie, Timothy felt ashamed. What she must have suffered he could barely bring himself to contemplate. His own mother had died giving birth to his younger brother. Losing her at the age of five had left him heartbroken, but his father said he must get over it; he was the son of a Laird, he had to behave like a man: there was no room for tears.

"Come to me," Timothy coaxed, holding out his arms. But Jeannie held back.

"Talk to me, Jeannie. I'm so sorry. Please tell me what happened, what did you do?"

The two of them sat down on the wall at the back of the graveyard, out of sight from the road. Solemnly, she relayed what had happened since discovering that she was pregnant.

"Can I see my daughter?" He asked.

"I-I-I'm not sure. We shouldn't really be seen together."

"Just once," he pleaded.

"I'll meet you here tomorrow: mid-morning," she agreed.

Timothy arrived early the next day. He realised that Jeannie wouldn't be able to wait for long, not with the baby: he didn't want to miss them.

Having had time to reflect on the situation, he felt worse than ever. How could he have been so selfish? He was well aware of the possible consequences of those idyllic moments, but it was only once — surely, they could not be so unfortunate. What Jeannie had endured was unimaginable.

He had kept out of sight as Jeannie had insisted, so he didn't see her until she appeared from around the side of the church with the baby in her arms.

"This is Kathryn," she stated, by way of introduction, "but we call her Kitty, Kitty Smith — my sister," she emphasised, looking at him.

"Our daughter," he smiled.

By way of acknowledgement, she handed the child to him. He took her gently in his arms; the name, Kathryn Campbell was etched on his brain: it had a pleasant ring to it. "Our daughter — Kathryn Campbell," he whispered, barely audibly. If Jeannie heard him, she did not comment. The tears coursed down his cheeks as he held the child for the first and last time.

Anyone seeing the three figures together that day might have wept too. But both Timothy and Jeannie knew that what they both wished for could never be. Any betrayal on either part would lead to the dishonour of both. Jeannie was fortunate — she could watch her child grow, loved and cossetted by her own family. Timothy, too, was spared embarrassment — free of all responsibility. The two could never belong to one another — he had to walk away.

"I'll never forget you," were his parting words. "You'll always be 'my girl'... 'My girls'" he corrected. "Thank you for sharing this time with me, for sharing our secret."

Watching Timothy disappear along the road on his bicycle was painful for Jeannie, but she was glad that they had met, that he knew the truth. Now she had to be brave, she had to face the future without him — living a lie. But she was lucky.

Maybe Timothy was lucky too, though there was many a time throughout his life when it didn't feel that way. He continued his education, attending the University of Aberdeen where he graduated in law.

CHAPTER 13
The Trust Fund

One Saturday, five years later, as he was passing the Episcopalian church in the local market town, Timothy Campbell stopped to watch as a wedding group emerged from the building. "Who's the lucky man?" he inquired of a group of bystanders.

"Edward Milne," came the response,

"He owns the hardware store in the town. Just bought a real nice house in East Bay. I believe his bride's from somewhere near there."

Timothy was curious — there was a familiar look about the attractive young woman in the ivory wedding gown. Fortunately, she was too focussed on her new husband to notice the prolonged gaze of the handsome dark-haired stranger amongst the crowd. A nudge from the man standing next to him brought Timothy out of his daydream, "You can't have her, she's already spoken for," came the rather cheeky comment.

Jerked into reality Timothy remarked, "Pity." He moved a little further back and redirected his focus on the whole wedding party, who were getting into position for a photograph — quite a complicated process. He recognised the bridesmaid — Jeannie's friend with the infectious laugh — but who was the little dark-haired girl by her side? Timothy felt the blood drain from his face as reality dawned. The child must be about five years old…

his daughter! *I must go, I must get away from here* he thought, but he couldn't move — he seemed fixed to the spot. He couldn't take his eyes off the child, a lively little 'imp', who didn't look too comfortable in her finery. An older woman, who Timothy took to be Granny Smith, bent down to straighten the little girl's dress and perhaps tell her to behave herself to have her photo taken. Timothy turned and walked away with a heavy heart. *Life was cruel*, he thought. How he wished things could have been different.

At twenty-two, Timothy was a graduate of the University of Aberdeen. He had obtained a position with a firm of solicitors in the city. His allowance from the estate, together with his salary, made him a wealthy man even at this young age. He realised that Jeannie, for a girl from a family of meagre means, had done rather well for herself: his concern was for his daughter. He decided he would set up a trust fund for her — maybe help with her education or in some other way in the future. He intended to keep an eye on her — from a distance, of course.

His thoughts were not merely the result of a moment of nostalgia, for he never forgot Jeannie. Despite the limited time they had spent together he would always remember her with affection. She was his first love: he had had to let her go — but his daughter was different. When he returned to work the following Monday morning, he went about the task of setting up a trust fund, which would be hers, no matter what else happened in his life.

The years passed. Timothy had several friends at university who, after graduating, entered the teaching profession. One of them, Brian, who had taught for three years in a secondary school, was appointed Headmaster of the primary school in East Bay where Kathryn (Kitty) Smith was a pupil. Sometimes Timothy met up with Brian, who lived in the schoolhouse. The pair chatted together over a drink or two and, now and again, Timothy persuaded his friend to tell him about his pupils: there is nothing quite like tales of the amusing antics of children to lighten a conversation! Normally the young headmaster focussed on the most mischievous of his students, but sometimes he commented on his 'star' pupil — a certain Kitty Smith. So, without actually prying, Timothy learned of the progress of his daughter from the age of eight.

One day, about two years later, Brian told Timothy of a grave concern he had for Kitty, who had quite suddenly changed from being a happy little girl into a sad, moody child. She insisted that she now lived with her Granny and Grandpa: she said she didn't have a mother any more, and she didn't have a father either. When questioned the girl clammed up. Timothy didn't know how to respond to this information. He couldn't interfere — he couldn't be the one to expose the truth, yet he felt responsible. Several months passed before Kitty's name was mentioned again, when Brian remarked that the girl had announced she had a baby brother, yet never talked about her mother. Brian said he had his 'star' pupil back

— not quite as happy as she was before, but better than she had been for a while.

At this point, Timothy decided he would try to help his daughter. From what his schoolmaster friend had said, the child must have discovered the truth, which had upset her. He also knew that his daughter was clever — perhaps the chance to continue her education at a private school in the city would give her a real chance to excel. With this in mind, he arranged for a letter to be sent from the solicitors revealing the existence of a legacy to fund her further education. Although he was a lawyer in the firm, he insisted his name was not mentioned. As a benefactor, he wished to remain anonymous.

The letter was sent directly to Jeannie Milne, an indication to her that the benefactor must know of her circumstances. She had her suspicions but mentioned them to no one. She passed the information onto her parents, who were reluctant to allow their granddaughter to attend a school in the city with the option of boarding during the week. Jeannie, however, was adamant that Kitty must be told and the decision must be hers. Her daughter had not coped well with the lie surrounding her birth, she was not about to deny her this opportunity: she would not lie to her again. Kitty was delighted at the idea of the boarding school. Her former sparkle returned as she prepared to leave home, albeit not permanently. Jeannie wrote to the solicitors accepting the offer from the unknown benefactor, intimating 'our girl is thrilled'.

If the donor was who she thought he was, he would understand the message.

For the next four years Kitty had the best of both worlds. From Sunday night, until Friday, she stayed at the school. At weekends and during the school holidays she could take advantage of the fresh air in the countryside and the coast with her old friends. Although she enjoyed learning, she was not intent on going on to university like a few of her classmates. Instead, she found employment in one of the banks in the nearby market town. It was a good job, especially for a female. However, by the time she was eighteen, she met her future husband, Alexander Anderson. They were married a few months later. Kitty continued working until just before the birth of their first child in 1919: a daughter, Isobel.

CHAPTER 14
From a Distance

In the meantime, Timothy had also married but, regrettably, his wife was never able to conceive so Kathryn, as he always thought of her, remained his only child. He never mentioned his teenage affair to his wife. Perhaps he should have done so when they first met but, as the years passed and the couple remained childless, the knowledge that he had a daughter would be too cruel to admit.

Surreptitiously, Timothy continued to follow the fortunes of his daughter, although he would never do anything that might arouse the suspicion of his wife. Any further practical help was, therefore, out of the question. He was delighted when he heard how Kathryn had thrived at the private school and pleased when he learned she had secured a position at the bank. However, he was a little disappointed at her choice of husband thinking that, with such a fine education, she could have done better for herself. Still, from what he knew of Alexander Anderson, a farmhand at a neighbouring farm, he was an honest lad and a hard worker. And, after all, he reasoned, Jeannie Smith was a girl from an ordinary working-class family and that had not prevented the attraction, which, he had always believed, was mutual.

For the duration of their married life, Timothy and his wife occupied a house on his father's estate. He was conscious of the necessity to become familiar with the running of the household and surrounding farmland, all of which would one day be his responsibility. However, his main occupation remained as a solicitor in the city. Every day, Monday to Friday, he would drive to the railway station in the market town and catch a train to the centre of Aberdeen, close to his office.

Sadly, before he reached the age of fifty, his wife was diagnosed with cancer from which she died within a year. His father, now well into his seventies, was not in good health, relying more and more on the support of his eldest son. Timothy's younger brother, forever a bachelor, had never shown any interest in the estate. He had moved to London as a young man, where he practised as a barrister. Timothy was troubled. He had no heir. Who would inherit the estate after him? As a lawyer, he could imagine long lost cousins grappling for a share: he had seen many a court battle. It was then that his attention turned once more to his daughter.

For several years Timothy was unsure of Kathryn's whereabouts, knowing only that Alexander had moved to the city, hoping for a better future for his family. Then, one day in 1936, a young lad presented himself for work at one of the farms on the Campbell estate. Timothy's father always left the farm managers to deal with their labourers: to hire and to fire; but the day that Alec turned up at the farm on his bicycle, Timothy happened to be there. He acknowledged the boy, who was approaching the farmhouse as he was leaving: there was a familiar look about him. A few weeks later he asked the farm manager, Jim Wilson, about the lad. "Best worker I've come across in a long time," came the reply.

"Tell me about him?" Timothy asked. "Who is he, where's he from?"

Mr Wilson, who had a fair knowledge of folks in the surrounding area, answered:

"He's Sandy Anderson's lad. His mother was one of the Smiths' girls out at Seaview Cottages near East Bay. Kitty Smith, she was. They moved into Aberdeen a few years back, but Alec yearned for the country life. He stays with Jeannie and Ted Milne in East Bay: bit of a mystery surrounding that lot! He calls Jeannie his Grandma." Jim stopped short, seeing a raised eyebrow from his listener. "Anyway," he repeated, "he's a real good lad."

Over the next four years, Timothy maintained a keen interest in Alec Anderson. He gleaned more information about the family; he had plans for the lad's future. "Keep an eye on him," he told the manager, "don't let him go."

Weird Mr Wilson thought, but who was he to argue with the son of the Laird?

The war, of course, interrupted everything. Alec, like so many young lads, was called up. "Very much against the boy's wishes," Jim had commented.

Within a week or two of Alec leaving, a tragedy occurred in the Anderson family, which was brought to everyone's attention by the headlines in the local newspaper. Alec's young brother, Stuart Anderson, barely three months old, had been taken from his pram. Timothy kept abreast of the progress of the search, frequently checking with a friend of his, a police inspector who was on the case, but no news followed. He was sorely tempted to introduce himself to his daughter, desperately wanting to offer her comfort, but he refrained. Maybe presenting himself to her at this time would cause her more stress. Someday he would find a way!

During the war years, the running of the estate fell increasingly on Timothy as his father's health deteriorated. Towards the end of the war, the Laird died leaving his son, who was still working as a solicitor in Aberdeen, Laird of the Campbell Estate. At sixty, Timothy considered retirement but decided to wait a little longer. His original plan had been to stay until he was sixty-five.

It was at the beginning of May 1945 that another incident occurred involving the Anderson family. Kitty's grandson, who lived with his mother Isobel, and great grandmother Jeannie, at East Bay, had a nasty accident during the end of the war celebrations in East Bay. Buried amongst the news of the festivities, the fate of the small boy was hardly visible, but Timothy noticed it. He later learned that the young child was recovering slowly in hospital in Aberdeen. About a month after the incident, Timothy made his way to the infirmary. He introduced himself, using his position as leverage to gain entry to the ward — not his usual approach — but he was genuinely

150

concerned and that showed in his face. The little boy took to him, asking if he would come to see him again. Timothy was cautious but managed to visit twice more, outside the normal visiting times. He wondered if this intrusion into the life of his great-grandson was perhaps rather reckless. Chris didn't mention these visits to any of his family at the time — there was so much going on at the hospital, so many people taking an interest in him: doctors; nurses; physiotherapists; as well as regular visits from relatives. When he did mention the elderly gentleman to Grandma Jeannie, she assumed it must have been the hospital chaplain.

Frequently Timothy considered approaching Jeannie, revealing his true identity, especially now that he was the Laird. But, how could he? They had promised never to betray one another and, desperate as he was, Timothy would never do anything that might cause problems for Jeannie. For her part, Jeannie knew that his name was Timothy. She was sure that he was the benefactor who had set up the trust for Kitty's education, but she had no idea that he was a landowner.

Soon after visiting Chris in hospital Jim Wilson, a farm manager on the Campbell estate, alerted Timothy that Alec, the Anderson boy, had returned from the war. He was currently with his regiment waiting for his demobilisation papers.

"Persuade him to come back when he is demobbed," Timothy instructed. Mr Wilson promised he would do his best.

Following his release from the army, Alec visited the farm once more. So far, he had not pursued any other areas of work, but he was determined to do so. In the meantime, he was willing to help out as necessary, especially with the main harvest imminent.

"What do you have in mind for your future?" Mr Wilson asked.

"Well," Alec hesitated, "I wouldn't mind managing a farm myself one day."

"You mean you're after my job?" Jim queried, with a twinkle in his eye.

"N-n-no, that's not quite what I meant" Alec responded, realising his blunder too late.

Jim Wilson laughed. "I'll have a word with the Laird," he said. "If you're as competent as you proved yourself to be before the war, you have my full support. We'll see what we can do."

For the next three months Alec toiled hard at the farm, often working from early morning until late into the evenings. After the horrors of the war, the Scottish countryside was the best antidote imaginable — he was exhilarated.

With the harvest over and winter looming, Mr Wilson called Alec to his office in the farmhouse. "The Laird has asked me to speak with you about your future on the estate. Would you be interested in running one of his farms?"

Alec was at a loss for words: he took a deep breath. "B-b-but I've never met the man."

"No, but he trusts my recommendation, Alec, and you *would* have to attend an interview up at the castle — Thursday, at two o'clock — does that suit you?"

"Y-y-yes."

"Dress your best," Jim added, "and don't look so worried."

Alec turned up for his interview promptly, looking more like a company executive than a farm labourer. He felt nervous as he followed the signs to the reception desk where his arrival was noted. As he waited to be called, he stared in disbelief at the stately hall with its elaborate furnishings and gilt-framed portraits: he had entered another world.

A few minutes later an elderly gentleman called him into a large room with a coal fire around which four, elegant, green leather-upholstered armchairs were arranged. Alec was directed to one of them, while his host sat down at another. A woman of mature years occupied the third chair, but the fourth remained empty. The gentleman, whom Alec had assumed to be the Laird, introduced himself as Mr Grant: he was, in fact, the manager of one of the other farms on the estate. The woman, Mrs Beatty, was the estate secretary; she had a notebook on her lap in which she scribbled furiously throughout the meeting. Mr Grant began by apologising for the absence of the Laird who, unfortunately, had been called away on business.

The interview went well. Jim Wilson, who thought very highly of Alec, had brought the lad to the attention of the Laird. He had noted Alec's ambition to broaden his outlook. He was sure that he had ability stretching far beyond that of a labourer: he was intelligent, competent, and was blessed with common sense. His experience in the army had taught him the importance of working with others.

Alec had questions of his own. What did the Laird have in mind for him? How was he to gain experience? What were his prospects?

Mr Grant explained that two of the three farm managers on the estate were due to retire in the next three years. A trainee manager was required to help out across the estate, to learn about the administrative side of the work, the buying and the selling, as well as the manual work. The successful applicant would ultimately take up a position as a farm manager. A cottage on the estate would be available for the appointee as part of the deal.

Alec was excited by this opportunity. Thinking about it later he realised that it was everything he wished for. On leaving the castle, he was told that the Laird would be in touch with him in the next few days.

When he arrived home that evening his Grandma Jeannie was anxious to know all about the interview, but Alec held back. He didn't want to raise his hopes just for them to be dashed should he be unsuccessful. Chris wanted to know if he'd met the Laird and was disappointed to discover that he hadn't.

At the time of the interview, Timothy Campbell was in his office in Aberdeen. He had decided against interviewing Alec, or the other candidates, himself. Alec must never believe that he had gained the position by any means other than his own merit. Although, as Laird, Timothy had urged Jim Wilson to keep an eye on the lad, it was Jim who had commented on Alec's competence in the first place. Nor had Timothy given any indication to Mr Grant that Alec must be given preferential treatment. Two other young men had interviews that same afternoon, but there was no competition. Without any help from Timothy Campbell, Alec Anderson outstripped them all. So it was that, though not made legal, the rightful heir to the entire Estate came under the auspices of his own grandfather.

Alec enjoyed his new role: he felt valued. In many ways, it was better than managing a single farm since it provided the opportunity to become acquainted with the workings of the whole Estate, which was precisely Timothy's intention in creating such a position. Strange though — for some considerable time after Alec's appointment, the Laird remained elusive.

CHAPTER 15
Charles Carter

Links with the Anderson family continued to play a part in Timothy Campbell's life, though the next encounter was quite coincidental. A few months after Alec's appointment as a trainee manager on the Estate, a gentleman in his early thirties turned up at the solicitor's office. His name was Charles Carter, a lawyer from London seeking employment and accommodation in the Granite City. Since Timothy happened to be available when he arrived, he was able to speak with him. Charles, who was a competent practitioner in English Law, was hopeful at the prospect of transferring to the Scottish system. Nevertheless, he understood that there would be barriers to be crossed to do so. Mr Campbell suggested he visit the University of Aberdeen in person to ascertain the additional qualifications needed to practise in Scotland.

As regards searching for a property in Aberdeen, either to rent or to buy, that was an area where the solicitor was able to oblige.

"What exactly are you looking for?" he asked.

"I'm not sure," Charles answered. "I arrived in the city yesterday. I have no idea about the property prices here or, for that matter, how your system works."

"Well," Mr Campbell answered, "we solicitors deal with everything to do with buying and selling, including advertising. I can show you what we have on our books.

It's not always a good idea to have the same solicitor as the vendor so, if you buy from our selection, you may need a different solicitor to act on your behalf. If you find a property through another solicitor then we would be happy to be of service. You may, of course, strike up an independent deal with a seller; but remember, here in Scotland, if you shake hands on a deal, it's as good as done. Should you agree to such a transaction, again we can be of service."

Mr Campbell proceeded to show his new client what was available. After only a few minutes Charles saw that the property prices were much lower than those in London. He said nothing but decided he needed to rethink his plans. Before leaving, he gave Timothy Campbell details of his workplace in London intimating that, for the time being, it was the best point of contact. Impressed by the young man and also curious, Mr Campbell asked, "What brings you to this part of the world?"

"Ah well," Charles responded, with tongue in cheek, "now that's another matter."

Feeling confident after his meeting with Timothy Campbell, Charles made his way to the University to glean information on qualifications in Scottish Law. The receptionist was able to inform him of the available courses but unable to indicate whether any exemptions would apply, given his knowledge and experience in the field. However, she made an appointment for him to see the Head of the Faculty of Law the following morning.

As he walked back to the centre of the city, Charles made several detours down side streets looking for 'For Sale' signs. After lunch, he wandered in the opposite direction — the West End — the select part of the city.

Back in his hotel room later that evening, he sat down to give serious consideration to his next move. He had already made some changes in preparation for his future, the first being the official name change. For most of his life, Charles Carter had been known as Ian Wright — the name assigned to him by his adoptive parents; the name on his adoption papers. After their misdeeds, which extended way beyond the tenancy fraud, he decided to disassociate himself from the Wrights; to rid himself of their name and return to his birth name — his *real* name — Charles Fraser Carter. It wasn't quite as straightforward as he would have liked, for Ian Wright would always linger there, in the background. It was the name on his qualifications — his degree. It was his name as an officer in the British Army. He couldn't eradicate it completely. But, he reasoned, it was *not* his name. From now on he was Charles Carter: it felt good.

Charles knew, from what he had been told by the Wrights, that his father had been killed in the First World War in 1914. His mother had died two weeks after giving birth in October of that year. Searching further, Charles discovered that, although he was born in England, his parents were from Scotland. They were married in Dundee in 1912. His mother was Margaret Fraser.

Although it was meeting Isobel that had first caused Charles to consider moving to Scotland, it was the deceitful antics of his adoptive parents and the discovery of his roots that urged him to carry out his plan. By reverting to his rightful name and escaping from his London life, he could make a new start. He hoped that he would find a future with the woman who had dropped into his life so unexpectedly; but, regardless, he wanted to leave the past behind.

He had not told Isobel of his intended visit to Aberdeen. She had made it obvious in her letters that he must not make any rash decisions on her account: the fact was that, despite a strong connection, they hardly knew one another.

After just one day in the city, Charles already felt a step closer to his goal: he could afford to buy a property in, or close to this northern city. He would contact Isobel after his appointment at the university and, if possible, arrange to meet with her at the weekend.

The following morning, as planned, he met with the Head of the Department of Law. With four years' experience before the war, together with his current employment, there were options to avoid starting from scratch, but there would still be a lot of work to cover. The Professor said he would accept a late registration for the new academic year in October. At some point, he would need to be assigned to a firm of solicitors for training purposes.

....

When the telephone rang in the grocer's store in East Bay, Isobel answered in her usual manner, expecting a normal business call. She was quite taken aback by the very formal voice of an English gentleman by the name of Charles Carter and further stunned when he invited her to meet him for dinner the following evening.

"Is this a hoax?" she questioned. "I'm too busy to…"

"It's Ian," he interrupted, "I'm in Aberdeen. I'll explain later."

Isobel was flushed and slightly shaken when she came off the telephone. But, once she had gathered her thoughts, she was excited about the meeting. She made arrangements so that she could travel into the city at the end of her working day on Friday — the next day. She could stay with her parents until Sunday. *What was the name he had given — Charles…? Whatever did he mean?*

Meeting Ian in Aberdeen seemed strange. She was delighted to be in his company and intrigued by what he had to tell her. How was she going to get used to calling him Charles? Yet, she liked the name — somehow it suited him. There was no doubt about the sincerity in his desire to make a future for himself in Scotland. He talked about discovering his ancestry; maybe he had relatives in Dundee? However, he explained, his immediate task was to relocate to Aberdeen. Between his remuneration from the army and his savings over the years, he had accumulated sufficient funds to buy a property in London. Those funds, he now realised, would go much further in Aberdeen. He could, for instance, buy a large property close to the city to divide into flats or bedsits to let out to students. This would give him an income to cover his living costs whilst studying. He would need to investigate the possibilities further, but investing in property could be his best option for supplementing his income whilst re-training.

As they spoke over dinner, Isobel began to feel relaxed in his company just as she had in London. He had obviously thought carefully about the practicalities of the move and, furthermore, he was not putting any pressure on her. After a delightful evening, Charles escorted Isobel to a taxi to take her to her parents' home, agreeing to meet again the following day. They spent most of Saturday and part of Sunday together. She needed to return to East Bay on Sunday afternoon to spend the rest of the day with her son and be ready for work on Monday morning. Charles was anxious to make plans for the next two days: he intended to look at all suitable properties within the city before returning south on Wednesday. He would keep in touch with Isobel by letter until moving permanently to Aberdeen.

Since first meeting Ian in the autumn of 1945, Isobel had revealed very little about him to her family. As far as they were concerned, he was simply a casual acquaintance. Even to her, after such brief encounters and residing so far away, she had to think of their association in the same way. Perhaps now was the time to divulge a little more. She had already told her parents about meeting 'her friend' from London. Now she felt she should be a little more open with her family, but without appearing too excited — after all, things might not work out: there was a long way to go.

Within a few weeks of their Aberdeen meeting, Charles made the move north. Initially, he rented a small flat near the city centre, whilst negotiating a property portfolio. As well as income from his investments, Charles was entitled to a grant and additional cash from trust funds. He approached Timothy Campbell for assistance in managing his affairs. Although having to study a second time for the profession, Charles was interested in the differences in the law between the two countries: studying came easily. As a competent solicitor in English Law, Mr Campbell was more than willing to accept him as a trainee Scottish Lawyer in his firm. From their very first meeting, the two men had struck up a rapport, each respecting the experience of the other.

In the meantime, Isobel bought a house of her own on the edge of the market town: a country cottage with three acres of land. It required renovation, which she set about organising immediately, having water and electricity connected and incorporating a kitchen and bathroom. However, she was not so enthusiastic about moving in. It was less convenient for her work. Both she and Chris were quite happy staying with Grandma Jeannie and Ted, despite her notion for a place of their own. Besides, the appearance of Charles in Aberdeen was already impacting her view of the future. Then, she had another idea — maybe her parents would like to move back into the country. She spoke to them. At first, they were against her proposal but, after giving it some thought, they concluded that it did make sense. Apart from Ernie, a medical student with his quarters near the hospital, the rest of the family were in the country.

Kitty pursued the possibility of a transfer to a branch of the bank in the market town: the place where she had been employed when she left school until Isobel was born. Much to her surprise, her request was granted. One of the assistants in the town branch was looking to move to the city. As for Da, he was sure he would find some work in the country — the three acres of land appealed to him: he could do something with that. They tried to negotiate rental payments for the cottage, but Isobel would not hear of it. They would be responsible for the other bills: it was not costing Isobel anything. The cottage was large enough to accommodate Chris and Isobel, should the need arise.

During this time, Isobel and Charles kept their relationship low key. Charles was determined to establish himself as a Scottish solicitor before making any commitment. Equally, Isobel did not want to be burdened with life-changing decisions until they were both sure of a future together. However, they enjoyed each other's company, met regularly, and grew ever closer. Jeannie noted a change in her granddaughter: a glow, a composure that had been missing. Her observation did not go without comment:

"And when are we going to meet the lucky man?" she would ask.

"Give it time, Grandma." She would respond.

"Well, don't miss your chance," Jeannie warned, "True love's not easy to find."

Isobel didn't need to be told. She was sure of Charles, but she was patient — the right time would come. For the next two years, between property deals and studying, Charles was fully occupied. Isobel too was busy, involved with managing the shop, caring for her son and organising the renovation of the cottage she had purchased. Then, in 1949, a sadness enveloped the family with the death of Granny Smith, followed by the tragic demise of Grandpa Smith.

By 1950 Charles, though still studying for exams, was spending more time with the law firm, where Mr Campbell had promised him a permanent position once he was fully qualified.

Charles arranged a special night out with Isobel to celebrate her birthday in May: she was thirty-one. The past year had been tough for her with the deaths of her great-grandparents — now was the time for change. Charles met Isobel at the railway station in Aberdeen in the late morning. They had some lunch at his flat in the city before strolling to The Duthie Park, a short distance away. There, in a quiet spot looking out across the lake, Charles stopped, took hold of Isobel's hand and, in the old tradition, stooped down on one knee and asked, "Will you be my wife?"

There was no hesitation on Isobel's part: her face was radiant in the afternoon sunshine as they ambled through the park and back to the city.

Charles had booked a corner table in a restaurant situated on Union Street, close to the city centre. A bottle of champagne had been placed on the table in readiness for their arrival. As they took their seats, Charles drew a small box from the inside pocket of his jacket. On opening it, Isobel gasped in amazement at the beautiful solitaire diamond ring within. Taking the ring, Charles placed it on the third finger of her left hand. At that moment a cheer went up from the staff waiting on the sidelines. The champagne was opened.

After one of the most memorable days of her life, Isobel was sad to say good-bye to Charles as she boarded the train for the short journey to the market town. She had planned to stay with her parents that night. Her father met her at the station to walk with her to the cottage on the edge of the town. Sandy and Kitty had settled well in the country. With chickens, a couple of goats and space to grow their own vegetables, Isobel's dad was in his element. He had also secured part-time work at Eddie's hardware store, so he was rapidly getting to know the locals. Also, his health had improved dramatically. His back still bothered him, but overall he was in less pain: the country life suited him. Isobel was satisfied with her decision: getting her parents away from the house in Aberdeen — the place that served as a constant reminder of the loss of their baby son — was good.

"You look richt pleased wi the sen!" her father remarked as they made their way home.

"Yes," she replied. "I'll tell you all about it as soon as we're home. I could do with a good cup of tea," she added, swaying very slightly from the effects of the champagne. *It was good stuff*, she thought.

They no sooner walked into the living room than Kitty, with her keen, sharp eyes, noticed the engagement ring.

"Well, well, well!" she remarked. "Come, show me. I take it your elusive gentleman friend may not be elusive for much longer!"

"I've asked him to come to meet you next weekend. I hope that's okay?"

"Nae afor time," Da commented with a grin.

"And this time we *will* be at the wedding!"

Isobel was delighted by her parents' light-hearted approach. She had enjoyed her day; she was overwhelmed by the proposal. Charles had proved himself so romantic for the occasion — it had been worth the wait.

The next day, when she presented the news to Chris, Grandma Jeannie and Ted, they too were thrilled. Chris was curious about his mother's friend. Isobel had talked to her son about him — usually at night when she tucked him up in bed, so she wasn't springing any surprises on him. She also spoke to Chris about his own father, showing him photographs of Nigel in his uniform. Chris was very matter of fact about meeting this 'new' man. He

166

asked if he could have his best friend, George, round to meet Charles, as he didn't want to listen to adults all day.

Isobel had to smile. "Of course you can, and you don't have to be 'stuck' with us adults all day: you can go out to play, as usual." Chris was visibly relieved.

Charles was coming out to meet Isobel's family the following Sunday. Jeannie had offered to cook the Sunday roast. Sandy and Kitty would join them. Isobel had arranged to meet Charles at the railway station but he phoned her at the shop on Friday to say he had bought a car. Not being aware that he could drive she was quite surprised.

They re-arranged their plans. She would still meet him at the station; he would take her for a spin in the car, pick up her parents and go together to East Bay. That way he would be introduced to her parents first — less daunting than meeting everybody at once. It suited him fine.

The day went well. Charles was charming, as always. He was amused by Isobel's son — a lively little character with a mind of his own; well used to adult company, yet eager to be off out to play with his friend. *Just as any young lad should be*, Charles thought.

The celebrations provided a welcome break following the sadness of the previous year, but it was not to last. Within a few weeks, Ted was taken ill. He was diagnosed with Leukaemia, from which he died six months later. Jeannie was distraught.

It was not until the death of Edward Milne (Ted) that Timothy discovered Charles had any connection with the family. Timothy saw the notice in the local newspaper, announcing the demise, along with the funeral details. On the same day, he overheard Charles ask the secretary to re-arrange an appointment booked for early Friday afternoon, as he would be attending a funeral at one o'clock. "Oh, I'm so sorry, Charles, was this a friend of yours?" Mr Campbell interrupted.

"No, no," he responded, whilst indicating to his elderly colleague to come into his office. Charles was never one for gossip at work: he did not want to say more in the presence of the secretary.

"Ted, the deceased is — well, was, almost family. I'm engaged to be married to his wife's granddaughter, Isobel."

Timothy Campbell stopped abruptly. He opened his mouth as if to speak, but no words came.

"Are you all right, Sir?" Charles inquired, somewhat alarmed.

"Y-y-yes, I'm so sorry, I must sit down, I'll be fine. And please, do call me Tim."

Although they had met more than four years earlier, in the spring of 1947, their relationship had always remained strictly professional. No longer a trainee, Charles was now an employee of the company. For some time, Timothy had felt that they could relax a little: he regarded the young man as an equal. Now, the moment had come. If Charles was to be married to his granddaughter, they needed to drop the 'Mr' and the 'Sir' (except when in the presence of clientele). And, somehow, Timothy would have to reveal his identity to the family that he had always regarded as his. He considered Kitty to be his rightful heir; Alec was managing one of the farms on his estate; and he had just discovered his colleague was to be married to Isobel. Since Isobel was clearly aware that Jeannie was her grandmother and not her aunt, the truth of Kitty's birth must have been exposed at some point.

He could say nothing to Charles about his own connections to the family. He could say nothing to anyone until he spoke to Jeannie, and now was not the time for that. He would have to be patient, at least for the next few months.

"Can I get you anything?" Charles asked, bringing Timothy out of his reverie, "A cup of tea; a glass of water?"

"No, no, really I'm all right," he answered, with a reassuring smile.

Charles returned to his own office, bemused. Something he had said had disturbed Timothy Campbell; of that he was sure.

Charles and Isobel were anxious to set a date for their wedding. The death of Tom had stalled their initial plans for the springtime — they would wait until later in the summer. In the meantime, they needed to make another important decision. Where to live? Charles had been looking at some large granite properties in the west end of the city, but Isobel was not impressed: she sometimes thought he had not moved away from the London mind-set. However, the more trips he made out into the country, the more he appreciated the fresh air and open spaces. Isobel, for her part, had concluded that she should give up the management of the village store — but what would she do? Charles would be away all day and Chris would be at school. Since Chris was just a few weeks old, Isobel had worked and, though not expected of married women, it was what she wanted. By the spring of 1951, with a wedding date set for the end of August, they found a solution. A hotel, in a village set back from the coast a few miles south of East Bay, came on the market. It was a bold move but it meant a new start for them both.

Charles assumed that he would pay for the property, funding the entire venture himself, but Isobel had other ideas. "This has to be a joint enterprise," she insisted. She had her own savings, as well as money left over from the sale of her house in Fulham: she had not used the entire proceeds for the cottage now occupied by her parents. Charles hesitated. He had been brought up to believe that men should take total responsibility in these matters. But his future bride was adamant. Following the war, when many women were forced into work, she maintained that the world was changing. "Okay," he relented. It was the right decision.

In June the invitations were sent out for the wedding. The ceremony was to take place in the small church at East Bay, the reception at a hotel in the market town. Guests were sparse on Charles's side; just a few work colleagues and their partners. He had no relatives. Isobel asked if he would invite the Wrights, but he declined. He had not told them of his engagement. He did, however, suggest that he ask Timothy Campbell to be his best man. "I know he's a bit old for this role, but he has been so supportive since I arrived here, and recently he has become a real friend as well as a colleague." Isobel had never met the man, but she could see no problem with that.

When Charles approached Timothy the next working day, his colleague was flummoxed by the request. He began to make excuses until he saw the look of disappointment on the young man's face. He apologised.

"I'm so sorry — of course, I would be honoured to be your best man. Please forgive my hesitation."

Charles put his colleague's initial uncertainty down to surprise. Neither had made many references to their personal lives, so it was understandable that Timothy was taken aback. Charles, of course, had no idea of the real reason!

CHAPTER 16
A Strange Reunion

Sitting at home later that evening, Timothy contemplated how he was going to deal with the problem. He could not just appear as best man at his granddaughter's wedding — he had to reveal his identity: something he had yearned to do for years, yet always avoided. He had to see Jeannie — but how? He could hardly turn up on her doorstep unannounced. It was highly unlikely that she would have a telephone, and trying to explain things in a letter was far too complicated. *I'll sleep on it* was the best he could come up with. Well, he slept on it for three nights before an idea eventually occurred to him. The shop in East Bay which, to his knowledge, Isobel still ran, must have a telephone. He would ring her with a request to speak with Jeannie or meet her — or something! In the end, he rang the store, not quite knowing what to say, but knowing he had to start somewhere.

He made the phone call from his office in Aberdeen, at a time when he knew the village store would be open. "Can I speak with Isobel?" he asked.

"This is Isobel speaking, how may I help you?" came the polite voice at the other end of the line.

"My name is Timothy. I wonder, could you pass on a message to your grandmother." There was a short pause before Isobel answered…

"Yes, I can. What would you like me to tell her?"

"Can you ask her to meet me at ten o'clock on Saturday morning?"

"Y- y -yes, I'll do that. Where shall I tell her to meet you?"

"Oh, she'll know," came the unexpected response.

"Oh — okay, and what was your name again?"

"Timothy — just say Timothy would like to meet her."

To say that Isobel was baffled would be an understatement. But she would certainly pass on the information to Jeannie. The gentleman on the telephone sounded very polite, rather posh in fact, but the conversation was — well, unusual. She didn't quite know what to make of it.

Isobel waited until Chris was in bed that night before she brought up the subject.

"I had a phone call today from a gentleman asking to meet you."

"Oh, yes," Jeannie responded, with sarcasm, thinking her granddaughter was teasing.

"No, really Grandma, a gentleman did phone. He was very polite and quite specific. He wanted me to ask you to meet him at ten o'clock on Saturday morning."

"And who was this gentleman?"

"He said his name was Timothy," Isobel replied. "I did ask a second time but he just said to say Timothy would like to meet you."

Jeannie turned pale — she felt numb; dumbfounded.

In an attempt to break the silence Isobel added, "I didn't know you had a secret admirer?"

Still, Jeannie made no response.

Isobel stared curiously at her grandmother, "Would you like me to make you a cup of tea?" she asked.

"Y-y-yes, please do," Jeannie managed to utter.

Together the two of them sat and drank tea — in silence. Then Isobel commented, "He didn't say where you were to meet."

"Oh, I know where to meet him," Jeannie answered, just as Timothy had predicted.

If Isobel was expecting an explanation to this mystery, she was sorely disappointed for, clearly, her grandmother was not giving anything away. Maybe she would be more willing to talk about this stranger once the meeting had taken place — that is if it did take place!

The next day, Friday, Jeannie was in a state of agitation, mixed with eager anticipation. It was fifty years since she had met Timothy at the graveyard when, with tears in his eyes, he had held their baby daughter. She was only fifteen years old and he, seventeen. Half a century! *Why now?* she thought. If there was any doubt that she would meet, it was short-lived. She knew she would be there. She knew *he* would be there.

On Saturday morning Timothy drove to East Bay. He parked his car by the side of the road, a short distance from the church. It was well before ten o'clock. He strolled across to the graveyard, out of sight of the road, to wait for 'his girl'. *What would she think of him? — an old man of sixty-seven with greying hair — hardly the young admirer of her youth.*

Jeannie, widowed six months earlier, dressed smartly, making a special effort for the occasion. At sixty-five, she still held herself well. Her hair was light in colour, though not the blonde it had once been. There was a sadness about her features — the loss of her parents and her husband in such a short space of time had taken its toll; yet she had much to be thankful for.

As she made her way around the church, her heart missed more than a beat. Hearing her footsteps on the gravel path, Timothy stepped forward to greet her. Facing each other, fifty years melted away. Taking her hand, Timothy led her to where they could sit on the wall at the far end of the graveyard, away from prying eyes. It was a bright sunny morning. They had much to talk about.

Although it was a strange reunion after so many years, it somehow seemed natural. Recounting her thoughts, Jeannie asked the question, "Why now?"

The response, "I'm to be best man at your granddaughter's wedding," was the last thing she expected to hear. "But," he added, "I would have come to see you soon anyway. I was sorry to hear of Edward's death."

Jeannie listened, intrigued by the story of his association with Charles Carter. She was glad that it had prompted him to see her. But, the main focus of that first meeting was Kitty. Timothy wanted to know all about his daughter. Jeannie told of Kitty's happy childhood, up to the time when she discovered that the Smiths were not her real parents, but her grandparents; that Jeannie was her mother, not her sister, as she had believed.

"She was so angry, she didn't speak to me for months," Jeannie recalled, "not until young Eddie, her half-brother was born. She started to call my mother and father Granny and Grandpa which, of course, they were: it caused a bit of a stir in the neighbourhood at first. The opportunity to go to the private school in the city, where she boarded during the week, was a blessing. At this point, Jeannie looked at Timothy. "That was you, wasn't it?"

Timothy confessed. "I didn't know how I could help her. I was not aware of the friction within your family, but I did know from a friend of mine, who was the Headmaster at her primary school, that she was a very bright girl — his star pupil. I just wanted to give her a chance."

More than an hour had passed when Jeannie said she must get home to prepare some lunch for her great-grandson, Chris. "Where do we go from here?" she asked.

"Well, the rest of your family need to know who I am," Timothy replied.

"Most of the family will understand our story — all, that is, except Kitty. Our daughter can be headstrong. I don't know how she will react when I tell her we've met. How can I get in touch with you? I don't even know your last name!"

"It's Campbell, Timothy Campbell. I'll give you my office number. Let me know how you get on with Kitty. Perhaps I can take you out for dinner next Saturday evening?"

"Yes, I'd like that." Jeannie nodded.

"I'll pick you up at half-past six."

As they parted Timothy once again took Jeannie's hand. "I'm so sorry for the agony I've caused you. I've thought of you often over the years. I hope we can be friends."

CHAPTER 17
Timothy Meets his Daughter

The next day Jeannie decided to see Kitty. She didn't want to leave it until next weekend, and her daughter would be working at the bank during the week.

Charles had arranged to pick up both Isobel and Chris on Sunday morning to take them into Aberdeen for the day. Chris was excited — he liked this man who was soon to become his stepfather. Jeannie asked Charles if he would give her a lift to her daughter's. It was not far out of their way.

"Have a good day!" came a chorus of voices as she stepped out of the car. They had no idea of the nature of her mission.

Here goes, Jeannie thought, as she entered the cottage.

"Hello, Ma! Good to see you," came the greeting from both Kitty and Sandy, as they heard the door creak, "the kettle's on."

Once settled, Jeannie became serious, "I have something to say," she announced. There was a pause as she gathered her thoughts. "I've just met your father."

"What do you mean?" Kitty retorted, "You've always claimed you didn't know who my father was."

Sandy caught his wife's arm. "Let yer Ma hae her say. Ye'r aye too quick wi' yer sharp tongue."

Jeannie continued, "All I knew, until yesterday, was his first name, Timothy. He went to a boarding school in

Edinburgh and talked with a posh accent. I suspected that he was the benefactor responsible for the trust that allowed you to attend the private school in Aberdeen. I was right. Honestly, that's it. It was Timothy who contacted me."

"And how did he know where to find you?"

"He knew I was married to Edward Milne. He had been passing the church on our wedding day as we came out of the church. Over the years he has seen references and heard news of the family."

"You mean he's been snooping on us?" sniped Kitty.

Jeannie was suddenly angry — "He's your father," she fumed, her voice raised. "Do you want to hear what I have to say or not?"

It was a long time since Kitty had seen her mother even slightly annoyed. She realised she had better listen.

"Charles Carter, Isobel's fiancé, is a lawyer with the same firm as Timothy. He has asked Timothy to be his best man at their wedding in August. That's why he had to get in touch with me."

Kitty still felt that this man, her father, whatever his name was, knew far too much about the family. He had deserted her as a child. What business was any of this to him?

Reading her thoughts Jeannie went on…

"When you were conceived, we were a couple of kids. I was only fourteen and Timothy sixteen. We were too young to be married, too young to make any decisions. Timothy never wanted to leave us, but there was nothing he could do. Don't you understand, even now? He provided for your education, otherwise you would never have been able to get a job at the bank."

Kitty relented. Her mother had a point; and she was in no doubt that Sandy was on her mother's side.

"I'll go and get the dinner on," Kitty announced. It was a legitimate excuse to distance herself from the argument and think things over.

Before Jeannie left, it was agreed that Kitty should meet her father before the rest of the family were made aware of the situation. Jeannie promised to suggest this to Timothy. It wasn't until she was back at her house later that afternoon that she realised she had not mentioned Timothy's last name to her daughter.

Jeannie contacted Timothy at his office on Monday afternoon to give him a brief resumé of her 'confrontation' with Kitty. She suggested a meeting between father and daughter the following Sunday, if that was possible. She would give Timothy a detailed update when they met on Saturday evening — their first proper date!

All that week Jeannie could think of nothing but seeing Timothy again. He was not the boy she had last seen fifty years ago, but she liked him: her original attraction had not waned. It was obvious that he had been concerned for her and Kitty over the years: he appeared genuinely kind and considerate. She fretted for days as to what she should wear on Saturday, raking through her summer wardrobe for something suitable for dinner with a 'gentleman'. Had she known of his real status she would, no doubt, have fretted a good deal more!

Similarly, Timothy looked forward to an evening out with 'his girl'. Funny, he had never stopped thinking about her in that way. It wasn't that he hadn't cared for his wife, but Jeannie was different. She was natural; down to earth; respectable in her way, but without the airs and graces of the 'well-to-do set' he had so often encountered in his capacity as a Laird. It was only then that it occurred to him — did Jeannie know that he was a wealthy landowner? Would that knowledge put her off? Still, he wasn't going to let that thought spoil their time together. His hope, his desire, was to get to know her better; to be a part of her family; to welcome her into his home, and... whatever?

Timothy picked Jeannie up on schedule as promised, early on Saturday evening. Two pairs of eyes watched surreptitiously from behind the net curtains in the front room. Isobel had quizzed her grandmother constantly about 'the secret admirer' she had met the previous Saturday; the man who was now taking her out to dinner. But Jeannie would not be drawn. His name is Timothy, was all she was prepared to say, telling her she would know soon enough. Isobel's curiosity was further aroused when Chris turned to her and said: "I've met him before. He's the nice man who came to see me when I was in the hospital."

"Oh! Are you sure?" Isobel was startled. "That was a long time ago Chris."

"I'm sure," Chris was adamant. "He smiled at Great-Grandma just like he smiled at me. We had lots of fun."

If Isobel was baffled before, she was even more baffled now. What on earth was going on?

Jeannie knew that her granddaughter and her son would have their noses pressed against the window: they would be watching as she made her way down the garden path and along the road with Timothy to where he had left his car, but she was not worried: they would discover the truth soon enough. In the meantime, this was her moment — their moment. Timothy's car was 'up market': not the sort of vehicle usually found on the streets of the little village. She felt like royalty as he held the passenger door open for her. The hotel/restaurant where Timothy had booked a table was about four miles away, in the direction of Aberdeen. It was very much like the place Isobel and Charles had described they were looking to purchase. In fact, it *was* the place they intended to purchase!

The evening was one of the most pleasant Jeannie could ever recall. Timothy treated her like a real lady, attending to her every need. How different things could have been, she thought. But, she reminded herself, Ted had been a good husband: she had been very fortunate.

Although he had held an interest in the family over the years, Timothy only really knew what was common knowledge: the births, the marriages and the deaths. Stuart's abduction had made headlines at the time: it had left Timothy feeling helpless. The child was, after all, his grandson. Chris's accident was embedded with the news of the VE Day celebrations, but it had not escaped his notice. He had dared to visit the boy in hospital — perhaps the most reckless move he had made. As for Alec, he was definitely the best candidate to manage a farm. Although Timothy wanted him for the job, he had taken great care to ensure that the decision lay with others; he had had no hand in the appointment.

That first evening together the couple, understandably, spoke mostly of Jeannie's family: the family from which, by circumstance, Timothy had always been estranged. If he was concerned by Jeannie's reference to Kitty's reaction to the knowledge that he was her father, he did not show it. He hoped that his daughter would come to terms with it and that, one day, she would accept him; but he could hardly blame her for her initial response: the news must have been quite a shock. It was only over dinner that Jeannie confirmed the arrangement for the two of them, father and daughter, to meet the following day. It was agreed that he would visit Kitty in her home at half-past ten in the morning. Sandy would leave them alone. "But you'll be there?" he asked Jeannie.

"No, no I won't. The two of you should be left together. But come round to my place afterwards. I'll cook a Sunday roast if that's all right with you?"

"That'll be great," he replied.

Now it was Jeannie's turn to ask the questions:

"Until last week I only knew your first name. Although, when you said you were Timothy Campbell, I recalled what you said as you held Kitty in your arms all those years ago. You looked at her and murmured, 'Kathryn Campbell'."

"I'm sorry, Jeannie, it was not my place, but I've always thought of her as Kathryn Campbell; it's who she should have been."

"Maybe it's time you told me a little more about yourself?" Jeannie interrupted his thoughts. "I know you're a solicitor and you drive a very nice car. I'll bet you live in one of those posh houses on the Queen's road in Aberdeen," she teased, with a smile.

"Well — not exactly," he responded. "I live in the country — in a castle."

Timothy grinned. Jeannie didn't believe him. She gazed at him, seeking the truth.

"No, really, Jeannie. I own a lot of land: I live in a castle."

There was a long pause as Jeannie tried to assess the situation.

"You mean you're the Laird?"

"Yes," he confirmed, "I'm the Laird."

"B-b-but I've just asked you to come for dinner tomorrow."

"Yes, and I've accepted your invitation."

"But, I'm not grand, I'm very ordinary."

He leaned across the table, took both her hands in his and very softly whispered. "Jeannie, it makes no difference to me. I want to know you. I want you to be my girl."

Timothy proceeded to tell Jeannie more about his life: his marriage, his profession, and his estate. As she listened, she realised that his life was much less exciting than she would have imagined for a laird. His closest relative was a brother in London who had no interest in the estate. Other than that he had a cousin in Fyffe whom he rarely saw, and some family of his late wife, who kept in touch from time to time.

Jeannie asked what he did with his time. He told her he had always loved his career as a lawyer. He had colleagues in the city and former school friends in different parts of the country. But equally, he enjoyed his life on his estate.

"I help out a lot in the garden in the summertime, I grow my own vegetables and cook, although I do have a gardener and a housekeeper. I have to oversee the whole estate, but mostly I leave the farm managers to get on with things: they are all very efficient, and that..." he hesitated, "includes Alec."

"You mean my grandson — our grandson — manages a farm on your estate?"

"Yes, and very well too. According to Mr Wilson, he was one of the best workers he had come across. He was very deserving of the appointment, which, by the way, I had nothing to do with. Aside from passing him on the farm road, I never met the boy until afterwards."

"So, does Alec know you're his grandfather?"

"No, I shouldn't think so. How could he?"

Having finished their meal, Timothy suggested they move to two armchairs at a low table set in a corner of the restaurant, where they might sit in comfort to have a coffee. With a little more understanding of each other, the pair relaxed. They spent the remainder of the evening conversing about things other than family.

When they arrived back in East Bay, Timothy escorted Isobel right to her door, where he kissed her gently on the forehead saying he looked forward to coming for lunch the following day.

Although Timothy had told Jeannie he was happy to meet Kitty on Sunday, he was more concerned about it than he had let on. He hardly slept that night, worried that his daughter might turn him away. Had he been a party to some of the exchanges Kitty and Sandy had had during the week, regarding the forthcoming encounter, he might have been a little less anxious. Sandy reasoned with his wife that the man could only mean well and, since he was to play a significant role in the nuptials of their only daughter, the biggest family celebration, other than funerals, that had occurred in a long time, she had better get used to the idea. Sandy and Kitty rarely quarrelled. They had suffered much over the years, with Sandy's poor health, the war, and the disappearance of their youngest child. The last two years had seen the deaths of her grandparents and stepfather. The appearance of her real father should be something to celebrate, not argue about.

Fortunately, the break of a week, between getting the news of her father's existence and meeting him, gave Kitty the chance to calm down. The initial shock of discovering her true parentage had never completely left Kitty. But her mother was right: the opportunity to spend four years at the private school in Aberdeen, where she had boarded during the week, was her saving grace; and that, she now understood, had been her father's doing.

As Timothy approached the door of his daughter's cottage he made a conscious effort to smile, while inside he was trembling. He didn't ever remember feeling like this in his life: perhaps because, more than anything, he wanted this relationship to work.

If there was any anger remaining within Kitty, it dissolved when she looked up at the elderly gentleman standing on the threshold. To the observant onlooker, there was no mistaking that they were father and daughter. For a few moments a silence hung in the air.

"Timothy Campbell," he stated by way of introduction.

"Dad," she replied. The ice was broken.

To say that the next hour went according to plan would be a mistake, for there was no plan. Father and daughter understood one another and, despite the past, there was a connection. All was well and the bond was strong enough to counter the next surprise when, unannounced, Alec arrived and, opening the door of the living room, came face to face with the Laird...

CHAPTER 18
Isobel and Charles

Timothy arrived at Jeannie's for lunch a little later than anticipated, but very happy at the way the morning had gone. Jeannie was relieved that Kitty had come to terms with events; though rather alarmed when she heard that Alec had arrived unexpectedly.

"It was fine," Timothy reassured her. "I emphasised that you had no idea I was a laird until last night."

"And are there any other surprises?" she asked, tongue in cheek.

"I don't think so," he stated firmly; forgetting, for the moment, about his meetings with Chris.

The Sunday dinner was almost ready when Timothy arrived. He offered to carve the meat and insisted on washing up afterwards. The meal passed smoothly. Isobel decided she must treat Timothy as — well, Timothy. Judging by some of the things he had told her the previous evening about his life, she was beginning to realise that her rather awesome idea of what it meant to be a laird was not quite as she had imagined. In the afternoon, Jeannie suggested they go for a walk, just keeping to the path round to the next bay, as neither was dressed for scrambling around on the rocks. The walk turned into a trip down memory lane as they followed the footpath, stopping on a grassy bank, where they sat down, looking out to sea.

"Would you like to join me for dinner next Saturday evening?" he asked, as they strolled back to the house.

"I'd like that very much," she replied.

"I could pick you up early in the afternoon. If you bring some suitable shoes, I'll show you around the estate first."

"And where will we be eating?" she questioned.

"Oh, I'll cook. It's a while since I entertained, but I'm sure I can manage," he stated positively, with a grin.

Jeannie invited Timothy in for a cup of tea after their walk. As they sat in the living room admiring the view of the bay from the large window, the front door opened and in came Isobel, Chris and Charles. Jeannie had not expected them back so soon.

Before there was time for any introductions, Chris went straight up to Timothy. "You're the man who came to see me in hospital, aren't you? I told Ma it was you last night," at which the child sat down on the settee, squeezing himself between Timothy and his rather startled grandmother. Isobel and Charles stood at the entrance to the living room, totally confused.

"I can explain," Jeannie stated, "well, I can explain most of it," she corrected, looking at her grandson. "This is Timothy Campbell. He's your grandfather."

Turning to Isobel and adding to the confusion, Charles indicated with his hand, "This is my colleague, Timothy Campbell."

"Is there any tea left in that pot?" Isobel asked, not knowing what else to say...

The following Saturday Timothy picked Jeannie up from her home shortly after lunch. Much to her surprise, the castle was hardly more than four miles from East Bay, although the Estate itself stretched well beyond. Timothy suggested they tour the area first before showing her around the castle and grounds. She changed into her walking shoes ready for a long trek, but Timothy directed her to a Land Rover parked round the side of the building. They drove along country roads, up and down rough tracks and passed farm buildings and cottar [iv] houses. Timothy stopped close to a wooded area on a hill slope. They walked for about half a mile along a woodland path to a clearing, from where they had a view across the farmland and over to the distant hills of Bennachie. Their next stop was a farmhouse. Instead of knocking on the door, as Jeannie had expected, they wandered past several byres and a milking shed, through a gate into a field of cattle. "This is Alec's farm," he announced. "I thought Alec might be around to show you himself. He's a dairy farmer, although he does grow some crops and keeps a few Jacob sheep."

As they returned to the farmyard, Alec emerged from the house.

"Ah, I thought that was your Land Rover!" he exclaimed. "Well, Grandma, it's good to see you. Have you time for a cup of tea?"

[iv] Farm labourer's cottages

190

"That would be lovely," she responded, looking to Timothy for approval.

The farm kitchen faced south. It was spacious, with a large wooden table set in the centre, flanked by several chairs.

"Time you had a wife." Timothy quipped.

"One day, Mr Campbell, "one day."

From the tone of the conversation, it was obvious that Timothy had teased the lad about this before. When Alec had first taken on the farm, he had been unsure about living in the farmhouse. The small cottage he had occupied before was quite adequate. However, he felt he needed to be on the job, so he let out the cottage, moved into the big house and hired a cleaner for two mornings a week, to keep the place in order and manage his washing and ironing. So far, it was working well. He wasn't in a hurry to be married — not yet!

Back at the castle, Timothy showed Jeannie around the gardens. There was a large, beautifully laid out lawn to the rear of the castle, surrounded by shrubs, trees and flowerbeds; but his pride and joy was the kitchen garden and the home-grown produce that he attended to himself.

The castle was, of course, far too large as a residence for a sole occupant: an observation that caused Jeannie to smile as she considered the recent dialogue between Timothy and her grandson. It did not go unnoticed. Her host gave her a guided tour of the whole castle before leading her into a section, which he referred to as his 'living quarters.' The rooms, with their wood panelling, high ceilings and beautiful furniture were grand but manageable. She imagined that the drawing room would be quite comfortable in the winter when the fire would be lit. However, it was the kitchen, not unlike her grandson's farmhouse kitchen, where she felt most at home. It was not just a place to cook, as her scullery at home, but a place to sit in comfort. Again she imagined how cosy it might feel in the wintertime, sitting round the open fire. Sensing her approval Timothy confessed, "This is where I spend most of my time."

The evening meal was superb: Timothy certainly could cook. Also, he stated proudly that everything was produced on the estate. The new potatoes and vegetables he had grown himself, the fillet steak was from one of the farms and the dessert, a fruit salad, consisted entirely of his own home-grown fruit.

Jeannie had always considered lairds as landed gentry, to be waited on hand and foot by their minions, not getting their hands dirty. How wrong she was — or wrong in the case of Timothy. She had been so taken aback when she had discovered his status, thinking that he was far too affluent to be involved with the likes of her; thinking that he would soon regret his desire to make himself known to her. But she was beginning to realise that she was wrong. Wealth may have its benefits but it had not brought Timothy what he wanted — a real home, a family.

Strangely, having visited his castle, Jeannie was feeling more comfortable with this man who was so much a part of her family. As for Timothy, he had no regrets about finding Jeannie. To him, she was still beautiful; she was still 'his girl'. During the next two months, they met regularly, becoming ever closer.

The plans for the wedding of Isobel and Charles were finalised and the remaining family members were made aware of Timothy Campbell's place in the family. If they thought it strange, they refrained from commenting, for they could see that Jeannie was happy.

The wedding in the little church at East Bay was delightful, followed by a meal and a ceilidh at a hotel in the town. The newlyweds spent their first night together at the same venue, but set off by car the following morning for a short break. Charles had organised a honeymoon in Inverness, where he had booked a hotel for a week. Neither Isobel nor Charles had ventured up to the Highlands before, but Charles had carefully mapped out the route and identified some of the places they might visit during the week. It was a carefree time for both, in the midst of their busy lives, that were about to get even more hectic. The completion date on the purchase of the hotel, which would also be their new home, was scheduled for the week of their return from holiday.

Chris, who had just begun his final year at primary school, was still staying with Grandma Jeannie, but he would join his mother and Charles as soon as they moved into their new home. For his eleventh birthday, he had been given a brand new bicycle, allowing him the freedom to cycle to and from East Bay at the weekends and during the school holidays. Most of his friends still lived in the village although, since the village school had closed, he had made friends with other boys who stayed out in the country.

Running the hotel was quite a challenge for Isobel and Charles, especially for the first year. Their particular skills were very much geared to administration. Ordering supplies and keeping the books in order was second nature to Isobel, after spending so many years managing the village store: Charles could cope with the legal issues but dealing with some of the practicalities was a different matter. The chef's day off proved tricky on more than one occasion during the first few months. Both had to turn their hand to the mundane chores involved in the daily routine, often being particularly busy in the evenings and at weekends. Although only a small hotel, with six guest bedrooms, there were moments when they wondered if they had taken on too much. But both were determined by nature: neither was going to give up easily. However, they were not going to succeed by running themselves ragged. It was not until after the New Year celebrations that the couple found time to sit down and consider how best to proceed.

When she was running the shop, Isobel rarely had any qualms about leaving her assistant in charge. With the hotel, she was reluctant: perhaps because they owned as well as managed the business. They both agreed that she needed to 'let go' — to be more trusting of the staff. Charles also needed some time out. He suggested they should have one night a week together, away from the hotel, or at least away from the work of the hotel, and that Isobel needed some time off during the week. The idea was good, the logistics more difficult. Unexpectedly, it was Timothy who came to the rescue. He had noticed, on several occasions, how tired Charles looked when he arrived at the office. He didn't need to be told what the problem was: he had spent years juggling his work as a solicitor and overseeing the estate. The secret was, as the young couple had already surmised, delegation.

"I was wondering," he said to Charles, "I have a young widow living in one of the cottages on the estate. Her husband died last year and, after being called up for national service, her son decided to sign on — he's now in the regular army. Mary is only around the age of forty. She is looking for a job and somewhere to live. Perhaps you could accommodate a live-in assistant?"

Charles pondered over the suggestion, hesitating for a few moments before answering. "That sounds like a good idea. I'll speak with Isobel tonight."

The more Charles thought about it, the more it made sense. However, whether this widow was the right person was something they would have to consider carefully.

Isobel, as he had anticipated, was reluctant at first. "We would have to interview her and, if she seems willing, give her a trial run. She might not want the job."

Mary, as it turned out, was thrilled at the idea. She didn't feel right about continuing to occupy what was technically accommodation for farmworkers, and she was desperately lonely: she needed to be with people.

Dressed in her Sunday best, Mary arrived at the hotel, bright and early, on a Saturday morning in February. The farmer had given her a lift into the town, where she had caught the local bus. Charles had offered to come for her, but she had declined, wanting to assert her independence.

Charles and Isobel had decided to talk to the candidate separately, comparing notes afterwards. Mary was nervous. Apart from helping out with the harvests during the war, she had not worked since her marriage, twenty years earlier. However, her job for six years had been in a boarding house, where she covered just about every aspect involved in the running of the place.

Both Isobel and Charles were impressed. Leaving their applicant alone for a few minutes, they decided to offer her a month's trial, working a few days each week when she would stay overnight, but not giving up her cottage until they were all sure. If she were happy with the offer, they would give her a guided tour of the whole place: she had so far only seen the public areas.

Mary was delighted. She would begin the following week, working Friday to Monday. February was the least busy time of the year for guests, although the bar could be quite busy at the weekends.

The appointment of Mary was the best decision the couple had made since taking over the hotel. It was a great relief to Isobel to have someone else living on the premises; someone who was competent, efficient and willing to turn their hand to anything. As for Mary, she could not have been happier with the arrangement. She had her own living quarters, a job and company.

Over the next few months, Timothy visited often, sometimes with Jeannie for an evening meal, but at least once a week for a drink. If they were busy, he would lend a hand, serving behind the bar. Then, one day, he told the couple to take the next evening off: he said it was time they had a night out, away from the place; he would easily manage. Isobel argued, but her grandfather was not taking 'no' for an answer. If the business was to survive, she needed to let go. Thereafter, once a week, Timothy relieved the pair of their duties, taking full responsibility. With Mary to help him, there was never a problem.

During this time, Timothy saw much more of his great-grandson. He was delighted to get to know him better. Chris, in turn, adored this new grandpa, who showed a genuine interest in him. The two of them would go for walks along the beach and the cliff tops. Best of all were his visits to the castle when Grandma Jeannie would often be there too and he could bring a friend. Grandpa would set them tasks to do in the castle grounds. They were allowed to walk or cycle around the estate, as long as they kept to the paths. Sometimes they ventured as far as Uncle Alec's farm, on the pretext that they had come to help!

Chris left primary school that summer. A capable student, he had gained a scholarship to attend grammar school in Aberdeen. Alternatively, he could go to the academy in the town, along with most of his friends. Chris wasn't sure — even though his Uncle Ernie had gone to the Grammar School and was now a doctor. He decided to talk to his grandmother, Kitty. She had no doubts: "Go to the Grammar School," she stated firmly. Until that moment Chris had no idea that Grandma Kitty had attended a private school herself.

His mother and stepfather also encouraged him, but Chris still hesitated. His friends from East Bay were all going to the local academy. It was his grandpa, Timothy Campbell, who finally persuaded him. He said he thought he would do well wherever he went, but there would be more opportunities open to him if he took up the scholarship: he was lucky to get the chance. Timothy also pointed out that the academy was much bigger than his primary school: he may not even be in the same class as his friends.

Chris thought about this. Going to school in Aberdeen appealed to him and, he reasoned, he would still see his pals in East Bay at weekends and in the holidays. Finally, his mind was made up. On visiting the Grammar School before the end of the summer term he noticed his uncle's name, a former head boy, engraved on a plaque in the entrance hall. He knew he had made the right decision.

The thought of his new school was not the only bit of excitement that summer. For several weeks his mother had not been very well, often suffering from sickness: it wasn't like her, she was normally so fit and healthy. Then, towards the end of July, she perked up. "I have something to tell you," she said to Chris, one evening at bedtime, "I'm going to have a baby." It took Chris a few minutes to process this piece of news before a broad grin crossed his face. "I'm going to have a little brother!" he exclaimed.

"A brother, *or a sister*," his mother corrected him.

That was even better — a little sister! Chris was thrilled.

CHAPTER 19
Jamie Meets Chris

About a week after hearing this news, Chris was messing around on the rocky beach at East Bay when a lad he had not seen before approached him. "Hello," he said. "I'm Jamie; I'm here on holiday from England. Are you on holiday?"

"No, no," Chris replied. "I live here — well, near here," he corrected.

Jamie looked at him, wide-eyed, "You live here, by the sea?" he questioned. "I've never been to the seaside before."

Straight away, the two boys struck up a friendship. Chris was used to strangers who stayed at the Bay during the summer holidays. Many came back year after year, often to stay with relatives: they were a part of the community. Others, like Jamie's mother and his aunt, had rented a cottage. Jamie had been to Scotland before but had always stayed with family in the city. This was a real novelty for him. Chris liked this new friend. Fancy coming here all the way from England, he thought. 'Oxfordshire'— he'd heard of Oxford, the famous Oxford University.

Jamie, who was a year older than Chris, was totally in awe of his companion. For the next two weeks they saw one another every day. They explored the beaches and roamed over the top of the cliffs to an old castle close to the cliff edge. They walked across the field to another castle, not quite so old, but which was cloaked in mystery. All sorts of spooky stories had been inspired by the place. Chris took Jamie to the burnt-out cottage where his great-great-grandfather had died. They clambered over rocks; talked to the fishermen; peered into the lobster pots. During the second week, Chris stayed with Grandma Jeannie so that he could spend even more time with his new friend.

After some of their dangerous escapades, it was, ironically, while they were on the beach at East Bay that Jamie slipped on a rock sustaining a very nasty gash to his leg. Chris whisked a handkerchief from his pocket to try to stem the flow of blood, but it wasn't looking good.

"Come up to my house," he said. "My uncle arrived this morning to visit Grandma. He's a doctor; he'll sort you out."

Jamie hobbled alongside Chris, up to the house overlooking the bay. "My friend's hurt," Chris called as he opened the door.

Ernie appeared at the living room door, then stepped back to allow the two boys to pass through. Taking one look at the leg he ushered Jamie out again and into the scullery. "Sit on that stool," he ordered, "let me see."

He grabbed a cloth from the draining board and cleaned the area around the cut, which was still oozing blood. "Nasty," he said. "It'll need a stitch or two."

"Are we going to the hospital?" Chris asked.

Ernie raked in his trouser pocket, pulled out his car keys and tossed them to Chris. "Fetch my black bag, it's on the back seat."

Chris did as he was asked.

Ernie cleaned the wound, dabbed on some liquid and proceeded to close the gap with stitches. Chris watched open-mouthed — glad it wasn't him that was injured. Jamie was very brave but very white-faced.

"Now, Master Crispin, get your friend a drink, and make some tea for us while you're about it," his uncle ordered, with a smile, "and don't look so startled, I'm a doctor; it's what I do."

"Where's Grandma?" Chris asked.

"She just popped out for a few messages; she'll be back soon."

"And what have you two been up to?" Ernie asked.

"Nothing," the boys declared in unison.

"Nothing!" Ernie repeated. "Well, I hope you don't get up to something if that's what happens when you're doing nothing."

"Honest, Uncle Ernie, we were just walking along the rocks."

Ernie smiled, tongue in cheek. He recalled some of the antics he got up to when he was a boy, and that didn't seem so long ago.

The colour was beginning to return to Jamie's cheeks.

"How are you feeling now?" Ernie asked.

"A bit better," came the response, "thank you doctor."

"You can call me Ernie, I'm off duty now. So — what brings you to this part of the world?" he asked.

In the space of ten minutes, Jamie told Ernie his life story, or so it seemed. It certainly served to distract his attention from his sore leg.

Jeannie was surprised to see the boys at home when she returned. Chris didn't usually appear until his stomach was rumbling. She was horrified at seeing Jamie's leg. Turning to Ernie, she suggested he see Jamie's mother to explain what had happened.

"Of course, Grandma, I intend to. He'll need to have the stitches taken out next week."

Later that morning, both Ernie and Chris escorted Jamie to the cottage his family had rented. Jamie's mother, Mrs Roberts, was alarmed at first, as Jamie proudly showed off his neatly stitched wound.

"Who attended to that for you?" she asked.

"I'm Ernest Anderson and this is my nephew Chris, Jamie's friend," Ernie interrupted. "I'm a doctor — a surgeon — I sorted Jamie's leg. He fell on the rocks."

"Oh, please, do come in," Mrs Roberts invited, directing them through to the living room. "I'm so sorry if he's caused you any trouble."

"Not at all Mrs Roberts. He is a very brave boy."

"So, you are Chris — Christopher Anderson?" Mrs Roberts questioned, turning to her son's new friend. "He's not stopped talking about you all week."

"No," Ernie chipped in. He's my sister's boy. He's Crisp…" Ernie stopped short, seeing the look on his nephew's face— he's Chris Leadbetter."

"And you're Doctor Anderson," she confirmed. "I'm so grateful to you, Doctor."

"He'll need to have those stitches taken out in a week or two. When are you travelling home?"

"We leave here at the weekend to stay with my parents in Aberdeen for a couple of days, before going back to Oxfordshire on Monday."

"I wish we could stay here longer!" Jamie exclaimed.

"You know I have to get back for my work, and Crispin will be longing to see you. Maybe we will stay here again next summer."

"Come on Chris," Ernie urged. "It's time we were getting back for lunch."

"Can I come to see Jamie this afternoon?" Chris asked.

"Yes, of course," his mother replied.

"They seem a really nice family," Ernie commented as they strolled back along the road. "It's a pity he has to go home so soon."

"Yes Uncle, I like Jamie lots. Thank you so much for helping him."

Chris only had Jamie's company for another two days, but they made the most of their time together. Before they parted Chris gave him his address and asked him to write to let him know if he was coming back next year.

"What's your name?" Jamie asked out of curiosity. "I thought Chris was short for Christopher, but I'm sure I heard your uncle call you Master Crispin."

"If I tell you, promise you won't tell any of my friends."

"I promise," Jamie assured him.

"I'm Crispin Leadbetter," Chris revealed. "It's not a common name in this part of the world — a bit too posh — my school friends would make fun of me if they knew."

Jamie was astonished but didn't let on. He didn't think that Crispin Leadbetter could be a common name anywhere in the world, not like his name. He was sure Jamie Roberts must be a more popular name, especially in Scotland. But, how was it he didn't know anyone else with the same name as his, yet he now had two friends, both called Crispin Leadbetter? *It's very strange*, he thought.

Jamie was sad to leave East Bay. It had been the best two weeks' holiday of his life — not that he had been on any other holidays, except visits to his grandparents and aunt in Aberdeen. Still, he was luckier than his friend at home. Poor Crispin never got to go anywhere. That thought sparked an idea in his mind...

For Chris, the summer holidays were nearly over. Meeting up with Jamie made him realise how fortunate he was. All year round he had the freedom to scour the beaches; to roam across the fields; to visit his new grandfather in the castle and, now that his mother was married, he even lived in a hotel.

CHAPTER 20
New Additions

Although he was looking forward to going to school in the city, Chris was apprehensive. He talked to his Uncle Ernie, telling him he was scared: worried about how he would get on with the city boys.

"You'll be fine," Ernie assured him. "I was scared too. Although I lived in the city, I was still leaving all my old school friends behind."

"Really!" Chris was astonished. He couldn't imagine his uncle being afraid of anything.

"Yes, really," Ernie told him. "I was petrified. Ma and Pa struggled to pay to send me there, and I had to work as a delivery boy to help out. I thought my classmates would all be posh, but they were just the same as I was— or just as different, whichever way you want to look at it. You're a clever lad, Chris, just as good as anyone else. Seriously, you won't have a problem."

Ernie was right. It was very strange at first, of course, but he soon settled into his new routine. He had no problem keeping up with the rest of the class, and was often top in Maths and English. He enjoyed sports and athletics. Usually, he managed to do most of his homework on the bus on his way home, leaving evenings and weekends free. As the summer drew to a close and the evenings became too dark for him to venture out, he began to help in the hotel, encouraged by Charles who gave him some pocket money for his efforts.

As Christmas approached, Isobel became increasingly tired. The baby was due in January but, from mid-December, she looked as if she was ready to produce at any moment. The last two weeks were exhausting. It was the second week in January when she went into labour. Chris had already set off for school in Aberdeen and Charles had left for his office. Following the festive season, the hotel was very quiet, with no guests booked in for that week. Mary, now very much a part of the family, was 'on hand' should her employer need assistance. She telephoned the cottage hospital in the nearby town, where Isobel had been booked in for her confinement, to let them know that they were on their way. She accompanied the expectant mother in a taxi, making sure that she was settled before contacting Charles. The midwife estimated that it would probably be several hours before the baby was born.

Charles tried to settle down for the rest of the day in his office, realising that there was nothing he could do if he dashed off to the hospital, as he was inclined to do. But, by lunchtime, Timothy ordered him to go. He could see that Charles was nervous, not concentrating on his work, and offered to deal with the only client booked in to see Charles that afternoon. He added that he would go straight to the hotel after work to help Mary so that Charles could stay at the hospital for as long as was necessary.

When Chris arrived home after school, he was bewildered to find that his mother was away, despite having been told that she would be going into the maternity ward at the local hospital for the birth. He pestered Mary for information, but all she could tell him was that he must be patient like everyone else, and wait for Charles to phone from the hospital.

Charles, meanwhile, was pacing up and down the corridor at the maternity wing of the hospital, becoming increasingly agitated.

"The baby will come in its own good time," the midwife told him. "Go to the café and get yourself something to eat," she urged. But Charles refused to go anywhere. Exhausted, he eventually flopped down on a seat outside the delivery ward. It was seven o'clock in the evening before a cry, emanating from the room, signalled the long-awaited arrival of his offspring. Several minutes elapsed before the midwife made an appearance to usher him into the room. She handed him a bundle wrapped in a shawl, "Your daughter," she announced, with a smile.

Taking the child in his arms, Charles breathed a sigh of relief only to be interrupted by the midwife telling him to have a quick word with his wife before she started to push for the next baby. Charles was momentarily stunned: "W-w-what are you saying?" he stuttered.

"I'm saying there's another baby on the way," she repeated, taking his daughter from his arms and allowing him a minute or two with his wife, before hurrying him out of the room to wait again. Fortunately, it wasn't long before another piercing cry was heard. This time it was the midwife who breathed a sigh of relief, as she once again opened the door to invite the proud father in. Charles glanced down at the two little girls lying in a cot, before going to his wife who was sitting up in bed looking calm though rather pale.

"Honestly, I didn't know," she said. "I really didn't know."

"There's no need to apologise," Charles remarked, attempting to cover his shock with a grin. He took both her hands in his and, kissing her gently on the lips, he whispered, "I love you."

After fifteen minutes, the midwife once again chased Charles out of the room.

"I've a lot of tidying up to do in here and your wife needs to rest. I suggest you come back tomorrow when you can spend a bit more time with her."

"Bring Chris," Isobel whispered, as they kissed goodnight.

Charles called the hotel from the hospital. He had two visits to make before returning home, but he needed to give Chris and Timothy the news first: he guessed they would be anxious, as indeed they were. Having lost his own mother when his younger brother was born, Timothy was more than a little nervous for his granddaughter. From the moment that Chris had arrived home from school, he had kept him busy, clearing tables, washing dishes, fetching in the coal — anything to stop the lad from asking him questions he couldn't answer. It was Timothy who picked up the telephone.

"They're fine, they're all fine. Can you put Chris on?" Charles sounded breathless.

Timothy let out a long low sigh as he handed the phone to his great-grandson. That they were all right was what mattered, but what did Charles mean by 'all'?

Tentatively, Chris took the phone. "Is Ma okay?" he asked. The reality of his mother being in hospital all these hours had made him almost as anxious as his great-grandfather, who had clearly been agitated, despite his attempts to stay calm.

"Yes," Charles replied, "she's well, but she's very tired. You have a baby sister," — there was a pause, before he added, "and another baby sister."

Chris blinked, "You mean there's two of them?"

"Yes, that's what I mean. Your mother had two baby girls. You have twin sisters! Now you can tell Grandpa the news. I'm going to see your grandparents, Kitty and Sandy, and Grandma Jeannie. I'll be home in about an hour — and I'm starving," he added

"Ma's had twins!" Chris exclaimed as soon as he had put the telephone down, "I have two sisters." Then, without thinking, he added, "Dad'll be home in an hour and he says he's hungry."

Timothy's eyes glazed over as he gave his grandson a hug. The reference to Charles as 'Dad', whether just a slip of the tongue or not, was an indication of how close he was to his stepfather. It was also a credit to Charles, who had accepted the boy as his own.

"Come on Chris, we'd better tell Mary the news and get something ready to feed the hungry traveller."

The next day Charles took Chris to the hospital. It was strange seeing his mother in her nightclothes sitting up in bed. He tiptoed over to give her a kiss, before turning his attention to the cot.

"Come and see," Charles beckoned.

Chris could scarcely believe his eyes at the sight of the two tiny babies, asleep side by side.

"Dad told me I had two sisters," Chris remarked to his mother, "but he didn't tell me their names."

Isobel glanced at Charles, noting the implication of the word 'Dad'. Neither commented, but from that day, Charles was Dad to three children.

"We thought we would call them Annabel and Rosemary; Annie and Rosie for short" his mother answered, at last. "What do you think?"

"I like those names," Chris responded. "But how will I know which is which?"

"In the hospital, they have little tags around their wrists. We'll have to think of something else when they come home. Maybe we could have a blue ribbon for Annie and a red one for Rosie."

"Come on, son," Charles said at last. "We've got a bit of shopping to do. Your parents will be in to see you this afternoon and I'll come back tonight," Charles assured his wife, as they departed.

"What do we have to shop for?" Chris asked.

"Well, we only provided for one baby. We'll need a twin pram, a bigger pushchair, more nappies and more clothes. Your mother has given me a list."

Isobel stayed at the maternity hospital for two weeks, allowing time for a good rest and recovery following the births. She appreciated the time to recuperate but was glad to be home. The next few months were hard work. How thankful Isobel was to have Mary.

Altogether it was an eventful year for Chris, with his move to the grammar school and the new additions to the family, and there was more to come. Just after Easter, he received a letter from Jamie to say that he would be staying at East Bay for two weeks at the beginning of August. He was looking forward to seeing Chris again. What he didn't tell him, partly because he wasn't sure, was that he was hoping to bring a friend with him...

PART III

SCOTLAND

CHAPTER 21
The Meeting

At almost twelve years of age, Stuart Anderson had lived his life as Crispin Nigel Leadbetter, knowing nothing of his true origin. At the end of his first year at the college, his supposed grandfather made an appointment to see the Headmaster before the end-of-year closing ceremony. Mr Smith was not pleased. He had a heavy schedule that day without having to waste time with this obnoxious man telling him how to run his school. It seemed Mr Leadbetter wanted to make life as hard as possible for the innocent boy, who was unfortunate enough to have this tyrant as his guardian. The school secretary had done her best to persuade the man to arrange a meeting for another day when the Head of the School would happily accommodate him. Crispin Leadbetter senior was incensed: he would not take 'no' for an answer. The last day of the term was the most convenient time for him since he would be attending the ceremony. He was not prepared to make two journeys. Mr Smith could barely contain his anger. In the whole of that year, neither of Crispin's grandparents nor any other family member — if there were any — had made the effort to attend important events in the school calendar. They denied the child the opportunity to return home for half-term breaks. Yet, periodically, there would be a telephone call from Mr Leadbetter demanding to speak with the Headmaster *immediately*.

Crispin knew that he had done well in his first year, yet it was with a sense of foreboding that he entered the large hall for the closing ceremony. It was the one occasion that his grandparents would be sure to attend and, as always, his grandfather would find something to criticise.

Following the prize-giving and a heart-warming rendering of the school song, years one to four were dismissed for the holidays. The older pupils, along with their parents, were invited to make their way to the library where tea would be served.

Crispin now faced the dreaded journey home by car — an ordeal that he had been relieved of since the end of primary school. As borne out by previous experiences, silence reigned. The grilling would come when they arrived home and he would be summoned to his grandfather's study.

As if on cue, no sooner had they entered the hall when the order came. "I'll see you in my room in ten minutes."

"Yes Sir," Crispin responded, politely.

Until he was inside the study, Crispin had no idea that his grandfather had had an audience with the Headmaster that morning. He stood, motionless, waiting for judgement to be passed. As anticipated, despite his good grades, Mr Leadbetter still managed to find fault. However, he dismissed him with a warning. He would be keeping a close eye on his performance over the next school year.

In reality, Mr Leadbetter had little to complain about. According to Mr Smith, Crispin was a good student: intelligent, attentive and diligent. He would do well.

As soon as Crispin left the study, closing the door behind him, he took the stairs two at a time up to the nursery, now converted to his sitting room, flopped down on the sofa and sighed. Whatever was he going to do for the next eight weeks?

Jamie was at school for another week. He would then be at home for a week before going to Scotland for a fortnight's holiday.

Crispin had never been on holiday. How he wished he could go away with his friend, but he couldn't begrudge him that pleasure. In a way, for Crispin, much of the school year was a holiday.

For one of the weeks that Jamie was away, Crispin went to stay with Henrietta and Raymond. They continued to take an interest in him, but Crispin was wary. He dared not reveal too much of his school life: he dreaded the consequences should a hint that he was happy reach the ears of his grandfather.

Crispin was relieved when Jamie came back, not just for his company, but also for the return of Mrs Roberts to her housekeeping duties. His grandmother complained endlessly about having to do all the chores herself.

Jamie was bursting to tell Crispin about his time in Scotland. Normally, he had only stayed with his grandparents in Aberdeen, so there had never been much to tell. This visit was different. He had loved being at the coastal village and finding a friend. He talked about the endless happy days he had spent with Chris on the beach and around the countryside. Crispin was agog as Jamie proudly showed off the stitches in his leg, telling him how Chris's Uncle Ernie had sewn up the gash. What he didn't tell Crispin was the strange coincidence of his new friend's real name. He had promised Chris he would keep that to himself.

It was after Christmas when Mrs Roberts received a letter from her sister to tell her she had arranged to rent the same cottage as before for the first two weeks in August. Jamie was delighted with the news. He suggested to his mother what had been on his mind for some time: that they invite Crispin to come up to Scotland with them. Mrs Roberts wasn't sure about the idea at first. Would Crispin want to, she wondered? Jamie was persistent. Crispin had never been on holiday, never been to the seaside; never seen the coast. Mrs Roberts had to agree that, despite his upbringing in a wealthy family, Crispin was, in many ways, neglected. It angered her to see the way that Mr Leadbetter treated the boy. Mrs Leadbetter, though not unkind to the lad, did not display the warmth that a grandmother would normally show — she was too wrapped up in her own lifestyle.

Mrs Roberts said she would check with her sister. If she agreed, then Jamie could ask Crispin when he came home at Easter. But she insisted that she would approach

Mrs Leadbetter herself, hoping that a positive outcome would be more likely if the request came from her rather than the boy.

Crispin, of course, was thrilled to be asked, but doubtful that he would be allowed such a privilege. Mrs Roberts was careful to choose the right moment to talk to Mrs Leadbetter. She knew that the idea would require the approval of Mr Leadbetter, but was not prepared to face him herself. Like Crispin, she kept out of his way as far as was possible.

Mrs Leadbetter was in favour of the idea, if only for the fact that it relieved her of the responsibility of the child for two weeks during the holiday: she could soon fill the gap with her own plans! Mr Leadbetter, as usual, was never agreeable to anything that would remove his grandson from a strict regime, but he had to concede that Mrs Roberts always managed to keep him in order and, for that reason, he did not react with the resounding 'no' his wife had expected. However, he was not giving in completely. The offer would only be accepted on the condition that Crispin's school grades came up to expectation.

Pleased that the request had not been rejected outright, Mrs Roberts updated her son who, in turn, shared the information with his friend. Crispin was thus prepared for the summons, which, he knew, would come. Standing yet again before his grandfather in the study, Crispin was careful not to betray his delight with a smile. Not that he had any difficulty, in view of the pending warnings he knew to expect. It meant that Crispin would have to wait until the end of the school term in mid-July before permission for the holiday would be granted.

Mr Leadbetter's grim adhesion to his own rules presented Mrs Roberts with a problem: she wanted to book seats on the train long before her employer would give his final approval. She was wondering how she was going to bring this problem to his attention when she, herself, was summoned to the study.

Feeling like a naughty child, she knocked, timidly, on the door. To her surprise it was Mrs Leadbetter who answered, immediately directing her to turn round and make her way to the sitting room. "We'll chat in comfort with a cup of coffee," she announced.

Mrs Leadbetter was not prepared to have her treasured housekeeper interrogated by her husband for making the generous offer to take their grandson on holiday. So the dreaded meeting turned out to be not so dreadful after all. Priscilla explained that they had discussed the proposal and, provided Crispin proved himself worthy of such a kind offer, he could join them for the two weeks' holiday. Mr Leadbetter then broached the subject of the cost. He would, of course, contribute in full to all expenses incurred. He asked the price of the rail tickets, which, he acknowledged, would need to be purchased in advance. Mrs Roberts professed that she would normally buy the tickets and book the seats three months before the journey: during the school holidays, the trains north were likely to be busy. Mr Leadbetter nodded in agreement.

"Mrs Leadbetter will have the money for you at the beginning of May. If Crispin's schoolwork is not of the standard we expect, the cost of the rail fare will be our loss."

Mrs Roberts breathed a sigh of relief as she escaped from the sitting room to make her way home. She was grateful that things had gone so well but aghast at the arrogance of the man, even as he demonstrated some goodwill. No doubt she would be provided with a set of instructions should the formidable gentleman be so kind as to allow his grandson to have two weeks' holiday.

Crispin was desperate to go away on holiday with Jamie, but dared not get too excited. His grandfather would not give his final consent until the last possible moment, keeping his grandson 'on his toes' throughout the term. Not that this latest threat made much difference. Crispin's greatest fear was being removed from his beloved school and his friends, to face a stricter regime elsewhere. He was thankful he found academic work relatively easy: studying was not a problem for him.

It wasn't until the last day of the school year, after Crispin had faced his grandfather in the study for a lecture on the importance of success and obedience, that permission was granted for him to go to Scotland.

In consultation with Mrs Roberts, Priscilla Leadbetter bought suitable clothing and footwear for her grandson. Crispin Leadbetter senior had furnished his wife with funds for his living expenses to give to the housekeeper before the departure: this included pocket money for

Crispin. Much to Mrs Robert's astonishment, Mr Leadbetter arranged and paid for a taxi to take the three of them to the railway station in London, thus taking much of the hassle out of the journey.

As he stepped into the waiting vehicle, waving goodbye to his grandparents, Crispin breathed a deep sigh of relief. Mrs Roberts smiled.

It was a long day, stretching into the early evening before they reached Aberdeen. Mrs Roberts had decided to travel by bus from the city since it would take them directly to East Bay, where her sister promised a hot meal for them on arrival. Although it was quite late by the time they had finishing eating, it was still broad daylight. The four of them decided to go for a stroll along the beach. It was the first time that Crispin had been anywhere near the sea, and still rather a novelty for Jamie. It was so good to breathe the fresh sea air, to listen to the water splashing against the rocks and hear the sound of the seagulls. As the daylight diminished, strange creatures swooped down towards the group, missing their heads by inches. "Bats," Jamie announced, showing off some of his knowledge from the previous year.

The two boys had imagined they would be chatting for half the night but fell asleep almost as soon as their heads hit the pillows. It had been a long day.

Chris cycled to East Bay the day that Jamie was due to arrive, where he had arranged to stay with Grandma Jeannie for most of the next fortnight. He was anxious to see his friend but the following day, being Sunday, he must first attend the service in the church with his grandmother, so it was after dinner before he made his way down to the shore. He saw Jamie at the far end of the bay skimming stones across the water but was a little dismayed to see that another boy was with him.

As he came closer to the two boys, Jamie turned round. Recognising Chris, he ran towards him greeting him with excitement.

"Who's your friend?" Chris asked, seeing the other boy looking on from a distance.

"He's my friend from home. Remember I told you about him last year. I'm sorry, I didn't tell you when I wrote because he didn't know until last week whether he would be allowed to come. You'll like him," he added. Chris wasn't so sure: he was a little disappointed — he'd looked forward to having Jamie to himself.

"Come on," Jamie coaxed, urging Chris to meet him.

As the two boys came face to face, the strangest feeling coursed through Chris's whole body: there was something familiar about this new visitor, though he couldn't quite think what it was.

"This is Crispin," Jamie announced, "and this is Chris," he said, as he introduced his two best friends.

Something inexplicable happened in the first moments of the meeting; it seemed that there was an immediate bond amongst the three young lads — the two, though unaware at the time, who were blood relatives, inextricably linked; and the third, who had unwittingly brought them together.

The boys spent the next few days exploring the beaches and the surrounding cliffs and countryside, with Chris as their guide. Then Chris said he would be cycling home on Wednesday after lunch, as he would be celebrating his thirteenth birthday with his family: he would be back on Thursday morning. He asked if they fancied visiting a Scottish castle later in the week — not like the ruins he had already shown them, but a real lived-in castle. Jamie and Crispin liked that idea.

"How can we do that?" they asked.

"Oh, just wait and see," Chris replied.

On Tuesday evening, as the boys parted, saying they would see each other in the morning before Chris went home, Crispin turned to Jamie and said, "It's my birthday tomorrow too, and I'll be thirteen."

"You should have said, I'd no idea, I'll ask Mum to make you a cake," Jamie suggested.

"No, no, I don't want to put your mum to any trouble," Crispin objected. "I just thought it a coincidence, Chris and I having the same birthday."

Jamie had still never revealed to Crispin that Chris was actually Crispin and that his last name was also the same.

As soon as they arrived at the rented cottage, Jamie announced that it was Crispin's birthday the next day. Crispin, exceedingly embarrassed, reacted: "I told you not to say anything."

Too late…Mrs Roberts and her sister looked at one another. They decided to organise a special birthday tea for Crispin. The boys would probably be out most of the day so it would be a surprise.

The following morning when the three boys met, Jamie wished his friend Chris a happy birthday leading the singing of *Happy Birthday* as they strolled along the beach. As soon as they had finished and bellowed out 'three cheers' he began again — this time for Crispin — much to the astonishment of a bewildered Chris.

The local store was well stocked, so purchasing the ingredients for a birthday cake was not a problem. By lunchtime, it was baked, iced and hidden away until teatime. With such short notice, a special birthday gift could not be obtained but the sisters did buy birthday cards and a very large box of chocolates: a treat that had been denied the nation until ten years of sweet rationing ended earlier in the year.

Crispin had a lovely day with Jamie and was delighted with his surprise birthday tea: he felt as if he really belonged. Meanwhile, Chris had an equally lovely day with a large family gathering at the hotel. During the celebrations he managed to have a chat with his great grandfather, Timothy Campbell, to ask if he could bring his two friends from England up to the Estate.

"Delighted," came the response, "I'll come to collect you if you like. Ten o'clock on Saturday morning at your Grandma Jeannie's."

Timothy was enjoying a cup of tea with Jeannie when Chris appeared with his two friends. A few minutes later they were clambering into the Land Rover, ready for a trip around the Estate before going to the castle. Their first stop was Alec's farm. Chris proudly showed his friends around his uncle's domain, leaving his uncle and great-grandfather to chat about farm business. Continuing the tour of the Estate they bumped their way along rugged roads and woodland paths, passing another two farms before heading for their destination.

By the time they arrived at the castle, it was well past noon.

"Time for some lunch," Timothy announced. "Chris, you can help; your friends are our guests. It's bacon butties all round."

Though simple, it was a hearty meal, made all the more pleasurable by this elderly gentleman, who obviously revelled in the company of these young lads.

In the afternoon, Crispin and Jamie were eager to see around the inside of the castle, so Timothy gave them a guided tour, while Chris disappeared out into the grounds. The two boys were intrigued by the place. Jamie, especially, was in awe of the grandeur: the oak panelling, the elaborate furniture. Crispin gazed at the paintings of the previous estate owners, ancestors of Timothy Campbell. "Are you a Lord?" Crispin asked.

"I'm a Laird," Timothy corrected, "It's the Scottish term for a landowner. I'm the Laird of this estate, which I inherited from my father, and his father before him: it's been in our family for many generations."

"So you're like a Lord and you live in a castle?" Jamie wanted to get all his facts right so that he could impress his school friends.

"That's about it," Timothy confirmed, with a smile. He had never considered it much of a privilege himself. There were times when he envied Jeannie, with her cosy house overlooking East Bay and the North Sea. They'd grown close since they met up two years ago; but their backgrounds, their lifestyles, were so different. He had contemplated being together all the time but, rattling about in his castle, however grand it might seem to these boys, was not Jeannie's idea of a home. In fact, to be truthful, it wasn't his idea either. The place needed a family; it needed life, not two ageing souls, although Jeannie had acknowledged that the private 'living quarters' were quite comfortable.

After seeing the inside of the castle, Timothy escorted the boys outside. Chris was engrossed, helping the gardener clearing up rubbish. Jamie made his way over to join his friend but Crispin lingered a while.

"So, your name's Crispin too?" Timothy remarked.

Crispin was not sure what he meant but answered politely, "Yes, that's right, Sir."

"And do you have any other names?"

"I'm Crispin Nigel Leadbetter," he whispered. "Jamie said it would sound very posh up here in Scotland, so I've not been telling everyone."

Timothy could barely disguise his surprise at hearing the name, or his amusement at the comment about it being posh.

"You're from Oxford, I hear," he said, wisely changing the subject.

"Yes; at least, I live in a village in Oxfordshire, but I spend term times at boarding school."

"I went to boarding school, too," Timothy revealed. "Do you like it?"

Somehow Crispin felt at ease speaking with this gentleman, who was so unlike the man he assumed to be his grandfather. He talked enthusiastically about his school and his friends, as they made their way across the garden to join Chris and Jamie. He said nothing of his family.

Timothy took the boys back to East Bay in his car, leaving the Land Rover in the driveway. He was taking Jeannie out for a meal in the evening. Mrs Roberts had invited Crispin to join them for an evening meal. It was a perfect end to the day.

Timothy and Jeannie had a lovely evening together, as always. He told her how much he had enjoyed spending the day with the boys. He was used to Chris turning up on his own or with one of his school friends, but these English friends were very different. He said nothing to Jeannie about the strange coincidence of Crispin's full name — but was even more astounded when she happened to mention that Chris and Crispin shared the same birthday. Time to investigate, he thought…

CHAPTER 22
Timothy Campbell Investigates

Timothy Campbell was troubled. Something didn't add up about this new friend of his great-grandson — or rather, it did add up. Crispin Nigel Leadbetter, he concluded, was not a common name, not even in England. Two of them with the same date of birth could not be merely a coincidence: it wasn't possible. But Timothy had to tread carefully. He must not reveal his suspicions without more evidence. He was fairly sure that Chris was unaware of the kidnapping of Stuart Anderson and, from what Crispin had said, he doubted Chris knew, as yet, that they shared the same three names as well as a birthday. Timothy was astute; after all, he was a solicitor. He might be able to glean further information from Chris — surreptitiously, of course.

Chris was sad when his friends went away, the more so because they couldn't promise that they would be able to return the following summer. Jamie was a year older than the others and would be leaving school next year. He was a bright lad, but he wasn't interested in academic subjects. His preferred option was trade school; to get an apprenticeship as a joiner or a plumber. However, he hoped to have a break before starting but couldn't be sure. Crispin wouldn't be able to come without him; and even then, it would all depend upon the 'wicked one'.

The next time Timothy turned up at the hotel, he went for a walk with his great-grandson, as he often did. "Well, Chris, you have some charming young friends," he commented. "Will they be back next year?"

"Jamie is hoping so but he can't be certain. I won't know until nearer the time."

Chris went on to explain the situation to his grandpa; that Jamie would be leaving school. Timothy had assumed that Jamie and Crispin were school friends so was surprised to hear of Jamie's plans and wondered how the two of them knew one another.

"Mrs Roberts, that's Jamie's mum," Chris clarified, "is a sort of part-time housekeeper for Crispin's grandparents. I think that's how they met, but they do live in the same village."

"And what about Crispin's parents?" Timothy ventured, hoping he wasn't coming across as too inquisitive.

"Crispin doesn't have any parents. His father was killed in the war before he was born — just like mine — and his mother died not long after. Crispin lives with his grandparents and they're not very nice; or, at least, his grandfather isn't." Chris stopped short... Maybe he shouldn't be saying these things to his grandpa. Then, seeing the grin on the elderly man's face, he carried on as if he were sharing a secret with a good friend: the way that Crispin and Jamie had shared their stories of the 'wicked one' with him.

Timothy listened but asked no more questions. He was amused at the way Chris confided in him but shocked at the revelations portrayed through his tales. If, as he suspected, Crispin was actually Stuart Anderson, *his* grandson, then he must act.

Changing the subject, Timothy asked about the 'scallywags', as he referred to Chris's twin sisters. There was never a shortage of comments on that subject. Chris adored the little girls but had to admit that, if it wasn't for the blue and red ribbons his mum stitched onto their dresses, he would have difficulty recognising which was which. Timothy reckoned it might be easier to distinguish between the two as they grew older.

Over the next few weeks Timothy collected together as much information as he could on the kidnap of Stuart Anderson, and the boy from Oxfordshire who was known as Crispin Nigel Leadbetter.

As regards the abduction, no trace of evidence had ever come to light. Considering that the baby was reported missing within half an hour of his disappearance, it seemed odd that nobody in the neighbourhood had seen or heard anything suspicious. Whoever was responsible had been careful to cover their tracks. A body had never been found, so there remained the possibility that the child was still alive. Since Timothy was not prepared to question the family about the incident, he had to rely on his own knowledge of the reported crime at the time, along with back copies of newspaper articles. He arranged an interview with the police department, but they were not at liberty to share information that was not already in the public domain. However, one small piece of evidence that he had not come across in his search, was brought to his attention during the discussion. Stuart Anderson had a small pale birthmark on the upper part of his right hand, close to his wrist: two triangular shapes the shade of a light-coloured freckle. According to the child's mother, it would hardly be noticeable to anyone who did not already know it was there. The investigation had reached a dead-end, although the file remained on record.

Coming across a boy with the same name as his great-grandson may well be mere coincidence, but Timothy could not believe that the exact correlation of all three of his names along with the date of birth could be attributed to pure chance. When chatting to Chris about his new friend, the further revelation that the boy's father had been killed in the war, and his grandparents had taken on the responsibility of raising him, appeared to support his theory. Having the child believe that his mother had died when he was born fitted in with the scheme: he would have to grow up in the knowledge that he was an orphan. As such it would be quite natural for the grandparents to take charge.

Gathering these facts was all very well, but Timothy would need more evidence to make a case. He had, of course, deduced that the Leadbetters had devised the conspiracy to abduct their grandson — but the plan had gone terribly wrong. Instead of their grandson, the victim of their crime was Stuart Anderson, the younger brother of their daughter-in-law. Did the Leadbetters know they had the wrong child? The kidnap, having taken place more than five hundred miles from their home, and in the middle of the Blitz, would hardly have made headline news in their neighbourhood: they would not want to draw attention to themselves by making enquiries. Timothy Campbell guessed the Leadbetters were unaware of their error. Even if they realised they had made a mistake, what exactly were they to do about it?

He decided it was time to share his thoughts with his colleague, Charles Carter, trusting that he would not trouble Isobel until the time was right. Charles, like Timothy, thought it highly likely that Crispin's friend from England was indeed the missing Stuart Anderson. Thinking back to the time when he first met Isobel in Fulham, he recalled her going in search of her sister-in-law, Henrietta, and husband Raymond, in Guildford, and her parents-in-law in Farnham. She'd had no success in either quest. It seemed both families had moved shortly after Isobel had returned to Scotland. Her solicitor, who had also been the solicitor for Henrietta and Raymond, said that as far as he knew, they had moved to Oxford in a hurry. He seemed to think there was something odd about the situation. Doctor Raymond Dobson no longer required his services; the house move involved an exchange with a relative or friend. As for Nigel's parents, Isobel had written to them twice shortly after arriving in Aberdeen giving them the address of her parents, where she was staying. The Leadbetters did not respond. A while later, once she settled at East Bay, she wrote again, but that letter was returned undelivered.

Charles commented that Isobel had been confused to discover that both families had moved, but neither had bothered to keep in touch or relay a forwarding address. She couldn't understand why none of the family wanted to stay in touch with Crispin — their only link with Nigel. The reaction when she visited the original home of the Dobsons in Guildford further added to the mystery. She felt, at the time, that she had met the current occupant before; but it was only afterwards that it occurred to her he was at her wedding.

Added to the information he had already gathered, Isobel's failed quest for her in-laws, and their seeming wish to disassociate themselves from her, reinforced the kidnap theory. However, both Timothy and Charles had to admit that the evidence they had gleaned so far was circumstantial. They would need to do more research to produce a solid case. Kitty and Sandy had suffered enough without facing a lengthy court battle — if they could solve this disgraceful situation themselves it would be the least painful outcome for everyone concerned. The two gentlemen agreed to reflect on the matter. They would give themselves a couple of weeks to come up with ideas as to the best way forward.

Allowing themselves the time to step back and consider everything served to convince both men of the validity of their theory, urging them to pursue the situation as a matter of urgency. Since the police had failed to solve the mystery of the abduction of Stuart Anderson, a confession from the Leadbetter family might be the only way to discover the truth. To do that they would have to prove, without any doubt, that there was only one Crispin Nigel Leadbetter, born on 5 August 1940, and he was right here in the North East of Scotland with his mother.

Charles knew that his wife kept all their important documents in the safe. He checked that she had Crispin's original birth certificate, hoping it had not been misplaced during her move north or, worse still, claimed by her former in-laws at the time of the registration: he guessed she might not have registered the birth herself. He breathed a sigh of relief on retrieving the genuine article. After taking a good look at the details, he replaced it. A copy could be purchased at any time in the future: that the original was in Isobel's possession could be crucial. Also in the safe were Isobel and Nigel's birth certificates, their wedding certificate, and information from the army about Nigel's death. The marriage had taken place in Guildford, which was also where their son's birth was registered.

In turn, giving all the relevant details, Timothy contacted the General Registration Office in Somerset House requesting a copy of Crispin's birth certificate. At the same time, he requested copies of the other certificates, which might prove useful to the investigation…. As he suspected, there was only one Crispin Nigel Leadbetter born on 5th August 1940.

It was agreed that Timothy should make the trip south to search for the missing relatives. It was easier for him to be away on business for a few days than Charles, who had family responsibilities. However, the day before he was due to leave, Timothy had second thoughts about keeping everything from his granddaughter. Perhaps he should at least seek her approval to look for the missing Leadbetters. Charles conceded; he too had been feeling a little uncomfortable about being so secretive. Neither wanted to upset the family or raise hopes about Stuart Anderson, but seeking the Leadbetters was different. So instead of going straight home after work, Timothy went to the hotel, arriving at the same time as Charles. Isobel, as always, was pleased to see her grandfather and invited him to stay for his evening meal. It was after dinner, once Chris had disappeared to his room, that Timothy broached the subject of his London trip. He explained that he was heading south on business and would she like him to have a look for her missing family? Isobel hesitated at first, before agreeing that, if it wasn't too much trouble, he could try. She gave him the address of the Dobson's original home in Guildford, saying she was sure it was Raymond's brother Frederick who had answered the door to her when she visited more than eight years ago. Her solicitor had told her that Raymond and Henrietta Dobson had moved to Oxford. Raymond Dobson was a doctor. As for the Leadbetters, she had no idea where they now lived but intimated that Crispin Leadbetter had his own accountancy firm. She was sorry that she could be of so little help but hoped he would have better luck than she'd had. As he was about to leave, she mentioned the name and location of her solicitor who had, at one time, acted for the rest of the family. She thought he would probably be retired, but it was worth a try.

Fortunately, Timothy, who was always well organised, had already packed his case, as he was much later arriving home than he had anticipated. However, he was glad he had spent so much of the evening with Isobel and Charles: he felt more at ease having Isobel's blessing to search for Nigel's family.

In addition to copies of the various certificates that he thought he might need in his quest; he had discovered from Chris the name of the village where his friend Jamie lived. It was also where the Leadbetters resided. Further details on addresses could be retrieved from the electoral roll, and telephone numbers from local directories.

On arriving in London, Timothy booked into a hotel close to the station: it was too late to proceed to Oxford, where he imagined most of his time must be spent. He had dinner in the hotel restaurant then rang his brother, Bernard, to arrange to meet up with him while he was in the city. The following morning, feeling refreshed after a good night's sleep, he decided to call on Isobel's former London solicitor. It had not been his original intention but the office was close by, and he might just gain a little more information — it was worth a try. He was quite prepared to find the man long gone, so was pleasantly surprised to discover that Mr Price, the longest serving partner in the business, was not only in his office but was available and willing to speak with this unexpected visitor. He explained to Timothy that he planned to retire in the spring, so was reducing his clientele, but was happy to have a chat with a fellow solicitor from north of the border. "I'm looking for my grandson," Timothy declared. "I believe he is in the care of Crispin and Priscilla Leadbetter."

"Ah, the Leadbetters!" Mr Price sighed. "Strange business altogether. I looked after the affairs of the whole family for many years, until around twelve or thirteen years ago. Mr Leadbetter and his wife moved without giving me prior warning. I knew nothing of it until another firm of solicitors contacted me with a letter, signed by Crispin Leadbetter, requesting I forward all files to them. I was stunned. A regular flow of business was generated by the accountancy firm, as well as family matters. It was a great loss, you understand?"

Timothy understood. "So that's the last you heard from them?" he queried.

"Not quite," came the response. "The other firm of solicitors was in Oxford, but Leadbetter Accountancy is in London, so there was no real reason for the transfer. After so many years of service, it would have been a matter of courtesy to let me know of their intention — not that Mr Leadbetter was ever the most courteous of gentlemen: he was arrogant and often rude. I was annoyed. I rang the Oxford solicitors seeking further explanation. Much to my amusement, I had been at university with their new solicitor. Of course, he was not at liberty to divulge the details but he did 'let slip' that they had moved to this village in Oxfordshire. Following the death of their son, killed in action in France, they had taken on the care of their young grandson."

"So, you had no more dealings with the family?" Timothy pursued.

"Henrietta, their daughter, and her husband Raymond, also ended their association with us rather abruptly; although they did, at least contact me. They were, apparently, moving house on an exchange basis with a relative or friend. Raymond, unlike his father-in-law, was always approachable. I thought it odd that he declined my offer to act on their behalf, even if the house move was a private arrangement."

"Do you remember when all this happened?" Timothy enquired.

"Let me see," Mr Price replied, getting up to check through some files. "October 1940. Yes, that's right. I lost two of my best clients within the space of a week but," he added, "I continued to act for Isobel Leadbetter until her house in Fulham was sold. That was something else that was a little strange. Why had the senior Leadbetters taken charge of their grandson when, as far as I could see, their daughter-in-law was perfectly capable of looking after her own child?"

"Off the record," Timothy stated.

"None of this is on the record, Mr Campbell. I told you, I'm not taking on any more clients. Anything you have to say will go no further unless, of course, you give your permission."

"Well," Timothy continued, "Isobel, my granddaughter, was and still is perfectly capable of looking after her son. She has been responsible for him since the day he was born. Until she remarried two years ago, they lived in the village of East Bay in Aberdeenshire."

"So, how can the Leadbetters claim to be looking after him?"

Timothy answered with eyebrows raised, "That, Mr Price, is what I intend to find out."

Timothy hesitated to say any more. It was enough that Mr Price was aware of the supposed existence of two boys of the same descent, born at the same time.

"So, let me be clear. Isobel's son is…"

"Crispin Nigel Leadbetter, born on 5th August 1940," Timothy confirmed.

"And, the Leadbetters claim to be raising their grandson, the same Crispin Nigel Leadbetter?" Mr Price quizzed.

"That appears to be the case," came the reply.

"And that, of course, is just not possible," Mr Price concluded. "So who is this child?" The two men looked at one another, shaking their heads.

"For the sake of both boys, I need to solve this mystery and I need to do so without causing undue stress to either of them in the process. You see my dilemma, Mr Price?"

"I do indeed."

The two men chatted for a few more minutes. Mr Price failed to see how he might be of assistance, other than to confirm what was already known; but Timothy said that that in itself would add credibility to the case.

Timothy was pleased he had visited the solicitor. Despite claiming there was little he could do to help, the information he had gleaned supported Isobel's story. It wasn't her imagination that her relatives were avoiding her; they had made a deliberate attempt to move without leaving any trace of their whereabouts. He was also curious as to how Raymond Dobson's brother fitted into the scheme. The house swap was feasible; the fact that the man had turned Isobel away from his door denying all knowledge of the previous occupant, was not.

Timothy had a coffee at the railway station before boarding a train to Oxford, where his first stop was the public library. Searching through the electoral roll he soon identified the Leadbetters, Crispin and Priscilla, and noted their address. He found the Dobsons, again without a problem, since Raymond was listed as 'Doctor'. He also looked up Mrs Roberts, which was more of a challenge. Several people of that name were listed and he didn't know her initials. Eventually, he whittled it down to two possibilities in the village that Chris had mentioned. He checked the telephone directory to discover numbers for the Leadbetters and the Dobsons, but no number for either of the Roberts.

He decided to have lunch in Oxford then take a taxi to the village, which was around five miles away. He gave the driver the name of the road where the Leadbetters stayed and a number, which he judged to be several houses away. Although he did not intend to pay them a visit, he wanted to identify their residence for future reference. Their home was an exclusive detached villa on the outskirts of the village close to the open countryside.

He guessed that Mrs Roberts' home would be closer to the centre of the village, so began to stroll slowly along the road in that direction. He asked a passer-by where he might find the first address on his list. He found it easily but, seeing that it was a large building, he decided to look for the second address he had identified. It was a semi-detached property halfway along a side street consisting of similar buildings. He walked up to the front door, wondering how to introduce himself, having given no prior warning of his visit. One ring on the bell brought the occupant to the door almost immediately. She was wearing a coat as if about to leave.

"I'm so sorry to disturb you. I'm looking for a Mrs Roberts. I met her son Jamie when he was on holiday in Scotland last August."

"I'm Mrs Roberts and I have a son, Jamie. And you are…?"

"My apologies, I'm Timothy Campbell. Your son visited me with his friend Crispin and my great-grandson, Chris."

"Ah, so you're the Laird that Jamie has talked so much about. Please, do come in."

As Timothy was about to cross the threshold, he hesitated, "You look as if you are on your way out? I really don't want to cause you any delay."

"No, no, please come in," Mrs Roberts repeated. "I arrived home a few minutes ago and haven't got round to taking off my coat. Can I get you a cup of tea?" she offered.

"That would be much appreciated, but don't go to any trouble on my account."

"It's no trouble, no trouble at all, Mr Campbell," she replied, showing him through to a comfortable lounge and inviting him to sit down.

Returning with tea and cakes, Mrs Roberts explained that she worked each morning as a housekeeper for a local family, returning home in the early afternoon, having prepared lunch for whoever happened to be there.

"Hmm," Timothy interrupted, "That's what I wanted to talk to you about, and please, call me Timothy."

"I'm Janet," Mrs Roberts responded. Looking at him curiously, she added, "You want to know about the Leadbetters?"

"My concern is for the child, their ward...?"

"Ah, Crispin is their grandson. As far as I know they took charge of him from birth. His father, their son, was killed in the war, around the time that Crispin was born and, sadly, their daughter-in-law died shortly afterwards."

"So that is what they tell everyone?" Timothy queried, seeking confirmation.

"Oh yes, it's common knowledge, you might say. Young Crispin always knew that his father, like Jamie's father, was killed in the war; but he was about six before he started to ask about his mother. According to Jamie, Crispin was very upset when he was told that his mother had died when he was born: Mr Leadbetter gave him a beating for crying. I've overheard the boys talking about Crispin's grandfather — they call him 'the wicked one'. I think sometimes they get a bit carried away, making things up. But, I have to admit, the man is a bully."

Janet paused. "Maybe I shouldn't be telling you this, but I *am* concerned for the boy. It's just as well he is away at boarding school during term time: the holidays are a nightmare for him. He seems to relax a bit when he's here with Jamie, but the only time I've seen him really happy was when we were in Scotland in the summer."

Mrs Roberts relayed the problem she had had persuading the Leadbetters to allow Crispin to join them for the holiday. She explained that Mr Leadbetter would not give his final consent until the last minute, even if it meant forfeiting the rail fare. She added that it was very likely Jamie would get a break this summer, between leaving school and beginning an apprenticeship. He wanted to visit East Bay again and invite Crispin along too, but the strain placed on the young lad by his grandfather would be unimaginable.

Timothy had heard much of this story from Chris, but hearing it from Mrs Roberts, who was in direct contact with the family, was even more upsetting. As for Janet Roberts, she had revealed more to this stranger than she would ever dare to say to anyone else — not least because she valued her job. Equally, Mrs Leadbetter, despite being a snob, appreciated her housekeeper, who was efficient and reliable.

"What are *your* concerns for the boy?" Mrs Roberts ventured.

"Well, Janet, this might sound strange but I want to know exactly who he is," came the baffling reply.

"He's Crispin Leadbetter — Crispin Nigel Leadbetter — to be precise."

"No," Timothy disclosed, "no, he isn't, and that's the problem."

"But, who else could he be?" Janet responded, taken aback by this alarming allegation.

"You've met my great-grandson, Chris?" he asked.

"Yes, he befriended Jamie the summer before last; they keep in touch by letter. Chris's Uncle Ernie attended to Jamie's leg when he fell."

"Chris's full name is Crispin Nigel Leadbetter. He was born on 5th August 1940," Timothy stated. "His father, Nigel, was killed in the war but his mother, Isobel, my granddaughter, is very much alive."

Janet Roberts was dumbfounded. She sat for several seconds, trying to make sense of what she had just heard. As confirmation, Timothy withdrew an envelope from the inside pocket of his jacket. He proceeded to show his shocked listener the copy of Crispin's birth certificate and the marriage certificate of the boy's parents. It bore the name of Crispin Leadbetter as Nigel's father.

"Isobel has the original certificates," he announced, "if further proof should be required in the future. The identity of the child in the care of the Leadbetters is a mystery that remains to be proved. It is possible that the couple genuinely believe the boy in their care to be their grandson. However, they are very much aware that their daughter-in-law is alive. When my granddaughter returned to Scotland with her baby, then just a few weeks old, she wrote to her in-laws twice informing them of her parents' address in Aberdeen, where she was staying. Her letters were ignored. She wrote again when she had settled in East Bay. That letter was returned undelivered. I have since learned that the Leadbetters and their daughter Henrietta and husband Raymond Dobson moved, at short notice, a matter of weeks after Isobel's departure. Neither family left forwarding addresses and both terminated long-term arrangements with their solicitor. It seemed odd to Isobel that, after making such a fuss over Nigel's offspring, they wanted nothing more to do with him."

"So, what do you think I might do to help," Janet asked.

"There's not much you can do," Timothy admitted. "Though, if possible, could you keep an eye on Crispin when he's home and do your best to bring him up to Scotland on holiday this summer? I'll give you my address and telephone number. Please get in touch if you find anything — well, anything *else* — untoward to report. I really must leave now. It would be best if Jamie didn't know of this visit."

Timothy was glad that he had managed to speak with Janet Roberts but upset at leaving her in such a bewildered state. He made his way to the centre of the village where he caught the next bus into Oxford and, from there, the train into London.

Despite acknowledging to Janet that there was little she could do to help regarding the identity of the supposed Crispin Nigel Leadbetter, the visit had not been wasted. It had served as confirmation that the Leadbetters believed their protégé to be their grandson, thus adding credibility to the theory that they had deliberately taken the child from his mother (or so they thought). Thereafter, they had lied to their friends, neighbours, and even their supposed grandson, telling them that Isobel Leadbetter was dead.

Timothy spent the evening relaxing at his hotel. He was pleased with the way his enquiries had gone. Although he had learned no more than he already suspected, it all served to strengthen the case. Hopefully, tomorrow would prove equally rewarding; after which he would be ready to discuss the matter with his younger brother, Bernard. He was meeting him for dinner the following evening.

Timothy made an early start in the morning, catching the train to Guildford. He headed directly to the public library to check the electoral register. He was looking for Raymond Dobson's brother, hoping that he still resided at the house he had exchanged with his sibling. Again his search was successful. A Frederick and Maria Dobson were listed at the address once occupied by Henrietta and Raymond; unless, of course, they had moved very recently. He checked the local telephone directory to find that the couple were at that address. Later that morning, once he had collected his thoughts over a cup of coffee, he went to a call box and rang the Dobsons' number. On hearing a woman's voice, he asked to speak to Frederick.

"I'm sorry," she replied, "my husband is at work, might I ask who's calling?"

"My apologies, I thought this was his business number, my mistake…thank-you." With that Timothy replaced the receiver, ending the call. This wasn't his usual way of conducting himself but he needed to be sure of his facts before presenting them to his brother. Since he had time to spare he located the address, a substantial semi-detached property situated about halfway along a tree-lined avenue. A fine location, he thought as he turned back towards the town centre. After a light lunch in a local teashop, he returned to his hotel in London, where he collated all the information he had accumulated so far.

He looked forward to spending the evening with his younger brother, wondering what he would make of the whole Crispin saga — hoping he would help solve the mystery. If anyone could get to the bottom of it, it would be Bernard. Timothy had great faith in his sibling, who had established himself as a Barrister in the U.K.'s capital. Not only was he an excellent lawyer, he also had 'contacts', and he wouldn't be afraid to use his influence.

The two gentlemen met at a grand hotel close to the city centre, where Bernard had booked a table for two — it was his choice. The brothers greeted each other in the foyer before making their way through to the elegant restaurant, where they were shown to their seats.

"What brings you to the big city?" Bernard asked, once they had done with the pleasantries and ordered food and wine.

"I'm looking for my grandson," Timothy announced.

"Your grandson!" Bernard exclaimed, "but you and Jane didn't have any children."

Now that he had his brother's full attention, he told of his teenage sweetheart and their brief moments of passion, with all the ensuing consequences.

"So," Bernard responded with amusement, "I'm not the only black sheep in the family."

Timothy was well aware of Bernard's meaning. His brother had never married but he had a very good 'friend', an eminent member of parliament. The two men had bought first-floor apartments in adjoining buildings.

251

Timothy was sure there was a connecting door between them!

Timothy continued his tale as the meal was served. He relayed the main events of the intervening years as he had followed the fortunes of the family — his particular concern for his daughter, Kathryn, his sole offspring. Bernard was pleased that his older brother had eventually had the opportunity to reveal his identity to his family, especially as he had obviously been warmly accepted.

"Now," Bernard interpolated, "what about this kidnap? I trust that is what you really want to talk to me about?"

"Yes," Timothy confessed, "And, if possible, your help."

He proceeded to unfold the incident of the abduction, the timing in line with Isobel's return to Aberdeen with Crispin in 1940, and his theory. The involvement of the Leadbetters and the link with the two boys, his grandson and his great-grandson.

Bernard, as his brother had suspected, was interested but realised it was a sensitive issue. Stuart Anderson would be particularly vulnerable.

"What information do you have on these Leadbetters?" he asked.

"This is what I have discovered so far," Timothy replied, producing a sheet of notes showing the names, addresses and telephone numbers of the Leadbetters and the Dobsons.

"Come round to my place for dinner tomorrow evening," Bernard offered. "I need some time to think this through."

The brothers, on finishing their meal, moved to more comfortable seats in an adjoining lounge and ordered coffees. It was good to be able to relax together, to share the experiences that had separated them by over five hundred miles, living at opposite ends of the country.

"You wouldn't think about coming back to Scotland?" Timothy ventured, knowing the answer before he asked.

Bernard was horrified at the very idea, "Live out there in the countryside, completely exposed!" he retorted. "No, no, here I can disappear into the crowd — my life's my own."

"But everybody knows you here Bernard." Timothy cajoled.

"They know me for what I do, not for who I am," Bernard responded, a little soberly. Besides I'm not interested in castles and countryside, although I admit Scotland *is* beautiful."

"Well, you must come up to see me sometime and meet my new family."

"I'll do that," Bernard promised.

The following evening Timothy made his way to his brother's apartment for seven o'clock, as arranged. Bernard kept his home immaculate: he had always been well organised, even as a young boy — he couldn't cope with things being out of place. The table was set when

Timothy arrived; the meal was ready and the wine cooled.

It wasn't until after dinner, when they sat down by the fire in the lounge, that the conversation turned once again to business. Having had time to consider the events around the time of the kidnap, Bernard was as eager as his brother to solve the puzzle. He agreed that Timothy's theory of mistaken identity was the most likely explanation, linking the abduction of Stuart Anderson with the Leadbetters. Bernard was willing to explore the case, not simply as a favour to his brother, but out of genuine interest. The previous evening he had been engrossed in the revelation of his brother's confession, along with the effect that those moments of passion had had on the rest of his life. However, it was the kidnap that had captured his attention. Now he needed to check the information gathered so far. To this end, Timothy went through the data he had collected. Bernard then turned his attention to the boy now in the care of the Leadbetters. Whoever he was, he was definitely not Crispin Nigel Leadbetter. Like Timothy, he recognised the delicacy of the situation. Whether he was Stuart Anderson or not, his wellbeing needed to be considered.

"I'll look into this," Bernard stated, "undercover, of course. Leave it with me. It may take some time, so we must be patient."

Timothy told Bernard that he would update Charles Carter on any developments, but remain discreet as regards the rest of the family, not wishing to build up false hopes. The brothers agreed to keep in touch.

The following day, Timothy Campbell returned to Aberdeenshire, satisfied that he had done everything possible to tackle the situation. He relayed his findings to Charles, before intimating that he had passed the information on to his brother Bernard, who had agreed to organise an undercover investigation into the case.

"Bernard, Bernard Campbell is your brother?" Charles was amazed.

"Yes, that's right. I reckoned if anyone could sort out this mess, it would be him — he's good. I take it you know him?"

"I was assigned to his firm when I was training in London before the war. I didn't have much to do with him but he's one of the best — established quite a reputation for himself in the City."

"I did mention you," Timothy responded. "He didn't say he had come across you."

"He wouldn't. I was Ian Wright at that time."

"Of course, I'd forgotten about that, having always known you as Charles Carter."

Isobel, of course, was curious to know if her grandfather had made any progress in the quest to find the Leadbetters. Timothy told her that Henrietta and Raymond had definitely exchanged houses with Raymond's brother Frederick and his wife Maria. They still resided at the property in Guildford. The elder Leadbetters, like their daughter, had moved in October

1940 without leaving a forwarding address. It appeared they were not in a hurry to be found.

"So, we still don't know the reason why?" Isobel questioned.

"I've left it in the hands of my brother. Hopefully, he will get to the bottom of it." Timothy assured her.

The winter was largely uneventful for the family, except that Jeannie was relying more and more on her relationship with Timothy Campbell. Now that her granddaughter was married and Alec had his own cottage on the estate, the house seemed empty. The summertime, with visitors to the village, was less lonely and the fact that her two brothers lived in East Bay helped, but the long winter nights seemed endless. Timothy too felt lonely, rattling around in his castle. Having turned seventy in the summer he had reduced his working hours, now attending the office on just three days a week, but reluctant to give it up altogether.

Then, one evening in January, having taken Jeannie out for a meal at a hotel in the town, they found the road to East Bay blocked with snow. Timothy knew he should have used the Land Rover but taking Jeannie out was always special — the car seemed more appropriate. The weather was turning worse, a biting north wind blowing snow from the fields across the road. Timothy reversed back onto the main road and headed towards the town, about a mile away. They returned to the hotel where they had eaten to request accommodation for the night. Only one double room was available. Turning to Jeannie,

Timothy offered to take her to her daughter's home a short distance away, but it was blowing a blizzard. "Just book the room," Jeannie urged. "It's not safe out there." Glad to be in from the cold, the couple ascended the stairs to the room they had been allocated.

And so, more than half a century after that evening in the churchyard, the two lovers, much older and a great deal wiser, passed the night enveloped in each other's arms.

CHAPTER 23
The Detective

Clive Short was a tall gentleman in his mid-fifties. He had a sharp eye and a broad grin, which he used to advantage: persuading his unsuspecting interviewees to convey more than they might to a person of sterner demeanour. Despite his general light-hearted sense of fun, his mood could change to reflect a more serious side to his character: an asset in his line of duty. Clive had worked with Bernard on several occasions, not only as a colleague but also as a close friend. The two men were often seen together, chatting over a drink in one or other of the more exclusive London hotel bars.

Bernard's story of the two boys, both known as Crispin Nigel Leadbetter, and the mystery surrounding the kidnap of Stuart Anderson, had Clive's immediate attention. He was more than willing to help his friend solve the case, especially as an undercover agent. Like Bernard, he was not easily defeated. Working outside his normal schedule it would take time for him to investigate the case. Nevertheless, he was eager to accept the challenge.

The link between the Leadbetters and the abduction appeared almost indisputable, but any element of doubt must be dispelled. He quickly concluded it unlikely that the senior Leadbetters would have been directly involved in taking the child, although they would undoubtedly have instigated the wicked deed. Discovering the reason behind the unprecedented hasty moves that the Leadbetters and their daughter had made in October 1940 was, he decided, his first task. He had a hunch that the Dobsons were somehow involved. The house exchange between the two brothers was puzzling — that is where Clive decided to begin.

By comparing the current electoral roll with the 1939 Register, he identified three households living close to the Dobsons in Guildford who had been there in October 1940 when the kidnap had taken place.

On a cold winter's day in mid-January 1954, Clive caught an early morning train to Guildford. He pulled the collar of his dark brown Ulster Coat up round his neck as he set off on foot, hoping to meet some of the Dobsons' neighbours. The first couple on his list resided a few doors along from the house where Frederick and Maria Dobson now lived. Being Saturday, the husband and wife were at home, but neither was able to offer any help concerning the occupants of number 25, either past or present. They had no memory of events surrounding the exchange of ownership.

Slightly disappointed but undeterred, he approached the house next door to the Dobson's. The woman living there was able to offer a little more help. She recollected how her erstwhile friendly neighbour, Henrietta Dobson, had snubbed her in the weeks before moving away, giving no indication of their intentions. She had seen the removal van and watched, dismayed, as the couple followed in their car without so much as a wave. Her current neighbours she described as keeping themselves to themselves: she barely knew them.

Never one to despair, Clive walked over to the house opposite the Dobson's. The widow, who occupied the property, had watched the stranger in the wool coat and Trilby as he had called on the two long-term residents of the avenue. She was delighted to see him cross the road to her house. Eager to know what was going on, she was at the door before he had the chance to knock. As soon as he introduced himself, she invited him in; showing him through to her sitting room, asking if he would like a cup of tea. While she disappeared into the kitchen he sat down on a comfy sofa, as directed, charmed by the warmth of this home as well as the welcome. The room, with a large bay window, was to the front of the property, offering a full view of her neighbours' residence across the road. As she returned with the tea tray, she introduced herself as Cynthia. Sitting in an armchair facing the window — which Clive concluded must be her favourite seat — it was clear that little would escape this lady's notice.

Proceeding with caution, so as not to upset the mood, Clive began: "It's a long time ago now, Cynthia, but can you tell me anything about Henrietta and Raymond Dobson, the couple who used to live across the road?"

"Funny carry-on that, altogether," she remarked. "What was it you wanted to know exactly?"

"I was wondering; did you notice anything strange around the time just before they moved away in October 1940?" Clive ventured.

"Why yes!" she exclaimed. "One afternoon — late afternoon, around teatime — a taxi drew up outside their house. Two people stepped out; a lady with a baby in her arms and a gentleman with a case… or maybe a large bag, a holdall, I'm not sure. I didn't recognise them at the time but a week or so later they moved into the house. They're still there now."

"Do you remember when this happened?" Clive asked.

Cynthia answered decisively, "Yes, it was the twenty-third of October, 1940."

"You're sure?" Clive was amazed that she could be so precise.

"Yes," she confirmed. "It was my son's twenty-first birthday. I was sitting right here thinking about him; feeling sorry for myself, I suppose; thinking what a wonderful day it should have been. He had been called up to serve in the army so he was away. My husband died when Johnny was only ten; so, for many years, there had just been the two of us. It was so sad. However, enough of that: at least Johnny came back — he survived."

Clive nodded; he understood. Of course she would recall such a date. "Do you remember what happened after that?" he queried.

"About a week later — or maybe less than that — Henrietta's parents arrived in their car. They stayed for an hour or so, then left with the baby. A few days after that, a removal van drew up. The furniture was loaded and off it went, followed by the Dobsons in their car."

"Did they say where they were going?"

"No," Cynthia replied, "and that was what was most odd. Henrietta was always friendly. In the summer of that year her sister-in-law, Isobel, came to stay. She gave birth to a baby boy. Sadly, Henrietta's brother Nigel, the father of the child, was killed in action. Isobel moved back to her home in London. From around that time, until they moved at the end of October, Henrietta ignored me. I had no idea of their plans to move, nor any indication as to where they had gone. The next thing I see is another removal van and the arrival of the couple I had seen getting out of the taxi with the baby — on my son's birthday. There was no baby with them."

"Do this couple have a family?" Clive was curious.

"Oh yes, they have two children. As far as I know, they were sent off to the countryside to stay with a relative for the duration of the war. They must have been about ten and twelve years old when they arrived here in 1945."

After another cup of tea and some general chatter, mostly about her son, Clive finally departed, leaving this lonely widow to her memories. In his job, he had often been grateful for people like Cynthia, who whiled away the time watching the comings and goings in their neighbourhood.

Back home in London, Clive analysed his morning's work. The information gained from the inquisitive widow was more helpful than she could have imagined: Stuart Anderson had been taken from his pram around eleven o'clock on the morning of the twenty-second of October 1940. Frederick and Maria Dobson had arrived at the home of Henrietta and Raymond Dobson at teatime on the twenty-third. It all made sense. The couple would have wanted to get as far away from the scene of the crime as quickly as possible. They would, he deduced, have made their way to Aberdeen railway station to catch a train south. However, it would have been too late to make the whole journey that day, especially given the restrictions during the London Blitz. So, they would have had to stop for a night at one of the other cities en route before completing the journey.

Clive then considered the rapid house moves of the families. As regards the Dobsons, they were clearly covering their tracks. Being a direct swap between the brothers, they would not have needed to wait for the completion of the sales and purchases of their respective properties before moving: but, what about the Leadbetters? How did they manage to organise a removal so spontaneously? It was two weeks later before Clive had the time to solve that issue. Searching through the 1921 census and the 1939 Register, he found the answer. The house currently occupied by Crispin and Priscilla Leadbetter had been the home of Mr Leadbetter's parents — it was his inheritance. Though maybe not crucial to the investigation, Clive Small was thorough: he didn't like loose ends.

His next quest was to approach the boarding school where the supposed Crispin Nigel Leadbetter was a pupil. He wanted to meet the boy in the hope of establishing a final and conclusive piece of evidence. If the child had a faint birthmark on his wrist, as described by his mother, the case for identity would be complete. Of course, such a mark may have faded altogether over time, so the absence of such a blemish would not negate the findings so far established. Naturally, Clive did not want to single out the boy, so any investigation would have to be done surreptitiously. However, having discussed the issue with Bernard, they had concluded that it would be politic to share some of the information with the Headmaster — after all, he was responsible for the boy's welfare. They need not, at this stage, disclose their knowledge of the abduction. However, that the child was not Crispin Nigel Leadbetter could be revealed, along with the information that the Leadbetters themselves may not be aware of the fact.

It was mid-February when Clive Small contacted the school to make an appointment to see Mr Smith: a date was set for later that month. The nearest railway station to the school was just over twenty minutes by Tube from central London. Being a little early, Clive spent the time he had to spare wandering around the area. For five minutes or so he watched an enthusiastic group of lads having a raucous game of rugby on a pitch set within the extensive area of the school playing fields. It brought back memories from his youth when he too had attended a boarding school. On entering the school building, Clive followed directions to the office to notify the secretary of his arrival.

"Ah, good morning Mr Small," she exclaimed, looking up, with a smile, to the tall gentleman who had made his presence known. "Mr Smith will see you in a few minutes. Please take a seat."

Mr Smith emerged from his office a few moments later, inviting the visitor to join him. "How may I help you?" he asked, after a brief introduction.

"I am investigating a mystery — a possible crime — relating to the identity of a certain Crispin Nigel Leadbetter."

"Master Leadbetter?" Mr Smith hesitated, unprepared to commit himself to any comment until Mr Small gave further explanation.

"Do you happen to have a copy of the child's birth certificate?" Clive, enquired, adding, "and adoption papers?"

"I'll ask my secretary to bring the boy's file," Mr Smith replied, rising from his seat and making his way towards the door. "Please excuse me."

It was a few minutes before Mr Smith returned with the file. "I've had a word with Miss Copeland, my secretary. She has opened the file at the relevant place. It appears that a copy of the birth certificate was seen but not left with us. The details, however, are recorded here. There are no adoption papers. Crispin has been with his grandparents since he was just a few weeks old. His father was killed in the war before Crispin was born; his mother died shortly after the birth. Since Crispin and Priscilla Leadbetter are his grandparents, they must have felt it unnecessary to adopt him — we have no records to indicate otherwise."

"That sounds all very credible — above board you might say but..." At this point, Mr Small withdrew an envelope from the inside pocket of his Ulster coat. He glanced through the bundle of documents contained within and extracted a birth certificate, which he placed on the desk in front of the Headmaster.

"This matches the information in the file," Mr Smith confirmed, unable to grasp the point that the detective was trying to make.

"The problem," Mr Small continued, "is that this birth certificate *does* match the details in your file. I am acting on behalf of Mr Timothy Campbell, a Scottish Laird. He is the great grandfather of Crispin Nigel Leadbetter — the real Crispin Nigel Leadbetter." He produced another document from the envelope: the marriage certificate of Nigel Leadbetter and Isobel Anderson. It bore the names of Nigel's parents — Crispin and Priscilla Leadbetter, adding support to the authenticity of the case. "Nigel Leadbetter, as you rightly stated, was killed in the war, but Isobel is very much alive. She lives with her son, Crispin Nigel Leadbetter, in Aberdeenshire. She has the original certificates as well as her deceased husband's papers."

Mr Smith was, momentarily, speechless. He rose from his chair behind his desk, "Please, Mr Small," he invited, "have a seat at the coffee table by the fire. I'll arrange for tea to be brought through; it seems this may take a little longer than I had anticipated... and do take off your coat; make yourself comfortable."

When Mr Smith returned, he too sat down by the fireside. Stroking his chin as he pondered the detective's words he queried, "So, who is the boy that the Leadbetter's claim to be their grandson?"

"That, Mr Smith, is what I have been hired to find out." Mr Small replied.

"Why have Mr and Mrs Leadbetter been so dishonest?" Mr Smith was anxious to know.

"Because, Mr Smith, they believe that the child *is* their grandson. However, they have lied about their daughter-in-law. They know perfectly well that she is alive but, thinking that they have her son, they have deliberately made it difficult for her to find them. Isobel, for her part, tried to make contact but without success."

The tea arrived, allowing for a pause in the conversation. The mood relaxed as the two gentlemen resumed their talk. The Headmaster was truly baffled. He believed the detective: he had no choice; the evidence shown made it clear that the child in his school, whoever he was, was *not* Crispin Nigel Leadbetter.

"This is a delicate matter," Mr Small continued. "As you no doubt appreciate, the wellbeing of both boys is of the utmost importance, especially that of the child in your charge. We have a fairly good idea of his identity but can reveal nothing until we are absolutely sure. If we are correct, we can attempt to work out a solution. If the child is not who we think he might be, then it could prove even more difficult. Whatever the case, the pupil you have here cannot continue bearing a false identity: something has to be done."

Mr Smith's expression changed from incredulity to concern. Every one of the boys in the school was ultimately his responsibility but, of all the boys, Crispin was the one who troubled him most. He was a bright lad, excelling in many academic subjects as well as sports, though he could be overly rough at times. He was popular with his peers, revelling in school life and polite with the staff but, according to his housemaster, there was another side to the boy. Whenever it came close to the end of a term he would recoil, enveloped in sadness: he dreaded the holidays. From his meetings with the grandfather, Mr Smith could understand the boy's anxiety. He found Mr Leadbetter rude and intimidating: a bully.

"How might I help?" he asked, "For clearly, that is the reason for your visit."

"What can you tell me about the boy, and the boy's grandparents?" the detective inquired.

Mr Smith, understanding the seriousness of the situation, proceeded to relay as much information as possible, including the sheer arrogance of the man he had assumed to be Crispin's grandfather — demanding an audience with him without notice; making accusations about poor standards and the lack of discipline in his school. He was, apparently, obsessed with his grandson's performance in mathematics: it was Crispin's destiny to take over 'Leadbetter Accountancy', carrying on the good name of the firm he had established, into the next century. Here, Mr Smith afforded a smile, "Crispin hates the subject, but he knows he will feel the heavy hand of his grandfather if he gains anything other than top marks — fortunately, we know that too," he added with tongue in cheek.

Mr Small understood the message. What a dreadful way to treat a child!

"I wonder," he requested, "would it be possible for me to meet the boy — with his class, I mean. Perhaps I could talk to them about detective work: identification; sketches; fingerprinting; that sort of thing. Maybe set them some tasks."

"I'm sure that can be arranged," Mr Smith responded, "exactly what the third year lads would like — especially with a real live detective!"

He suggested Mr Small contact him by telephone the following week to fix a date. The focus of the interview must, of course, remain confidential, so the Headmaster agreed that the proposed lesson would be promoted as his idea.

The detective was satisfied with the outcome of his meeting with the Headmaster: it had given him an insight into the character of the kidnapped child. It was comforting to know that the boy was cared for in the school environment. A date for him to engage with the third-year class was organised for early March. Mr Small found himself looking forward to the experience. He enjoyed his work as a detective and hoped that he might inspire some of these teenagers with his enthusiasm. Maybe there would be a future recruit amongst them!

A few weeks later, complete with a Gladstone bag containing materials for the lesson, Mr Small entered the school for the second time. The boys were primed to be on their best behaviour for the gentleman who had kindly volunteered his time, though nothing could suppress their excitement as the morning progressed. On methods of identity, the inevitable question arose as to how it would be possible to distinguish between Henry and George, the identical twins who were in the class. Crispin still had difficulty, even after sharing a dormitory with them since the age of seven. There followed a discussion on fingerprints and, as Mr Small had anticipated, the pupils wanted to have a go using the professional ink.

So far, the detective had not asked the pupils to give their names so, apart from the twins, he did not know who they were. He did, however, have a class list so, as they worked in small groups, taking each other's fingerprints, he circulated, checking each individual with the record. Crispin was working with two other boys. Mr Small, with his keen eyes, noticed the two triangular birthmarks on the boy's upper wrist: they were quite small and faint, but nevertheless, distinguishable. By the time Crispin Leadbetter announced his name, the detective had already ticked him off on the list.

At the sound of the lunchtime bell, the form teacher entered the room to dismiss the class. But, before making their exit, one of the boys formally thanked Mr Small on behalf of them all. Not only had the morning achieved the goal of confirming, without a shadow of doubt, the identity of Stuart Anderson, but it had also been one of the most satisfying experiences of Clive Small's career.

Mr Smith was anxious to know how the morning had fared. The detective was able to report that it had been successful on two counts. Spending time with the boys had been a pleasure, and he now had the evidence he needed to complete his investigation into the real identity of Crispin Nigel Leadbetter.

Although eager to learn the details, Mr Smith realised that the detective would first have to report his findings to his client. Mr Small gave his assurance that he would be furnished with the outcome of the investigation in due course. He intimated it unlikely that he would return to the school, suspecting that the next visitor would be Timothy Campbell.

Leaving the school behind, Clive Small was eager to write up his report and discuss his findings with Bernard. He was sure that his friend would be relieved to know the results of his enquiries, especially the outcome of his morning at the school. His crafty plan to meet the boy had enabled him to identify the final piece of the jigsaw, thereby strengthening the case. Back at his desk, he set to work on his official account of the investigation, which he forwarded to Bernard before arranging to meet him a few days later.

Bernard was pleased with the detective's findings: it was a job well done. In any normal abduction case, with so much incriminating evidence, the next step would be an arrest. In this case, a much more diplomatic approach was required, and that would take time. The delicate manner in which his friend had undertaken the various enquiries could prove invaluable in the next stage. Without meeting the culprits, Clive Small had gained an insight into the characters involved. In alerting the supposed Crispin Nigel Leadbetter to his true identity, the particulars not included in the report would, perhaps, be vital. It seemed obvious from what the detective had gleaned from the Headmaster that the boy did not have a happy home life: it had been noted that he lived in constant fear of his grandfather, dreading the holidays. (This was evidence that supported the comments made to Timothy by the housekeeper, Mrs Roberts.) However, that the boy was happy at school was indisputable. So, how would all this affect him?

A few days after talking things through with Clive, Bernard contacted his brother on the telephone, before sending a copy of the report. Timothy was, naturally, pleased to have the evidence he sought. Now he must consider his next task. Stuart needed to know the truth and, at almost fourteen years old, it was crucial that he should be a party to the facts as soon as possible. Bernard assured his brother that he would continue to help in any way that he could. Living in central London, he suggested he might be able to provide a 'safe haven' for the boy should the need arise. "Do give him my details when you break the news," Bernard urged, "the school's little more than twenty minutes away on the Tube."

Timothy agreed to keep his brother up to date on any developments. At some point, it was likely that a warrant would be needed for the arrest of those responsible for the kidnap. Should that time come, he would need Bernard's help.

All data and reports pertaining to the case were filed in Timothy's office, which he now only attended three days a week. The one person with whom he shared the information was Charles — and, for the time being, only in an official capacity. After giving much thought to the situation, Timothy Campbell decided that he would contact the school, relay the information regarding the kidnap to the Headmaster, Mr Smith, and make arrangements for a visit in May,

CHAPTER 24
Crispin Nigel Leadbetter makes a Decision

Crispin Nigel Leadbetter, as he was known, returned to the home of his supposed grandparents for the Easter holidays. As usual, he did not look forward to the break from school, being in constant fear of his grandfather ruining what should be a happy time with his friend, Jamie. Even the prospect of another holiday in Scotland did not help, for once again, 'the wicked one' stipulated conditions on the generous offer from Mrs Roberts. Crispin must continue to prove himself worthy of such a privilege — he must excel in his grades; he must be better than his peers; he must gain prizes for his academic achievements.

Crispin was sick of Mr Leadbetter's threats. He had proved himself time and again at school, always maintaining high standards, yet never receiving a single word of praise from the man. Thank goodness for Jamie and his mother. He was always made to feel so welcome in their home: it was so different from the oppressive atmosphere at his grandparents'. What troubled Crispin most was the fact that Jamie would be leaving school in the summer so, after the holiday in Scotland, if he were allowed to go, he would have no respite at all during the vacations.

A few days before he was due to return for the new term, he was called to his grandfather's study. Since he had already endured the lecture about only being allowed to go on holiday with Mrs Roberts and Jamie on condition… he wondered what this summons might mean.

Mr Leadbetter began: "If I do consider you worthy of going to Scotland in the summer, I have a surprise for you when you arrive home."

"Yes Sir," Crispin responded after the pause that followed. He wondered what sort of 'surprise' awaited him since he could not recall his grandfather using that term before.

Mr Leadbetter continued, "You will fourteen. You will accompany me to my office each day for the remainder of your holiday. It will be good experience for your future with the company. Now, what do you say to that?"

There was another pause before Crispin managed to reply, in the way in which he knew was expected, "Thank you Sir."

"You are a very lucky young man," his grandfather commented. "It will be a great privilege for you to become part of my team: there's many a young gentleman who would be grateful for such a splendid opportunity. Now — dress smartly for dinner this evening, I have invited two of my colleagues to join us."

Crispin's heart sank as he left his grandfather's study. He must keep calm during the coming weekend, before returning to school on Monday for the start of the summer term. Although he had always known that his destiny — a life of monotony in an accountant's office — had been the plan, he was stunned by its imminence. True, he had at least another year at school but the idea that, from now on, he would have to spend the holidays in the presence of his grandfather, was too awful to contemplate. By the time he reached his room, the anger rising in him was as powerful as the deep sorrow he had felt at the age of six when he was told of his mother's untimely death. But he was no longer the boy of six who had been so cruelly beaten by 'the wicked one': he was thirteen, he was almost as tall as his nemesis and, he guessed, much stronger — he would never be punished in such a way again. As the unbidden hot tears threatened to overcome his demeanour, he resisted the temptation to flop down on his bed and cry out in fury. Instead, rising to his full height, he walked sedately over to the window. Looking across the open fields — out to the world beyond the residence that was designated his 'home' — he made a decision: he would not return!

I will keep calm, I will behave like the 'little gentleman' Mr Leadbetter expects me to be, he told himself, as he prepared to meet his grandfather's guests at dinner. Crispin Nigel Leadbetter recognised the pomposity of those who resided within the walls of this godforsaken place: he could conform. But to him, it was not real life. Jamie's home was real: it had warmth. His school was real: it was like one big happy family. Granted, there were grand occasions: formal events, ceremonies to which V.I.P.s were invited and strawberry teas — times when they were expected to conduct themselves with decorum. But the pretence did not intrude into everyday life. Even Mr Campbell, the Laird he had met on holiday last summer, lived in the real world, despite his home being a castle. The dinner that evening was every bit as awful as Crispin anticipated. How could he ever contemplate living this sort of life?

Fortunately, Crispin was able to spend much of his final weekend with Jamie. He told his friend of his grandfather's expectations, how he was to accompany him to the office during the school holidays. He also alerted Jamie to the stipulations regarding the longed-for holiday. As expected, he would only be allowed to go to Scotland for two weeks in the summer depending on his school report. It must show that he continued to attain the highest standards.

Mrs Roberts was likewise summoned to Mr Leadbetter's study. Her offer to have Crispin join herself and her son for a fortnight's holiday was acknowledged. It would be accepted on condition that Crispin's achievements were worthy of such a privilege. Once again, he assured her that he would forfeit the money for the rail tickets should he decide that his grandson had not fulfilled his part of the bargain. Janet Roberts never failed to be astounded at the arrogance of the man. As agreed, she had never mentioned Mr Campbell's visit to Jamie nor had she made any reference to the problem of Crispin's true identity. However, Jamie had commented on the strange coincidence of the name of his friend, and that of the boy he called Chris whom he had met in East Bay.

Mrs Roberts hoped that the mystery surrounding the two boys would soon be solved, although she was concerned for what might become of the boy she had always known as Crispin Nigel Leadbetter. She was glad that Timothy Campbell had left his contact numbers. Should the boy be denied his forthcoming holiday, she would be in touch with him immediately.

Crispin pondered over whether or not to tell Jamie that he had no intention of returning to the home of his grandparents. If he had conjured up a definite plan he would, perhaps, have had the confidence to let Jamie into the secret. As it was, he had little idea of how to get away, so decided it best to keep things to himself. However, of one thing he was certain: he *would* have his holiday at East Bay. So as he said farewell to Jamie on Sunday afternoon, his parting words were: "Don't worry, I'll see you in Scotland." It was a weird comment, leaving Jamie somewhat puzzled. Whatever did his friend mean?

As with many children in the post-war era, Crispin was encouraged to save. He had his own bankbook. At the beginning of the school year, his grandfather deposited money with the school for this purpose, and for pocket money. Each week Crispin went to the school office to be handed his weekly allowance, paying the specified amount into his bank via the school, and keeping the rest as spending money. Crispin did not usually use all of this money, so he placed what was left over in a purse in his locker. This term he would save as much as he could.

His trunk was only sent home at the end of the school year, so Crispin had brought home a satchel with his schoolbooks and a duffle bag with a few items of clothing. As he repacked to return to school, he put some extra casual clothes into the bag. He looked around his room for anything that he didn't want to leave behind. He found some school photographs and placed them in his satchel amongst the books. There was nothing else that was of any interest to him. His life was not here; he had never felt that he belonged. There was the faintest tinge of sadness as he said goodbye to his grandmother before getting into the taxi that had been ordered to take him to the station. She had not caused him harm — well, so far, not to his knowledge! As for his grandfather, he had said a final farewell the previous evening with a formal shake of his hand. He had already left for his office earlier that morning: Crispin hoped never to see him again.

CHAPTER 25
My Name is Stuart Anderson

Once the new school term was underway, Timothy Campbell telephoned the school, politely requesting to speak with the Headmaster. Since Mr Smith was in a meeting at the time, the secretary suggested he would return the call as soon as he was available. She took Mr Campbell's name and number.

Mr Smith had been expecting the call. He was anxious to speak with this gentleman who had instigated the investigation into the mystery of a pupil in his care: the boy whom he had always believed to be Crispin Nigel Leadbetter. Mr Campbell, he was assured, was great-grandfather to the real Crispin Nigel Leadbetter. The Headmaster, naturally, was keen to know the identity of the boy in his charge.

Never having met the Headmaster, Timothy was reluctant to convey too much information over the telephone. However, he felt sufficiently confident to confirm that the boy was definitely not the child that Mr and Mrs Leadbetter supposed him to be. "His real name is Stuart Anderson and, bizarre as this may seem to you, he is my grandson," he announced.

Mr Smith was confused. "So, the child we have here is Stuart Anderson — your grandson — and the real Crispin Nigel Leadbetter is your great-grandson?"

"Yes, that's right," Timothy replied. "There is, of course, much more to this situation. The findings of Clive Small in ascertaining the identity of the boy can now be submitted as evidence in a criminal investigation. Since you are responsible for the child during the school term, I can disclose more about the case but would prefer to do so in person."

Mr Smith understood. He added his concern for the child, realising that Mr Campbell would also need to see his grandson.

A visit to the school by Timothy Campbell was organised for mid-May when he would meet Mr Smith and make arrangements to break the news to his grandson. Only Charles Carter was made aware of the true nature of his colleague's impending trip south. If all went well, Timothy hoped to share everything with Jeannie and, most importantly, Kitty and Sandy.

Timothy set off for London in a tentative mood: so much rested on the outcome of this trip. Once more he booked into a hotel in the city centre, declining his brother's offer to stay with him. Since Bernard would be working during the day, Timothy decided the hotel would be more appropriate. He could meet up with his brother in the evenings.

His visit to the school had been arranged for Friday morning, allowing Timothy the next day to rest after his journey and give further consideration as to how best to tackle meeting his grandson. Ultimately, he concluded that planning was not the answer: he would have to trust his judgement by the reaction of the boy at seeing him turn up at his school. He looked forward to joining Bernard and the detective, Clive Small, for a meal in the evening. The report that Timothy had received from Clive on the investigation was informative, revealing all the facts necessary to justify an arrest should that be deemed the way ahead. However, there were some amusing details — not pertaining directly to the case — that had not been included. The informal evening provided the opportunity for the detective to share some of these details: anecdotes from the inquisitive Cynthia, who lived opposite the Dobsons; some of the references from the Headmaster about his encounters with the indomitable Mr Leadbetter; and, best of all, the cunning plan whereby Clive had gained access to the third-year class by taking a lesson.

Although not facts that would be applicable in a court of law, many of these details were useful for Timothy Campbell to know. They gave an insight into the nature of the school he was about to visit, the philosophy of the Headmaster and his staff, and further evidence of the overbearing 'grandfather'. He felt more relaxed about his forthcoming visit.

It was a warm sunny morning in the middle of May as Timothy Campbell made his way to his grandson's school, south of the city of London. He was glad to escape from the stuffy atmosphere of the Tube, into the daylight. He had no difficulty locating the large Victorian building with its generous playing fields, barely a ten-minute walk from the station.

He was cautious as he approached the main entrance to the building, hoping that he would not accidentally encounter his grandson before his scheduled meeting with the Headmaster. The secretary was expecting him — realising that he was an important visitor, though not a party to the real significance of his presence in the school. Mr Smith was ready to receive him immediately, unable to disguise his curiosity about the mystery surrounding the young teenager in his charge.

He directed his guest to a comfortable armchair by the coffee table, where he joined him a few minutes later, after requesting tea to be brought to the room. He anticipated that it might take some time for Mr Campbell to explain the details he had been unwilling to disclose over the telephone.

Timothy hardly knew where to begin in recalling the saga of the abduction of Stuart Anderson; so, by way of introduction, he confirmed what he had revealed in the telephone call earlier in the month: the pupil in the school, known as Crispin Nigel Leadbetter, was actually Stuart Anderson — his grandson.

As the story of the kidnap unfolded, Mr Smith could barely contain his anger. He tried hard not to interrupt as Timothy proceeded to recount the despicable deed that had led to Stuart's miserable existence with the arrogant Mr and Mrs Leadbetter, but there were moments when he could not stop himself. To break with the narrative and allow the shocked Headmaster to absorb the facts, Timothy presented items of evidence that he had brought along to verify the case: first, the article in the Aberdeen Press and Journal reporting the abduction of Stuart Anderson in October of 1940. Later, he produced a copy of the birth certificate of Stuart Anderson, pointing out that Kathryn Anderson, the boy's mother, was also the mother of Isobel Anderson. Mr Smith understood from the information taken from *Crispin's* birth certificate that Isobel Anderson was the mother of Crispin Nigel Leadbetter. The Leadbetters had claimed that she had died shortly after her son was born. Timothy stressed that Isobel was very much alive and bringing up her son, the real Crispin Nigel Leadbetter — she was Stuart's sister.

"What a tragedy!" Mr Smith exclaimed. "The whole of the Anderson family devastated by these wicked people."

Timothy registered his listener's concern. It was obvious that he was upset for all those involved. "It has been terrible for them," he agreed, "especially my daughter Kathryn and her husband. And now," he continued, "I must talk to Stuart to make him aware of his true identity."

"I can't imagine how the child is going to respond to the revelation, especially coming from someone he has never met before." Mr Smith looked sympathetically at Stuart's grandfather.

"Oh, I'm so sorry." Timothy interjected, "I should have mentioned earlier — I *have* met him." He proceeded to explain the strange circumstances that had resulted in the boy visiting him at his castle; while emphasising that, at the time, neither he nor the boy had any idea of their connection. Stuart was still ignorant of the fact.

"In that case, perhaps you would like to see Crispin…hmm, I mean Stuart, here in my room, where you will not be disturbed. I have plenty of other things to be getting on with." Timothy agreed: it would be ideal.

At that moment the bell rang signalling the end of the morning break. Mr Smith left his visitor and went out to find the boy before the start of the next lesson.

Crispin was somewhat alarmed as the Headmaster stopped him in the corridor on the way to his geography class. "There's a gentleman in my office, waiting to see you," he announced, "and, don't worry it's not your grand-d-d…it's not Mr Leadbetter," he stuttered, remembering that Mr Campbell *was* the boy's grandfather — his real grandfather. "Just knock on the door and go straight in," he added, much to the further confusion of the unsuspecting teenager.

With satchel slung over his shoulder, his hair blown by the wind, his tie loosened from around his collar and scuff marks across both knees, a puzzled Crispin Nigel Leadbetter made his way to the Headmaster's Office — a place that usually meant trouble. He knocked on the door, as instructed, but hesitated before gently turning the knob and pushing it open. A tall, elderly man stood facing him as he entered the room. Crispin stopped, wide-eyed; and stared at the Laird he had met last year on his memorable Scottish holiday — his only holiday, ever.

Equally at a loss for words, Timothy responded to this strange union in the way that seemed most appropriate at that moment. "I'm your Grandpa," he announced.

With complete trust and requiring no further explanation, Crispin moved towards Timothy who responded with open arms, welcoming the boy into his embrace. The bond between grandfather and grandson was sealed.

"Come, sit down," Timothy invited, directing Crispin to the comfortable armchair, recently occupied by the Headmaster, while he returned to his place on the other.

For the next half-hour Crispin listened, with incredulity, as his grandfather unfolded the story of his kidnap, with its disastrous consequences for the family.

"So I'm not Crispin Nigel Leadbetter, (he needed to double-check, to make sure he had interpreted everything correctly) and the wicked Mr Leadbetter is not my grandfather?"

"No, he is not. He is no relation of yours," Timothy confirmed with a smile.

"And my name is Stuart Anderson?"

"Yes, that's right."

"And my mother is alive?"

"Your mother and your father are both very much alive," Timothy repeated, "as is the woman the Leadbetters told you had died after giving birth to you. She is your sister; the mother of the real Crispin Nigel

Leadbetter whom you met when you were on holiday last year."

Stuart Anderson was stunned, yet relieved to learn the truth. It would take him some time to come to terms with the situation, to fathom his relationship to all the members of the Anderson family, and to understand how it would affect his future: there were so many questions he needed to ask.

"I like my school," he stated, "but I don't want to go back to the Leadbetters'. It's not my home, it's never been my home," his voice rose in anger, "I hate them all!"

"We have a lot more to talk about," Timothy responded, calmly. "It's Friday. How about we ask Mr Smith if you can stay with me for the weekend?"

"I'd like that, but I'm playing cricket on Sunday afternoon," Stuart replied. "Can we be back for that?"

"Yes, of course we can," his grandfather replied. "Now, if you're okay, I suggest you have lunch with your friends and attend your afternoon classes. It'll probably be best if you continue to be known as Crispin for the moment, and keep most of this to yourself for the time being: there is a criminal investigation into the case. You can tell your friends that your Grandpa from Scotland is here to visit you."

Before leaving the Headmaster's study, Crispin looked at his new Grandpa and, with the broadest grin, remarked, "Thank you for finding me."

Timothy Campbell was delighted with Stuart's reaction to the news. It appeared that his grandson was relieved, rather than upset, to learn that he wasn't the person he thought he was. He was glad that the boy had found comfort and friendship at his school, but it could not possibly compensate for a miserable home existence. Although Timothy had gained some idea of the child's home circumstances from Mrs Roberts, as well as from the Headmaster of the school, he now had confirmation from the boy himself. Hopefully, he would learn more in the next day or so as he got to know him better: he looked forward to that. As he sat pondering the events of the morning, there was a knock on the door signalling the return of Mr Smith. He had seen Crispin making his way to the refectory and was anxious to know the outcome of the meeting.

Like Timothy, the Headmaster was delighted at how Crispin had responded to the news, but concerned as to how to proceed. It was clear that the boy was immersed in the life of the school; so whisking him away, especially at this point in the school year, would not be sensible. However, it was also obvious that he would be reluctant to return to the home of his erstwhile 'grandparents'. Timothy explained that the boy had been invited to spend a fortnight in Scotland with his friend Jamie, at the beginning of August. He thought that if he were persuaded to go back to the home of the Leadbetters for the first week of the summer holiday, that would be the ideal solution, keeping the battle with the family at bay until the boy was well away from them.

Mr Smith agreed. Besides, if the Leadbetters were arrested for the kidnap, it would be best that the story break in the vacation, rather than during the school term. However, both agreed that it had to be Crispin's decision.

Timothy declined Mr Smith's offer to have lunch at the school. He preferred to get out for some fresh air and find a café in the vicinity. He would return at the end of the school day to collect Stuart and take him into London, commenting he had already promised to have him back on Sunday morning so that he could participate in the cricket match in the afternoon. Before parting, he gave the Headmaster a copy of Stuart's birth certificate along with the address of his parents. This information would be kept in an envelope marked confidential, and only accessed in case of an emergency. The two gentlemen agreed to keep in contact throughout the rest of the term, regarding the welfare of the child.

CHAPTER 26
Stuart and Timothy

At the end of afternoon school Crispin, or rather Stuart, changed out of his school uniform into more casual clothes, packed his duffle bag with items for his overnight stay in the hotel, and met his grandpa at the main entrance. Mr Smith waved them off, with his blessing, saying he would see them at the cricket match on Sunday. Stuart looked questioningly at his grandpa, who confirmed that he would attend the match to cheer him on. He understood, from the Headmaster, that it was the final match in a tournament with other local schools: it was an important event. So, for the first time ever, the overwhelmed teenager would have someone there to support him. He could hardly believe how much his life had changed in a few hours. It was with an enormous sense of relief that he set off to spend some time with a real live relative. For this weekend, he would be Stuart Anderson and, hopefully, after the end of the term, he would be able to leave Crispin Nigel Leadbetter behind!

During the afternoon and evening, the two relative strangers had plenty of time to share something of their life stories. Stuart held nothing back in relaying the dreadful time he had spent with his abductors. He tried hard to control the anger he felt at discovering the truth about his situation but, as his grandfather pointed out, the truth was his salvation. Knowing that Stuart would go through many different emotions in the coming weeks, he displayed an understanding that comes only with the passing of the years: it marked the beginning of a unique bond that so often exists between grandparents and their grandchildren.

In relaying the tale of his connection with the Anderson family, Timothy Campbell did not hide anything from the young lad. Stuart's whole life had been a lie, even his identity. The frankness of the elderly gentleman helped bring the two closer. Here was someone that Stuart could trust; a Laird, no less, whom he didn't have to address as Sir; a real gentleman who genuinely cared for him and from whom he did not shrink in fear.

Despite living close to England's capital, Stuart had only ever visited London on rare shopping trips with his grandmother and Aunt Henrietta. He had never seen any of the famous sights. Timothy suggested they spend the next day visiting some of these places, many of which were within walking distance of the hotel. He also wondered if Stuart would like to meet his great-uncle Bernard: the man who had arranged for the investigation into the kidnapping. Since Stuart was particularly keen on this idea, Timothy rang his brother. Bernard invited them both to his home for a meal the following evening.

Waking up in the hotel room, having slept on a bed settee in the same room as his grandpa, Stuart thought he must have been dreaming. It took him a few minutes to fathom out how he came to be in this place. What had happened? A call from his grandpa, "Wakey, wakey! We don't want to miss breakfast," brought him to the present.

It was real; yesterday was real. Rubbing his eyes, he sat up. "Good morning, Grandpa!" he said, acknowledging the elderly figure, already up and dressed, gazing out of the window onto the street below.

"Good morning, Stuart," his grandfather responded.

Stuart disappeared into the bathroom, wondering how long it would take for him to get used to hearing his real name.

As soon as he was ready, the two of them made their way downstairs to the dining room for breakfast. This really was like being on holiday, he thought. It was the first time he had had a weekend away from boarding school during term-time. Not that he minded being at the school, but it was good to be like the other boys: to have somebody care enough about him to give him a break.

The day went well. They spent a couple of hours in the British Museum, but the weather was too good to be inside all day. They wandered down to the Thames, to Tower Bridge and the Houses of Parliament; had lunch, and strolled back through Hyde Park, returning to the hotel in time to relax for an hour before making their way to Bernard's for an early evening meal.

Bernard, as always, was a most hospitable host, welcoming his guests with open arms. He had especially looked forward to meeting Stuart Anderson, the boy whose identity he had played a part in confirming. The introductions were no sooner over than there was a knock at the door.

"Ah, we have another guest," Bernard announced and, turning to Stuart, he added, "I believe you have met him before."

Opening the door, a tall gentleman bearing a broad grin entered the room.

"Mr Small!" Stuart gasped, in astonishment.

"The very man," Bernard acknowledged.

The evening could not have gone better. Here was a group of distinguished men who, unlike Stuart's erstwhile relatives, did not put on any airs and graces — there was no need. Stuart felt more comfortable than he had ever felt when he was at home. These people were interested to hear what he had to say: they treated him with respect.

It was only now that Stuart realised that the detective, who had so generously offered to take his class for a lesson, was there as part of the investigation into him. He was eager to know more.

"How did you discover I was Stuart Anderson?" he asked, once the nature of Mr Small's mission to the school had been disclosed.

The detective asked Stuart to show his hands. "Now," he requested, "turn them over so that we can see the back of your wrists." Stuart did as he was asked.

With the forefinger of his right hand, Mr Small touched the birthmark on the back of Stuart's right hand. "There," he said.

"But how did you know? I hardly notice that mark myself."

"It was in your mother's report when you were kidnapped," the detective explained. "When I walked into that lesson, I had a class list but no way of matching the names to the faces. I identified you purely by that mark. Had it faded completely, as might well have been the case, it would not have ruled out your real identity but, since it was visible, it left no shadow of doubt as to who you were."

"Wow!" Stuart exclaimed, "So you were spying on us?" he added with a grin.

"I was just doing my job," Mr Small responded, in his own defence, "but I thoroughly enjoyed taking the class."

"And we loved having you," Stuart commented, "It was inspiring. It left me thinking what an interesting job it would be."

The evening went well for Stuart, although it did leave a question mark regarding what the next move should be. His grandpa was guarded about putting forward his proposal; that 'Crispin' might continue his life as normal, returning to Oxfordshire with his supposed grandparents at the end of the school term. If he could bear to stay with them for a week, until his holiday in Scotland, the abduction would not be revealed until he was well away. After that, he need never see them again.

It was with caution that Timothy presented this plan, realising that it was unlikely to be acceptable to his grandson. As predicted, Stuart's immediate reaction was one of horror at the mere thought of having to endure another minute in the presence of the Leadbetters, let alone a whole week. In his eyes, as in the eyes of the three gentlemen in whose company he found himself, they were criminals — dangerous, wily deviants who could never be trusted. However, he did understand the logic of his grandfather's argument. Bernard concurred that such a consideration made sense but, like his brother, admitted that he would not insist Stuart undertake such action: it had to be the boy's decision.

Stuart was anxious to complete the year at his boarding school, including the end of term closing ceremony. He worked hard and was proud of his achievements, even if Mr Leadbetter wasn't. He wouldn't wish to spoil the event in any way and could appreciate that a confrontation before that could be catastrophic. So, much to the amazement of everyone, he agreed that he would try, although he could not promise. The next few weeks, with the thought of having to face his erstwhile family, would be a challenge.

Bernard offered to keep an eye on his great-nephew. His home in central London was relatively convenient for the school. He suggested Stuart be furnished with his contact details and use his house as an escape route, should that become necessary.

When they arrived back at the hotel, Timothy assured his grandson that he would understand if he was unable to comply with the plan. In order to help if he should find himself in a difficult situation, he gave him money to cover his rail fare to Scotland and extra for expenses; a copy of his real birth certificate; the address of Kitty and Sandy, and his own contact details.

Stuart did not let on to his grandpa that, before meeting him yesterday morning, he had already decided never to set foot in the Leadbetters' home again. He had racked his brain trying to think exactly how to carry out his escape but, other than a determination to see Jamie in Scotland, he had not been able to ascertain how he would manage, nor what he would do once the holiday was at an end. Now, most of the work had been done for him. However, he would not dismiss his grandfather's idea: he had a few weeks to mull it over.

Sunday was a glorious day — ideal for the final match of the cricket tournament. It was a superb game: Timothy was impressed at the skills displayed by the boys, especially his precious grandson. Stuart was delighted by his grandfather's presence; all the better as his team won!

It was with some sadness but much hope on both sides, that they parted company at the end of the afternoon. "Remember," Timothy said, "Bernard's in London if you need him and I'm just a telephone call away. Mr Smith knows the whole story should the Leadbetters cause any problems in the meantime."

CHAPTER 27
The Truth Revealed

Timothy returned home to Scotland feeling more positive than when he had left a few days earlier. It was a relief to find his grandson not only alive and well but appreciative of the efforts that had been made to reunite him with his blood relatives. Although saddened that the boy had endured such a miserable home life, he had, at least, found a home of sorts at his school. There, he had plenty of friends amongst his peers, as well as the concern of adults under whose care he had fallen. That Stuart had displayed anger when made aware of the truth, was understandable. Hopefully, there would be some compensation to be gained from his birth family when they finally met.

After the long journey, Timothy made his way to the castle intent on having a good night's rest before visiting the home of his daughter and her husband. He was bursting to let them know that their son had been found — that the story behind the abduction had been solved. However, he wanted to feel refreshed: there was a lot of explaining to do; many questions that they would want answered.

The next morning Timothy ventured into the market town, having decided to warn his son-in-law of his impending visit. Kitty was normally home from the bank shortly after five o'clock. Sandy suggested Timothy join them for supper around six o'clock — a meal that he would be cooking. The unusual advance notice alerted Sandy to suspect that there was something serious on Timothy's mind.

"What's he been up to now?" was Kitty's immediate reaction to the news of her father's imminent visit. His active involvement in the affairs of the family intrigued his daughter. After her initial burst of indignation — that he was interfering in their lives — she had come to realise that his interest was genuine: it was borne out of a desire to become a part of their circle. She had grown to accept and love the elderly Laird who was her father.

Timothy still found it strange to give a cursory knock on a door and walk into a house without waiting for anyone to answer, but that was the way with all of his 'new' family. Even if the residents were not at home, their door would not be locked. He was told just to go in, make himself a cup of tea, and wait! On this particular day, being fine and warm, the door was ajar, and he knew that Kitty and Sandy would be there. "Come in," came a familiar voice from the living room. Greeted with a friendly smile, as always, he felt immediately at home. He had no sooner sat down when Kitty's curiosity got the better of her.

"Well, what brings you here?" she asked.

"There's a delicious smell coming from the kitchen," was his response, indicating that the reason for his visit would have to wait until after they had eaten.

Once the meal was over and the three of them were relaxing in the living room with a cup of tea or, in the case of Sandy, his usual pint mug and pipe, Timothy was ready to break the news.

"I've found your son, Stuart," he announced, "He's alive and well and looking forward to seeing you soon."

For a few moments, the information did not register with either Kitty or Sandy. They had endured the pain of the loss of their son for so many years; all hopes of ever finding him had long since been dashed. A resistance had been built up to protect them from further hurt: this declaration could not be real.

"I've found Stuart," Timothy repeated, seeing the bewildered looks on their faces, whilst, at the same time, tears welled up in his eyes. "I've met him; he wants to come home."

Seeing her father struggling with his emotions, it dawned on Kitty that what he was saying must be true.

"You've seen him?" she probed.

"Yes, I saw him at the weekend. He's at a boarding school in England," Timothy emphasised.

At this, the questions flooded from his anxious audience.

"Where? When? How?"

Timothy began to relay the story from the day of the kidnap: the awful truth that the wrong child, their beloved baby Stuart, had been taken. As the story unfolded, Kitty and Sandy were increasingly horrified. How could their daughter's in-laws have contemplated such a wicked deed? For their sins, they had brought up the wrong child, but that was little compensation for Stuart Anderson or his parents. Once Timothy had finished telling the sorry tale of how Stuart had fallen into the hands of the Leadbetters (his nephew's grandparents), the focus of concern for Kitty and Sandy turned to their son. How was Stuart, where was he and, most importantly, when would they see him? Timothy continued the saga, telling of the strange coincidence of his meeting with a boy called Crispin Nigel Leadbetter, born on the same day as Isobel's son. It was then that he had decided to investigate. The evidence had been gathered and only recently collated, unequivocally confirming his suspicions.

Looking to his shocked listeners, Timothy reassured them that Stuart was fine: they would see him soon. "He is coming up here at the beginning of August with his friend Jamie," he revealed, "and he will not be going back to live with Mr and Mrs Leadbetter. He has a copy of his real birth certificate and your address. You'll need to have his room ready," he added, with a smile.

Kitty suppressed the urge to dance for joy. Both she and her husband were stunned by the news and, perhaps understandably, cautious in their reactions: the revelation that, after almost fourteen years, their son had been found safe and well, seemed too good to be true.

"Does Isobel know?" Kitty ventured to ask.

"No, the only person who knows is Charles: copies of all the documents about the case are filed in the office.

Even he doesn't know how well things went on my visit south. Would you like me to speak with Isobel or would you prefer to break the news to her yourself?"

"I think *we* should tell her," Kitty answered, indicating herself and Sandy, "but perhaps you should be there as well," she added. "There will be lots of details she may want to hear, and I'm afraid I'm finding it difficult to take it all in."

"Might I suggest we go to the hotel sometime on Saturday," Timothy answered. "I'm going there tomorrow evening to help out, so I'll ask what time would be best for her — to fit in with her busy schedule!"

"Maybe Ma should be there too," Kitty proposed, "after all, this is a matter for all the family. I take it she knows nothing about any of this?"

"No," Timothy responded. "I couldn't tell any of you until I was absolutely sure. Had my suspicions been unfounded, it would have been too painful to imagine."

"Fit aboot the wee loon?" Sandy interrupted, with reference to Chris. "A dinna s'pose he even kens aboot the kidnap."

"True," Kitty agreed, "I don't suppose he does. It all happened when he was just a tiny baby."

"Aye, an tae think they took the wrong un! It'll be a rale shock tae oor Chris, "Sandy commented.

"And, of course," Timothy emphasised, "Chris already knows Stuart or, at least, knows him as Crispin." He was shaking his head at the number of people affected by the selfish actions of his granddaughter's in-laws. Isobel would be devastated.

Before Isobel's parents and grandparents were due to arrive on Saturday afternoon, Charles, indicating that he had an idea what the meeting was about, suggested he take the twins out for some fresh air: Chris was keen to go with them. Isobel already realised there must be some important announcement, since Timothy was asking her parents and Grandma Jeannie to meet together. Her husband's seeming prior knowledge further mystified her but she could never have anticipated what was about to be revealed.

Isobel listened in amazement as her ma and da disclosed the news that their youngest son, who had been taken from them so cruelly almost fourteen years ago, had been found safe and well. However, as the story unfolded, her delight turned to horror. As her grandfather had anticipated, the relief of learning that Stuart was fine turned to distress when she discovered the truth. She had never held her in-laws in high esteem, viewing them as middle-class snobs, but she would never have suspected them of instigating such a wicked plot. How could they keep the boy they assumed to be their grandson from his mother? Now, of course, everything fitted into place — the unanswered letters, the unprecedented house moves of her in-laws without leaving forwarding addresses, the denial of Raymond's brother as he had turned her away from Henrietta's former home. Having absorbed these unsavoury details, it was another aspect of the story that upset her even more: she was beset with guilt, blaming herself for bringing all this grief on her parents. If she had not fled from London with Crispin to seek shelter in her parents' home, this tragedy would never have happened.

For the family, many aspects of the story were unclear. Filled with mixed emotions at hearing the news, they had not absorbed all the facts on the first telling. They turned to Timothy to repeat the details about his meeting with the boy calling himself Crispin Nigel Leadbetter; the young lad who had unknowingly come face to face with the real Crispin Nigel Leadbetter and innocently revealed his name to the man who was his grandfather. They wanted to know all about the investigation, and especially about Timothy's recent visit after the truth had been uncovered.

Hearing the sound of Charles and Chris returning with the twins, it was time to end the formalities. It had been an odd get-together. Jeannie and Kitty could see that, despite the good news, Isobel was upset. She would now have the onerous task of relaying the story of the kidnap, as well as the recent turn of events, to her son, who knew nothing of his long lost Uncle Stuart.

As they were leaving the hotel, Timothy and Jeannie suggested that Kitty and Sandy join them for an evening meal in Aberdeen. They arranged to meet them at the railway station and take a train into the city. Timothy had already booked a table for two, for himself and Jeannie, but he didn't think there would be a problem about accommodating two more guests. It was a relaxing evening for the four of them: the grateful parents now more settled in the knowledge that their beloved son was safe.

For Isobel the 'good news' was so marred by the disclosure of the involvement of her in-laws in the abduction, accompanied by her feeling of guilt, she was unable to rejoice. Both Charles and Chris were alarmed by her distress following the family meeting. Charles, already aware of the facts, understood what was wrong, but Chris had no idea: he had to be told. Later that evening, after the twins were in bed, Isobel succumbed to her son's persistence.

To Chris who, so far, had no idea that he had an uncle just two weeks older than himself, the whole story held a certain fascination. Since he had never suffered the loss that his older relatives had endured, he did not have the same reaction. When he learned that his friend Crispin, whom he had met the previous summer, was his missing Uncle Stuart, he was eager to know more. From what 'Crispin' had told him about the Leadbetters, together with this information about their part in the abduction plot, he was thankful that he had escaped the ordeal: it sent a cold shudder through him, realising that it was he who was the real target of the kidnap. He had never known these grandparents and, knowing what he knew now, he didn't want anything to do with them. Unlike his mother, having met Stuart and spent a fortnight with him and Jamie, he knew that his uncle had survived — he had good friends and an amazing tale to tell. Would he have fared so well?... He wondered! Chris was anxious to have a long talk with his great-grandpa who, he understood, had spent some time with Stuart the previous weekend: perhaps he would be able to tell him more about his plans for the future. His mother told him that Stuart intended to come up to East Bay with his friend, Jamie, in the summer, but parts of the story, as she relayed it to Chris, were blurred: she was so distraught.

It was a blessing to her that her son appeared relatively unperturbed about the involvement of the Leadbetters in the affair. Apart from expressing his disgust, and commenting that he never liked the name 'Leadbetter', he shrugged his shoulders and assured his mother that it wasn't her fault.

Over the next few days, Charles tried his best to console Isobel but, despite her son's positive reaction, it was several weeks before she came to terms with the facts and, even then, she had not fully recovered from the shock.

CHAPTER 28
The Escape

I'm Stuart Anderson, the young teenager still known to all his friends as Crispin Nigel Leadbetter, kept reminding himself. He would be very glad when he could leave his false identity behind and begin life anew as the person he really was. However, the one thing that troubled him was the thought of never returning to his beloved school. At almost fourteen years of age, he had spent seven years — half his life — with the same peers: they had become his family; they *were* his family. Although he yearned to be united with his blood relatives, he would miss these close comrades.

The thing that didn't trouble him at all was the thought of his final departure from the loathsome Leadbetters. Before the visit of the Scottish Laird, his own grandpa, he was already planning his escape: *I'm never going back,* he had told himself before the end of the Easter break.

Although his grandpa said he would never force him to return to his dreaded 'home', Stuart could see the sense in the argument to carry on as normal, to spend one week there before going up to Scotland on holiday with Mrs Roberts and Jamie. Furthermore, he did not want to let his grandfather and great-uncle Bernard down. But the problem that niggled away in his head was the awful thought that Mr Leadbetter would refuse permission for him to go on holiday — then what would he do? As the end of term drew closer, Stuart concluded that however much he wanted to please his new grandpa, he really couldn't entertain the idea of returning to Oxfordshire: a plan began to formulate — he had an idea!

With a change in his circumstances looming, Stuart was more determined than ever to excel in his end-of-year exams, as well as on the sports field. In all his years at boarding school, no one had come to the annual sports day to cheer him on — but this year was different. Much to his surprise, two people turned up: his uncle Bernard accompanied by the tall, cheerful, private detective, Mr Small. Both supporters were amazed at the boy's prowess in his events: they clapped and cheered as he went up to receive his prizes. Instead of tagging along with one of his friends and their family for the regulation cream tea at the end of the afternoon, Stuart joined a relative of his own.

The final day of the school year dawned at last. 'Crispin', as he was still known to his classmates, was filled with a mixture of excitement and sadness, tinged with fear — would his cunning plan work? He would find out soon enough! The morning rehearsal for the closing ceremony, which was to take place in the afternoon, went well. Crispin's position in the line for year group awards, dictated alphabetically according to surnames, was ideal. He worked out his strategy. It was proving difficult for him to keep his growing anxiety from his friends, especially Sam, who tended to be more sensitive than most. Although Crispin always fell into a sombre mood at the approach of the school holidays, somehow this time was different: something was afoot — Sam just knew it.

Fifteen minutes before the ceremony was due to begin the hall was already packed with the families of the boys, including the Leadbetters, who were seated at the far left close to the back. Apart from the boys who were in the school orchestra, the pupils were waiting in their classrooms for the signal to make their way to the hall in the order prescribed during the morning's practice. The dignitaries, who would join the platform party, were being organised into a queue in the sequence they would enter the stage on the stroke of two o'clock, once all the boys were in their places.

Crispin, who did not notice his grandparents as he entered the hall, wriggled in his seat, wondering if he dared risk scanning the audience to locate them. "They're near the back, over in the left section," Sam whispered (he was sitting next to Crispin). Crispin nodded to his friend, mouthing 'thanks', as he risked a glance in their direction. All he could see was the top of his grandmother's hat. *Good*, he thought, *I'm almost out of their sight.*

The ceremony began with a hymn and the school prayer, followed by the introduction of the V.I.P.s, and the Headmaster's speech, which covered the highlights of the school year. Eventually, it was time for the prize-giving beginning with the first year. They lined up along the right aisle to access the stage at that side. Every pupil received their end of year certificate, while several received specific awards for excellence in different areas of the curriculum. They exited the platform from the left, making their way round the back to wait until the rest of the class joined them. The whole year group re-entered the hall through a door to the right of the stage to return to their seats.

The same procedure was repeated for the second and third year. Aside from his end-of-year certificate, Crispin had a special award — a small shield, for the best overall academic student of his year. Having received his award, he made his way down the steps to join his class line round the back of the stage. Immediately, he nudged Sam. "I don't feel so well," he said, "I'm going to lie down for a while." With that, he walked away, disappearing through the back door to make his way to his 'house' at the end of the sprawling school building. Taking the stairs two at a time he entered his dormitory, catching his breath. He whipped off his blazer, shirt and school tie, and tossed them into his open trunk at the end of his bed. He donned a pale blue shirt, mid-blue tie and dark jacket, which he had left in his locker along with his ready-packed duffle bag. He added his satchel and year-group shield to the trunk before closing the lid, locking it and placing the key in an inside pocket of his jacket. He cast his eye around to check that he had not left anything behind, before racing down the stairs and out of the building into the warm afternoon sunshine. From there, he strolled nonchalantly through the back school gate and along the road to the railway station. He was almost sure he had not been seen. Apart from the secretary, whose office he had circumvented, the whole school was assembled in the hall.

He had only a few minutes to wait for a train to take him into the city centre. Within three-quarters of an hour of leaving the school hall, he was purchasing a one-way ticket to Aberdeen. The next train north was leaving in ten minutes. It would take him as far as Newcastle where he would have to change for Edinburgh. He had no idea when he would reach Aberdeen, but he was relieved to be on his way.

....

The ceremony in the school hall was drawing to a close as the train, taking Stuart Anderson north, pulled out of the station — Crispin Nigel Leadbetter was gone!

Mr and Mrs Leadbetter stood chatting to those around them as they waited their turn to exit the hall: being at the back they were amongst the last to leave. They expected Crispin to be at the entrance to his 'house', ready to join them for the journey home. Mr Leadbetter was irritated that the boy was late. Sam hurried past the awesome couple to greet his parents who were standing just a few feet away. He thought it was strange, seeing the Leadbetters. He had been anxious to check that Crispin was feeling better; so when he saw that everything was as it should be — the empty locker, the locked trunk — assumed that his friend had already left the building. Had the Leadbetters been normal parents, he would have approached them to enquire; but they were not, so he ignored them and hoped that all was well — poor Crispin!

Several minutes after the last of the boys had left the building, carefree at the thought of the weeks of freedom ahead, Mrs Leadbetter was becoming anxious. It was not like her grandson to act in a way that would upset his grandfather. She had been proud of seeing him collect his special prize as the best academic achiever in his year; surely he wouldn't risk doing anything to spoil that moment. "I'll see if I can find him," she announced, as she disappeared into the building, leaving Crispin senior at the entrance in case the boy should turn up.

The place was eerily quiet. Priscilla had not been inside before. She began her search by opening the doors on the ground floor. Apart from one, which appeared to be a common room, the rest were classrooms. There was a corridor off to the left of the entrance hall leading to the rest of the school. The living quarters, she concluded, must be on the two upper floors. She made her way up the wide staircase to the first floor. Although the doors to the dormitories bore plaques adorned with gold lettering indicating the year group, she opened each one regardless and took a good look around. The doors that were devoid of such a notice led to bathrooms and store cupboards. Priscilla continued her search, ascending the stairs up to the second floor. Again she looked into every room. At last, she came to the door labelled 'Year 3'. Breathing deeply she entered, warily: this, she realised, was where her grandson spent much of his life. She walked down the middle, observing the labels on the trunks that were ready for collection at the foot of each bed. She had no trouble locating Crispin's space. Just like the others, the bed was stripped; the locker was empty aside from the key, and his trunk was closed and secured. There was no sign of her grandson.

Leaving no door unopened, she scoured the remaining rooms, before descending the stairs to be greeted by her husband, now visibly shaking with anger. It was more than half-an-hour since the closing ceremony had ended.

"Perhaps he has gone straight to the car park," Priscilla remarked. "Not very likely, but worth a try." They made their way around the back of the school building to the regular car park and the playground, which had been designated an overspill parking area for the afternoon. Having circled the entire building, all to no avail, they returned to the main entrance. A slow trickle of fifth and sixth form leavers and their parents were emerging: they had remained after the ceremony to partake of afternoon tea in the library. The Leadbetters decided to return to Crispin's house in the hope that they might see the housemaster. He would surely be there to check the dormitories once all the older boys had left. This time they waited in the foyer until, as they had anticipated, the housemaster descended the stairs and saw the agitated pair. He had never met them before but had heard about them. Mr Leadbetter, in his usual offensive manner, demanded to know the whereabouts of his grandson.

"He left the closing ceremony with his year group," the bewildered master assured them. Like the Leadbetters, he had not noticed that Crispin had disappeared after receiving his certificate and prize.

"Well, we haven't seen him. We've looked everywhere." Mr Leadbetter's voice boomed.

"I'll check his dormitory again," the housemaster answered, as he raced back up the stairs, not listening to further comments from the angry grandfather. He had already made a thorough search of the building so was unsurprised to find no sign of the boy, or any other boy.

"He's not here," he announced, as he once again approached the couple.

"This is preposterous," Mr Leadbetter spluttered, "you must know where he is."

The housemaster ignored the accusation. He suggested they follow him to the office to report the matter to the secretary.

As soon as she heard the name Leadbetter she was on her guard — this man was 'trouble': he was not one to be defied. The master intimated that Crispin Nigel Leadbetter could not be found. It seemed he had disappeared after the ceremony, not waiting for his grandparents.

Without waiting for a response, Mr Leadbetter insisted that he must see the Headmaster immediately.

"I'm sorry, Mr Leadbetter," came the reply, "The Headmaster has already left."

Crispin Leadbetter senior was incensed. "What do you mean, he's left? He's supposed to be running the school."

The secretary remained calm. "It's the end of term, Mr Leadbetter, the pupils are all away: Mr Smith is entitled to a holiday. He is celebrating his silver wedding anniversary at the weekend; he'll be back in a fortnight."

"I don't care what he's celebrating," Mr Leadbetter snapped, "our grandson is missing and I want answers."

"The Deputy Head is still here. I will ask if he will see you in his room," the secretary responded, quietly. "Just one moment please," she added, as she left her desk to alert the unsuspecting gentleman.

Mr Harris, who was Head of Maths as well as the Deputy Headmaster, was rather deflated at the news that the Leadbetters were demanding an audience with him. In retrospect, he had breathed a premature sigh of relief as the last of the boys had left the school building — the end of another school year! In a few hours, he could go home and relax. Although he would technically be on call for the next two weeks until Mr Smith returned, the pressure of the school term was off, or so he thought.

Mr Leadbetter remained annoyed as he and his wife entered the domain of the Deputy Headmaster. To Crispin Leadbetter, this man was second best — he had wanted to see the Head. Assuming, correctly, that Mr Harris knew who he was, he made no attempt either to introduce himself or to hide his displeasure. Even though they had both seen their grandson on the platform in the hall as he collected his award, Mr Leadbetter laid the blame for the disappearance squarely on the school. He claimed that they were solely responsible. Mr Harris tried to point out that, once the boys had been dismissed from the ceremony, their welfare passed automatically into the hands of their parents or guardians. At this, the irate grandfather's mood became threatening. The boy had better be found: he would take the matter further; he would sue the school for neglect.

Mr Harris, too, was becoming annoyed. In an attempt to keep his cool he tried to calm the situation. He assured the couple that he understood how upset they must be. He was sure the boy could not be far away — he would undertake a thorough search of the premises. If that failed, he would inform the police.

At the mention of police, the Leadbetters were alarmed. Changing his approach, Mr Leadbetter emphasised there was no need for that. Perhaps Crispin had made his own way home. He turned to leave...

Mr Harris was baffled by this sudden change in attitude. "Please let me know if you find him at home," he requested. "If I haven't heard from you by seven o'clock this evening, I will *have* to alert the police."

"You are *not* to get in touch with the police," Mr Leadbetter repeated, between gritted teeth.

"You have the school telephone number. I will be here until seven," The Deputy Head called, as the Leadbetters departed.

Mr Harris was no fool. The Leadbetters, he was sure, would not hesitate to accuse the school should Crispin not be found or, God forbid, should anything untoward have happened to the child. It was his duty to call the police: it was not a choice. Before making a search of the whole campus, Mr Harris asked the secretary to retrieve Crispin's personal details from the file and leave them on her desk. He would stay by the telephone in her office after she left at half-past five. He had plenty administrative duties to attend to while he waited for the phone call.

A thorough search of the area in and around the school was, of course, unsuccessful. As the secretary was leaving, the cleaning staff arrived. If the boy was lurking in any nook or cranny, they would find him. As requested, the information about Crispin was on her desk. She had not retrieved the brown envelope marked 'private and confidential': she could not know how relevant it would be to the current situation.

Crispin and Priscilla Leadbetter barely spoke to one another on the drive home to Oxfordshire. They both knew what was on the mind of the other. If the police were called and Crispin's disappearance was reported in the press, they dreaded to think what the outcome — for them — might be!

When they arrived home to find no sign of their supposed grandson, they did not call the school.

At exactly seven o'clock in the evening, Mr Harris picked up the telephone in the secretary's office and rang the police....

....

By seven o'clock that evening, Stuart Anderson was well on his way to Newcastle. For most of the journey, he had gazed out of the window, relieved that his escape from his erstwhile captors had gone according to plan.

He guessed that they would be furious that he was not waiting for them as they left the ceremony — but that was not his problem. He had no intention of letting them know where he was or even that he was safe. As far as he was concerned, that was for them to find out. Tomorrow he would be with his mother and father who, for almost fourteen years, had suffered the loss of a son, not knowing whether he was dead or alive. Stuart retrieved his birth certificate from the envelope in his jacket pocket. *Fourteen*, he thought. Tomorrow was his birthday, his *real* birthday; he would be fourteen. At Newcastle, he managed to buy a sandwich and tea from a platform vendor, before boarding a train to Edinburgh. He arrived at Scotland's capital too late for the last train of the day to Aberdeen. However, a porter told him that the next train, the night sleeper, would be stopping in the early hours of the morning: "You won't get a compartment with a bed but you might get a seat — it's worth a try."

Stuart settled down on a bench, thinking he would just wait for the first regular train of the day. However, after more than three hours and feeling tired and uncomfortable, he heard the night sleeper as it chugged into the station. He decided to take the porter's advice: he would ask. He made his way to the platform and, clutching his Aberdeen ticket, he approached the guard's van.

"Missed your train, did you?" the guard queried, looking at the ticket.

"Yes," Stuart mumbled, not wishing to go into a long explanation.

"On you get," the guard invited, "Follow me, there's a free compartment in the next carriage, with an unreserved bunk. You look as if you could use a few hours' sleep." Stuart could scarcely believe his luck. There was a small wash-hand basin in the compartment, so he was able to have a quick wash and brush his teeth. He undressed and slipped between the sheets — bliss! Twenty minutes before the train was due into Aberdeen there was a knock on the door: a wake-up call from the guard. It was half-past seven in the morning as the train rolled into the station. Stuart had slept soundly for several hours. Anxious as he was to see his parents, he decided it was a little too early in the morning to descend on them. He found a café near to the station where he ordered a full Scottish Breakfast. Rested and fed, he had a stroll around the harbour before catching a bus to the market town where his parents lived.

It was almost ten o'clock in the morning when the tall sandy-haired youth walked into the local bank in the market town a few miles west of East Bay. With a nervous grin, he went up to a teller and asked to see Mrs Kathryn Anderson. "Who shall I say is asking?" the young girl enquired.

"I'm her son," Stuart replied....

....

Although Stuart had been discovered alive and well at the end of May, Kitty was not expecting him home for another two weeks. When the young teller told her that her son was asking to see her, she assumed it was Alec. She came out of her office into the customer area to find out what he wanted, but the only client in the bank appeared to be a sandy-haired youth around six feet tall. She turned back towards her office, thinking that the girl must have been mistaken. "Mum," came a deep voice from the young man, "It's me — your son, Stuart."

For a few seconds, Kitty stood frozen to the spot until, filled with pent-up emotion, the tears blotted out her vision. Stuart stepped forward towards the attractive middle-aged woman; her dark-hair showing hints of grey — his mother. Gently, he embraced her.

"Happy Birthday," were the first words she spoke, as he loosened his grip, "Let's go home."

Kitty retrieved her jacket and handbag from the office and told her assistant she would be back on Monday —

her son was home. No further explanation was needed: the bank staff knew all about the kidnap.

On the way to the cottage, Kitty stopped at the local baker's shop, where she ordered a birthday cake to be collected later that day. Being a regular customer the baker knew her well. This was a very special request — they would do their best! For the next two days, Stuart remained solely in the company of his parents, who just wanted to have their son to themselves for a while. On Saturday, they thought perhaps they should alert the rest of the family to the return of their youngest offspring. In the morning, Stuart and his dad walked the three miles or so up to the castle. If Timothy was at home, he would ring Isobel at the hotel and, no doubt, drive to East Bay to see Jeannie.

Timothy was not surprised to see Stuart. He did not blame the lad for sneaking away from school to avoid the Leadbetters. "A cunning plot," he remarked with a grin, "and I don't suppose they know where you are?" Stuart shrugged his shoulders in response. *That can wait for another day*, Timothy thought. He would give Bernard a ring tomorrow.

Timothy contacted Isobel with the news of her brother's arrival — she was thrilled to learn that he was home at last. High tea, from five o'clock until seven o'clock on Sunday, was the best they could do for a family gathering at such short notice: it was the height of the summer season. Stuart and his dad accepted a lift home with Timothy, calling in at Alec's farm on the way.

After dropping his son-in-law and grandson off in the town, Timothy continued on to East Bay. He would be spending the rest of the day with Jeannie.

The family celebration the following day was delightful. Isobel had managed to contact her brother Ernie who, much to her delight, was off-duty and would be able to join them. So it was that Kitty was united with her family: her mother and father, her three sons, her daughter and grandchildren. Stuart, of course, was delighted to meet up with his friend, Chris — his nephew — the real Crispin Nigel Leadbetter!

....

Mr Harris was not surprised that the Leadbetters failed to contact him by seven o'clock on the day of his disappearance, as he had suggested: it signalled to him that the boy had not returned home.

The police sergeant, who responded to his call to report Crispin's disappearance, was confused as much as concerned, as the Deputy Head recounted the tale. The reaction of the grandparents at the mention of involving the police seemed more of a mystery than the missing boy. Since all of the pupils had, by now, gone their separate ways, locating them for information would be time-consuming. "Did he leave anything behind in the dormitory, any clues as to where he might have gone?" the police sergeant asked.

"No," Mr Harris confirmed, "everything was in order; nothing left lying around; his trunk closed and locked ready to be collected."

"Don't let the trunk go," the sergeant urged. "I'll make out a missing person's report right now, but we'll not take this further until we have contacted Mr and Mrs Leadbetter. It sounds as if the boy has deliberately chosen to make himself scarce. Did he have any particular friend that he might have confided in?"

As well as Crispin's description and the details of his home address and telephone number, Mr Harris also gave a contact number for himself. He promised to get in touch with the boy's housemaster to ask for any information that might help with an investigation. Before going home, he went to the dormitory, placed a sheet over the trunk and attached a large piece of paper marked, DO NOT REMOVE.

The following afternoon a plain-clothed detective, together with a uniformed police officer, approached the Leadbetter's home in Oxfordshire. Tentatively, Priscilla Leadbetter opened the front door a few inches: it was held in place by a chain, as she had no intention of allowing the men inside.

"We are looking for Crispin Nigel Leadbetter," the police officer stated. "Is he here?"

"Yes," she lied — on the instructions of her husband.

"May we speak with him?" the detective asked.

"He's asleep," Mrs Leadbetter responded, "He's not feeling well; I don't want to disturb him."

"We have a warrant to search the premises," the officer announced, as he retrieved the item from his jacket.

The terrified Mrs Leadbetter changed her tune. "He-he-he's not here, she stuttered."

"We still need to search the property," the officer insisted.

Left with no choice, she let them in. They went into every room throughout the property but did not rummage through cupboards and drawers, as the detective was tempted to do — that might well happen later. Satisfied that there was no sign of the boy, they made themselves comfortable in the sitting room (uninvited) to question her as to the whereabouts of her grandson. She said she had no idea where he was, insisting that the last she had seen of him was in the assembly hall the previous afternoon. Neither the police officer nor the detective was prepared to accept her story: she had already lied to them. For the next hour they probed deeper and deeper — if she didn't know where he was, why did she not want the police involved?

By the time the men left, Priscilla Leadbetter had reached breaking point. Why had she lied? Why had they kidnapped the child? For almost fourteen years she had lived with guilt — although never so guilty as to seek out her daughter-in-law and return Crispin to his rightful home!

When Crispin Leadbetter senior arrived home from his office to find his wife distressed, he tried his best to console her. Perhaps it had been foolish to attempt to avoid the police: maybe that had made matters worse. Surely Crispin could not be far away. He assured Priscilla that their grandson would be home in a day or so. After all, where else would he go?

During the weekend, Mr Harris contacted Crispin's housemaster who commented that the boy did not appear to have a happy home life. He hated the holidays, always dreading the end of term. He mentioned that if any of Crispin's classmates knew where he might be, it would be Sam. He offered to try to get in touch with him.

Sam was alarmed to hear that his friend was missing. He told the housemaster how Crispin had not returned to the hall after receiving his prize, saying that he didn't feel well. He added that his friend always feared going home, but this time was different: he seemed agitated rather than afraid. Sam had no idea where he might be.

On Monday morning three incidents took place that moved the case rapidly to a conclusion:

The police department contacted Mr Harris to request his presence at the school. Two officers met the Deputy Head at the premises. Firstly, they opened Crispin's trunk. It had been neatly packed, apart from a white shirt, school tie and blazer, which had been flung carelessly on top, along with his satchel and the year-group shield. Next, they asked for any other information on the missing boy that might be useful. They followed

Mr Harris into the school office to retrieve Crispin's file. The officer in charge opened the brown envelope marked 'confidential'. The three men looked in disbelief at the birth certificate. The missing boy was Stuart Anderson — not Crispin Nigel Leadbetter.

Stuart Anderson, on the advice of his grandpa, Timothy Campbell, went into the police station in the market town with a copy of his birth certificate in his hand. "I'm Stuart Anderson," he announced. "I was kidnapped from my home in Aberdeen in October 1940. I believe you were looking for me!"

Bernard Campbell contacted Clive Small who presented his report on the kidnapped Stuart Anderson to the police department in London. Their investigation into the boy who had disappeared from his school the previous Thursday afternoon was solved.

On the evening of the following day, just as Crispin and Priscilla Leadbetter were settling down to their evening meal, a police van drew up outside their house.

Seeing two police officers approaching, and finally anxious for some news of their missing grandson, they both went to the door. They were rather uneasy when the officer in charge asked them to step outside the house, but that was nothing compared to the way they felt a few seconds later when he announced: **"I am arresting you on suspicion of the abduction and detention of Stuart Anderson. You do not have to say anything but..."**

EPILOGUE

Bewildered, the deceitful pair were directed, handcuffed and protesting, into the back of the van. Mr Leadbetter was found dead on arrival at the police station, stricken with a massive heart attack. Mrs Leadbetter was subsequently found guilty of the heinous crime. She was incarcerated for fourteen years: the exact length of time she had kept Stuart Anderson away from his family. Frederick and Maria Dobson pleaded guilty to their part in conducting the kidnap. They too were imprisoned, though for a lesser duration. Similarly, Henrietta and Raymond received shorter sentences as accessories to the crime.

Before his untimely death, Crispin Leadbetter had made a Will in which he left his business, 'The Leadbetter Accountancy Company', in trust to his grandson, Crispin Nigel Leadbetter — a child who was barely a month old the last time his grandparents had seen him. Mr Leadbetter's obsession with the firm, and the 'good name' of Leadbetter, was central to his existence. His beneficiary felt this legacy should rightly fall to his uncle, Stuart Anderson, who had been the one to suffer over the years; but Stuart was glad to be away from his Oxfordshire home: he wanted nothing more to do with it.

Always a keen mathematician, Crispin intended to pursue a career in accountancy, so the legacy was not wasted on him. However, so disgusted was he by the behaviour of his paternal grandparents, he changed his name by deed poll to Christopher Nigel Anderson and, with it, the name of the Accountancy firm! Until he was old enough and qualified, his Great-Uncle Bernard kept a close eye on the firm, which continued to thrive in the competent hands of the current staff.

As James Roberts set off on holiday to Scotland with his mother, the awful truth of the abduction of his friend 'Crispin' was headline news. James was confident that he would soon meet his two pals. He looked forward to seeing them both, as well as hearing the details of the scandal. As the boy who had unwittingly introduced the uncle and the nephew, he was welcomed whole-heartedly into the family circle: he and his mother, who eventually returned to Aberdeen to be with her family, remained close friends of the family in the years to come.

....

In the early autumn of the same year, another wedding took place in the little church at East Bay. The 'mature'couple, looking as radiant as any young bride and groom, celebrated with a reception in a Scottish castle, with caterers, a dance band and entertainers hired for the occasion.

Acknowledgements

My thanks to Russ Naylor for his support, proof-reading and editing; and for his encouragement and enthusiasm throughout the writing process.

Thanks also to Gill Hallgate for her support and comments.

About the Author

Louie Elizabeth Parker was born in Kingston Upon Hull in 1947, where she lived until the age of twenty. In 1968 she moved to Leeds and trained for the teaching profession. For more than six years Louie taught at a primary school on an estate designated as an education priority area. It was a challenge! At the end of 1977 she moved to Aberdeenshire, where she spent the next thirty-nine years. During that time she taught in country and village schools, lectured at the Northern College and gained the Degree of Master of Education. She spent the last seven years of her career as a primary school headteacher.

Louie's second novel, *The Chris-Cross Episode*, is set predominately in North East Scotland inspired by the time she spent with her late husband Alexander <u>Alan</u> Crawford Parker, an Aberdonian by birth.

louieelizabethparker.com

Another publication from the author:

TWENTY YEARS FROM HOME
by Louie Elizabeth Parker

Twenty Years from Home follows the life of a young child seemingly abandoned by her irresponsible parents who, as students, are tempted by a hippie lifestyle. Her widowed grandmother, determined not to make the same mistakes she feels she must have made with her daughter, decides to go back to 'basics'. She leaves her middle-class existence in the city to bring up the child in a run-down cottage in the Scottish countryside. For twelve years they have no electricity, no telephone and only a cold-water tap in the kitchen. The toilet is an outside privy.

But what has happened to the parents? Why did they desert their families, their precious offspring and their promising careers?

It is a story of kindness and cruelty; love and foolishness; revenge and shame.

Printed in Great Britain
by Amazon